GREEN MEADOW

JENNY HALEY

DEDICATION

For Dad, who believes in me.

CONTENTS

BAILEY ROSE, M.D. SERIES

CHAPTER ONE

Most of the frenetic ride to Dr. Montgomery's office was spent in silence. Madge, his fiancé's maid, had come to fetch him alone, and she steered the rig skillfully at a break-neck pace through the city streets, her brown eyes bulging with panic and her bonnet strings flapping. Montgomery's office was on Evergreen Street, about fifteen blocks from the courthouse. In the time it took to travel it, Jacob's mind reeled at an equally frenetic pace, trying to make proper order of the utter mess of his life. He had found his childhood love, Bailey Rose, after fifteen years; the little girl raised in a brothel in the heart of San Antonio's Red Light District had overcome a life of deprivation to become a doctor, returning to serve the fallen women and children. He had found her, but not before one stupid night of drunkenness with Caroline had sealed his fate: he had impregnated a woman he didn't love, and now he was bound to her, for life. He sunk his head into his hands, utterly despondent. Bailey had just been acquitted of murder: it should be a time of rejoicing; she should be in his arms right this minute. She had shot a man fifteen years ago in self-defense, a man who had been revealed to have been kidnapped and horribly abused as a child along with Bailey's mother. Bailey was free now; free to walk out of that courtroom after months in jail, and he needed to be with her! What in God's name was he doing in this carriage?

1

Being trapped in his own miserable life, that's what. He would be marrying Caroline soon; they were having a baby in a few short months, and then he would begin his term as the youngest mayor in the country. And all he desired—all that he *needed*—was to be on the train back to Bluebonnet Ranch, Bailey in his arms.

He sat up then, reminding himself. Caroline was ill; his unborn baby might be in danger. It was time to step back into his life.

"What happened?" he asked gruffly.

Madge whimpered. "I'm sure I don't know, sir. I found her myself an hour ago. I went to her room to take her a tray, and she was shaking on the bed, flopping around like a fish. Scared the daylights out of me. Then she just went limp, and we couldn't get her to wake up. Now, she's had headaches and long days of sleeping sickness before, but never a fit like this, you see. Jerry, the stable boy, got her and her mum to the doctor's right away, and then Mrs. Vogler sent me to fetch you. I suspect it has something to do with the diphtheria, don't you think?"

Jacob gulped, his face flooding. He had never been a good liar, so he said nothing, knowing his omission made him just as duplicitous. And what did Madge mean, Caroline had headaches and sleeping sickness? She had never told him about that.

He was halfway out of the rig before Madge had it completely stopped, and tore into the office. The waiting room was strangely empty, and he wondered what kind of medical office Montgomery ran, being closed in the middle of the day.

"Mrs. Vogler?" he called, his voice echoing. The waiting area looked much like the Rose Clinic, he noticed with a pang. "Dr. Montgomery?"

"We're back here, Mr. Naplava," called Montgomery, and he strode through the waiting room down a narrow hallway, looking right and left into various small examination rooms until he found what he was looking for. Mrs. Vogler sat next to a bed upon which lay Caroline, white and still. Dr. Montgomery stood at the other side, taking her pulse.

"Hello Jacob," quavered Mrs. Vogler. "I'm so glad Madge

found you."

He slowly approached the bed, staring at the girl who lay there. Her eyelids were twitching and her chest rose and fell, but the rest of her was absolutely still. Her blonde-white hair had been braided to the side and rested over her shoulder, making her look five years younger than she was. He felt a surge of pity for her and wondered if she had divulged her pregnancy to her mother. Mrs. Vogler's next words put that question to rest.

"I don't know what on earth is wrong with her," she cried. "She's had episodes before where she gets upset and then sleeps for a few days, but nothing like this. It must be the diphtheria." Jacob felt as low as he ever had.

"Mrs. Vogler," said Dr. Montgomery gently. "You've been here for an hour. Why don't you let Madge take you home to rest? Caroline's vital signs are very strong; she's resting now. I have every confidence that she's going to be just fine and will wake up any time now, fully recovered, just like the other times. Let young Naplava here stay with her for a while. We'll send word immediately if there's a change."

It took some convincing, but the elegant woman finally took her leave, assisted to the rig by an attentive Madge. Dr. Montgomery and Jacob followed them out, bidding them farewell in the waiting room. Montgomery then sighed and gestured Jacob into his office.

"What about the baby? Is he okay?" Jacob blurted as they made their way to the small room. Montgomery remained silent, pointing at a chair.

They sat and stared at each other. "She didn't have diphtheria," Jacob began.

Montgomery waved his hand impatiently. "I know. She told me about the plan."

Jacob's face flooded with shame. *The plan.* It sounded so nefarious.

"Then what the hell is wrong with her? And is the baby okay?"

"I honestly don't know what's wrong with her. But you should know that this has happened before. Many times!

3

Caroline has struggled for years with this condition, ever since she and her family came to Texas; since I've known them, anyway."

Jacob stared at him. The doctor wasn't mentioning the baby, which was not a good sign, and a flush of dread began somewhere in his chest and spread to the rest of his body.

"The baby. Is he dead?"

There was a crash as the entry door in the waiting room was flung open with enough force to drive it into the wall behind it, jangling the bell jarringly. They both jumped.

"Hello?" called a woman's voice, and she sounded familiar.

"Hello there? Where's the doctor?" she called, and Jacob had it. Alice! Anton's Alice! He jumped to his feet and ran to the waiting room, followed by Dr. Montgomery.

They both stopped in their tracks, shocked into immobility for entirely different reasons.

Alice Barnes stood with her feet spread wide, one hand clamped firmly around the wrist of another woman who appeared to be just a few years' Alice's senior. The other girl stood sobbing, her golden hair coming loose from a bun and hanging in strands around her face. It looked as though a struggle had occurred and Alice had come out on top.

Dr. Montgomery uttered a sound that could have been "No!" or a moan of pain. He began to back up, his eyes bulging with fear, but Alice pointed at him.

"You might want to think about not moving another step," she hissed, and Jacob gaped at her.

"Alice! What the hell is going on? This is Caroline's doctor! And she's sick—she's back there laid out on a table, unconscious!"

Alice's expression softened as she regarded Jacob. He was her favorite Naplava boy by far, except for Anton, of course. She considered herself an excellent judge of character, and this man was as good they came. "Oh, Jacob, I think we all better sit down," she said gently, and still with the angelic smile on her face, shoved the girl roughly into a chair, then lowered herself gracefully beside her.

She pointed at Montgomery again. "Sit," she ordered, and he sat, as did Jacob, who was beginning to realize that this was perhaps the strangest day of his life thus far.

Alice took a deep breath and looked at each of them, her eyes finally resting on Jacob. She shook her head admiringly. "I've never in my life seen a man with prettier eyes," she said unexpectedly. "Everyone moons over Anton—and he *is* pretty—but I think you might be the looker in the family." He stared at her, flushing, and could not think of a thing to say.

"Alice," he finally managed after a terribly awkward pause. "What is going on?"

"Well, this is all quite simple, really. Brace yourself, Jacob. Ready?"

He stared at her, wondering if she had lost her mind.

"All right then. Jacob, Caroline Vogler is not pregnant."

The words fell into the room like a hard rain, drenching him in icy fingers, robbing his breath. Montgomery produced a guttural sound and sunk his face into his hands, and the other girl's chin dropped to her chest in shame.

"I'm sorry. Alice, what did you say?" he finally managed after several long seconds, his voice choked.

"Caroline isn't pregnant and she never was. She lied to trap you into marriage. Montgomery here is in on it. And so is this sorry girl, Honey Lane. Caroline disguised herself as a matronly older woman, Mrs. Hall—she wore a wig and stuffed her clothes and everything, I saw her with my own eyes, Jacob—and she gave Honey a thousand macaroons, with the promise of a thousand more upon delivery. You see, Honey here is expecting a baby, and Caroline's been paying her to get her checkups with Montgomery. When the time comes for her to deliver, Caroline was just going to come here and pretend to go into labor and *oi- la*! There's a baby!" She flipped one hand in the air to demonstrate the simplicity of the plan.

Jacob stared at her, the blood draining from his face and settling somewhere deep where a hot ball of rage had begun to form.

"I saw Caroline meeting with Honey at San Fernando's a month back and I didn't have the whole story yet, Jacob, or I would have told you. Caroline was in disguise—oh, it was a good one, and I never would've known it was her until I heard her speak and followed her home and saw the dark wig and clothes and stuffing in the carriage. But I figured it all out and tracked down Honey at Harding House. You see, Honey was going to adopt that baby out anyway, and for two grand, it was just so easy to say yes, wasn't it, Honey?"

The girl sobbed louder and shook her head violently. "I told you, I changed my mind. I was trying to get the money back she gave me so I could tell her no. I want to keep my baby! Oh, can I, Dr. Montgomery? I don't have to give it to Mrs. Hall—I mean, Miss Vogler, do I?"

Montgomery groaned again, apparently incapable of forming an answer, his eyes bugged with fear. He was certain that the big Naplava boy would kill him.

There was another long, strained silence, Jacob trying to remember how to breathe, the girl sobbing, and Montgomery groaning.

"No, Miss Lane," Jacob finally said with a kind voice. "You don't have to give your baby to Miss Vogler. You keep your baby, and don't worry about paying back that money." He smiled gently at her, even as the ball of rage expanded, pushing against his heart and making it pound with a furious rhythm.

"Oh, thank you, Mr. Naplava! Thank you! I'm ever so sorry. I didn't know she was tricking anyone. I thought she was a nice older lady who just wanted another baby and couldn't have one. And she's not even married!" She ended on a wail, and Jacob grimaced, feeling the ball pushing everything else out of the way.

He stood, balling his fists. "Alice. Would you please take Honey back to Harding House and make sure she's fine? There will be no charges filed against her, and if she chooses to tell Reverend Eckles, that's up to her. None of this is her fault."

Alice stood, yanking Honey with her, not quite ready to

relinquish her prisoner. "Why, of course I will, Jacob, but are you sure?"

He nodded tersely. "Yes, I am certain. I'm indebted to you, Alice. Really, I am. Thank you." He took a step forward and gave her arm a squeeze, smiling into her eyes, and she was surprised to feel her heart flutter a bit. She'd have to confess to Anton that she had just a tiny crush on his younger brother. She was pretty sure Anton had just a tiny crush on Lindy, so they'd be even!

She smiled and saluted. "At your service! Anything for a brother of Anton's, of course." She whisked out of the office, pulling Honey with her, endeavoring to be a bit gentler now that the drama was over and Jacob seemed to be most forgiving.

Jacob did not feel forgiving—well, maybe toward that poor hoodwinked girl, but not toward the blubbering man in the chair behind him. And certainly not toward the serpent who lay coiled in the bed down the hall. He felt murderous.

He turned to the doctor; Montgomery was full-on weeping now, sure that he was about to die. "How did she get you to do it?" he finally said, his voice deadly quiet. "Was it money?"

The doctor only shook his head, unable to speak. For long moments the only sound was his sobbing, punctuated by hiccoughs and snorts.

"Did she pay you?" he asked again, his voice gaining volume. He heard a roaring in his ears from the rage and failed to notice quiet sounds from the hallway beyond.

"Y—y—yes," Montgomery finally blubbered.

An onerous thought occurred to Jacob and he ground his teeth together so fiercely he felt shooting pains in his jaws. "Did she pay with *favors*, too?" he forced himself to say, and leaned forward to pull the man to his feet by the lapels. "Did she?" His whole body was shaking now, from the inside out, the ball of rage pushing at his skin, his face, contorting his features, lending him strength beyond his considerable norm.

"Yes," wailed the doctor, and Jacob threw the man with such force back onto the chair that he tipped backward and fell to the floor with a crash, and lay there, unmoving, the toes of his boots pointing at the ceiling, still whimpering. Jacob crouched down and put his face one inch from the doctor's.

"You will be gone by tomorrow morning. Get out of this city, forever. Get out of the state. If I ever see you again in the state of Texas, I'll kill you. Do you understand?"

Montgomery's head bobbed on his shoulders like a floppy doll, relief rendering him limp.

Jacob straightened and tried with all of his willpower to stem the rage surging inside of him. He failed. Every muscle in his body was on fire: his blood surged, his heart raced, his eyes bulged. He needed to hit something before he walked back into the room down the hall. He turned and put his fist through the wall with such force that his knuckles traveled through several layers of paint and plaster. He gasped and pulled his hand out of the wall, sinking to the floor and cradling it for a moment. It was broken for sure, and bleeding like a son of a bitch.

He bowed his head and let the fury wash through him in wave after sickening wave. Caroline wasn't pregnant. She had tricked him, all this time, using the vilest means imaginable, exploiting others to get what she wanted, and he had been the colossal dumbass who had fallen for the oldest trick in the book.

He allowed himself a moment to think about what might have been. Bailey, his sweet girl, his one love, with him in the hen house the night of the barn dance, *oh, Lord.* If not for Caroline he would have been on his knee that night proposing to Bailey, begging her to marry him. She would have said yes. And right now, already—because he would have walked her to the church within a week, *the next day,* if she would have let him—he would be her husband. *Bailey's husband.* That's who he had been born to be; he was more certain of that than he had ever been of anything in his life. How unforgivably he had hurt her, loving her, making her love him, all the while intending to marry Caroline. Even today, he had left her. My God, what did she think of him now? Where was she now? He felt a primal need to get to her. But there was something he must take care of first.

He drew a bolstering breath and got to his feet. Montgomery still lay in a heap on the floor, but with a sharp command from Jacob he leapt up and scuttled out the front door, still blubbering. "Leave your rig," growled Jacob after him, and the man squeaked like a mouse and ran on foot from the building.

Jacob turned to look down the hallway, his anger sufficiently dissipated. All it took was to think of Bailey, and the world regained balance and made sense again. *Just get it over with.* He straightened and strode quickly down the hall; he would wake her and tell her he knew everything. He would give her the same ultimatum he had given Montgomery: leave this city. Leave this state. Remove yourself from my sight or I will ruin you. Ruining Caroline would not involve lifting a hand against her, which of course, he would never do, no matter how tempted. He would send Alice with a story to Hedelga Jones for *The Express*, and Caroline's life in her precious high-society world would be over. He would give her one day to get out of town or she would suffer a social death.

He took a deep breath and entered the room.

She was gone.

CHAPTER TWO

He found Montgomery's rig tied up out back and made straight for Anton's; his family was staying there, and Johann would know where to find Bailey. *Bailey.* Her name looped like an endless hosanna in his brain. He would put that wooden ring back on her left ring finger where it belonged and beg her to forgive him, to marry him. What if she said no? What if his actions today had sealed his fate? He had to get to her!

He tore into Anton's stable, barking orders to the stable boy and sprinting into the house. He burst through the door and found the family in the parlor to the left; clearly, they had just arrived, as Lindy and Marianna were shrugging out of their wraps.

Everyone turned to stare and the room grew silent.

"Jacob! How is the baby?" Gacenka blurted. Jacob's gaze darted to Johann.

"We all know, little brother," Johann confessed.

Jacob clenched his jaw, dreading what he would have to say next. He took a deep breath and expelled it. "She's not—she never was with child," he forced himself to say. His face flooded, fueled by anger and embarrassment. "It was all a trick. Alice figured it all out. She found the girl Caroline paid. It was a girl at Harding House; Caroline *bought* her baby."

He allowed his gaze to travel to each family member; every

one of them was frozen in place with dumbfounded expressions on their faces. Everyone except Lindy, who looked not the least bit surprised. It was she who spoke first.

"It's not your fault, Jacob."

He waved his hand impatiently. "Yes it was. I was a blasted moron, falling for that. I should have seen it." His eyes shifted to Johann and a note of urgency crept into his voice. "Look, none of it matters now. I've got to find Bailey! Johann, where is she? Did she say where she was going when you talked to her after the trial? Surely not back to St. Ursuline's with the press following her?"

There was another uncomfortable silence. Johann cleared his throat and looked at the floor. "Ah. Well. By the time I could push my way to her, she was gone, brother. She had totally vanished. I think Cunningham must have snuck her out somehow to fool the crowd."

Jacob's heart fell. She didn't get his message then, that he would find her.

"Jacob! What happened to your hand?" Marianna suddenly exclaimed. Jacob looked down: his hand was already turning blue, the knuckles bloody. Pain was shooting up to his elbow and he gritted his teeth.

"I punched a hole in Montgomery's wall. Caroline's doctor," he clarified.

"Oh, my son," Gacenka murmured, moving forward to examine it.

"Ma, I don't have time. Look; I've got to find Bailey! She'll fix it up for me." He paused long enough to lean down to kiss his mother on the cheek. "Anton, when Alice comes back, thank her again for me, will you? I owe her everything. She's a keeper, that girl." He flashed a smile at his brother as he backed out of the room, and then he was gone, just as abruptly as he had entered.

But he utterly failed in his search: his first stop was St. Ursuline's, but she hadn't returned there, as he suspected. Her clinic was dark and empty, and a quick conversation with Gabriella and Thomas at Harding House proved futile as well.

"I'll bet she left with her family," Gabby said gently, cradling her baby. Jacob stared at the infant, his heart hurting, hoping beyond hope that someday Bailey would be holding their child just like that.

Thomas nodded gravely. "Yes, my guess is that she's bunking with them tonight, or maybe..." he stopped abruptly, his face coloring, and he cleared his throat and looked at Gabby.

"Maybe she's on the train to Pennsylvania," Gabby finished for him, gazing at Jacob.

Jacob stared at her, adrenaline beginning to flow again. "I'll find her. I'm going to find her! Where do you supposed her family was staying?"

"It's hard to say, but if I had to guess, they'd be at the Menger," Gabby mused.

"Right," he said, and he was already halfway down the steps on the way to his rig before the word was even halfway out of his mouth.

Gabby and Thomas watched him go, then looked at each and burst into laughter.

"She doesn't stand a chance!" Gabby said gleefully. "They may be getting married before we do!"

Thomas wrapped his arms around her and the baby and nuzzled her neck. "I don't think so," he murmured. "I was thinking that tomorrow might be a good wedding day; what do you think?"

She turned and kissed him full on the mouth. "We have to wait for Bailey," she whispered. "She has to stand up with me."

Thomas groaned. "Well, then, if you'll excuse me, I think I'll go help Jacob look."

"No, my love. That's his—how do you say it—*quest*. And besides, I thought we'd canoodle tonight on the porch swing and watch the stars."

"If you insist," he said with a teasing tone, rolling his eyes as though canoodling with her would be a terrible bore, and just barely ducked her punch as he followed her back inside.

Jacob spent two more hours combing the city. The Millers were not at the Menger: they had been, but they had checked out. That piece of information took him straight to both train stations, but after a conversation with the ticket masters he was sure they had not left town. They were hiding from the press; that much was obvious. There had been at least twenty reporters camped in the lobby of the Menger, and almost that many at the Havana, Gaslight, and Crockett. He began looking at the lower-rent establishments on the southwest side of the city, to no avail. He had inquired at every hotel, boarding house, and hostel in town, as well as ducking his head into several restaurants. They had just simply vanished, and at last he finally had to admit to himself that the Millers must have found refuge with a family in town for the night.

He made his way back to Anton's, stabled Montgomery's tired horse and drug himself into the house. He found Johann, Anton, Wenzel, and Miguel still awake in the kitchen, drinking beer and playing Taroky with a battered deck of cards. They sobered at once when he entered, concern creasing their faces.

Anton swore softly as he looked at Jacob's hand. "I guess you didn't find her then. That looks plenty bad, Jacob. Let me wake Libby and have her take a look."

Jacob sank into the chair and didn't even bother to answer. Wenzel filled a mug and pushed it in front of his brother, and Jacob removed his hat and gratefully took a long draught. He sat back, tipping his head and staring morosely at the ceiling.

"I don't know where the hell she is. I looked everywhere. She probably hates me anyway."

The four men glanced at each other, worried. Jacob was not one to feel sorry for himself.

"Don't be an asshole," Johann finally said bluntly. "She doesn't hate you. She loves you, idiot. But she thinks you're with Caroline; why would she leave a trail? She's just giving you space."

Jacob shrugged and took another long drink. He banged the mug down and glared at his brothers. "Since I can't find Bailey tonight, I'm going to find Caroline. She'll be going away, *permanently*."

"Jesus, Jacob," Anton whispered. "You can't kill her."

Johann rolled his eyes at Anton. "He's *banishing* her, genius. Kicking her out of town." He looked at Jacob with his eyebrow raised. "Right? That *is* what you meant, isn't it?"

"Yes," Jacob snapped. "That's what I meant. I want her gone, out of Bailey's sight, out of my sight. I won't even be able to look at her when I find her; the sight of her will make me sick. But I just want to get it over with." He rose from the chair suddenly and jammed the hat back on his head. "See you later," he said simply.

Wenzel rose and followed his brother from the room. "Jacob. Wait a minute."

Jacob turned, patient even in the midst of his hurry to get the unsavory duty over with. He probably wouldn't be able to find Caroline anyway: she wouldn't have just gone *home*, would she have? He realized suddenly that he had no plan to speak of.

"What is it, Wen?"

Wenzel stared at him for a long moment and Jacob forced himself to stay quiet. Wenzel was obviously thinking very hard about something, and Jacob had learned to never interrupt that process. He finally spoke. "Why don't you write Bailey a note, and I'll look for her while you're hunting down Caroline? There's hours of daylight left. Heck, maybe she'll even come here. You might just miss each other somehow."

Jacob nodded, a grin beginning to light his face. "That's perfect, Wen! Hey! Maybe you can get the birds to tell you where she is." He was only half-joking.

Wenzel shook his head. "Naw. These city birds just talk about food."

Jacob laughed and felt immeasurably better somehow. "Give me a minute, okay?" Wen nodded and sat down in the parlor, and Jacob ran upstairs to his guest room to write a letter, keeping it brief and to the point.

My dearest Rosie,

I'll tell you everything, my love, as soon as I can find you. I'm looking for Caroline now; she'll be leaving the city—the state—hopefully, the country—forever, and then we'll be together forever if you'll have me. She is not pregnant, nor was she ever pregnant; it was all a lie. How could I not have known? What an unforgiveable moron I am. I love you more than anything, anyone in my life. I'm so, so sorry, Rosie. Please forgive me. Can you? Wait for me just a little longer, will you?

Yours forever,

Jake

He ran the letter downstairs and Wenzel tucked it into his pocket. "I'll find her, Jacob. I promise."

"Could you maybe give her some flowers with the note?" Jacob asked sheepishly, feeling a little desperate. "Bluebonnets, if you can find them?"

"Sure will."

"Thanks, brother. I love you, you know," he blurted, surprising himself, not sure where those words had come from at this moment. He enveloped his brother in a hug, a rare show of emotion between the two of them, and Wenzel hugged him back, hard.

"I love you, too."

Jacob stepped back and nodded a few times, and feeling uncharacteristically emotional, made a quick exit. He found a fresh horse, and foregoing a rig, set off for Caroline's, determined to put this whole stupid stage of his life behind him.

With no other ideas and a keen need to keep moving, he made his way to the Vogler estate, expecting to find Mrs. Vogler but not Caroline. Mr. Vogler was still out of town, thank God. He tied his horse out front and pounded on the door.

No one answered. A chill of foreboding began at the back of his scalp and worked its way down his spine. The butler, or sometimes the doorman, always answered the door immediately, day and night. He looked around him, befuddled. Odd that a stable boy hadn't come out to greet him and take his horse. The Voglers kept a full staff: stable boy, doorman, butler, cook and her staff, head housekeeper, and at least two maids. Where was everybody? He pounded again, the brass knocker vibrating against his palm, and waiting another two or three moments. Nobody came.

He tried the door and was shocked to find it unlocked. He pushed it open slowly, his brain screaming *caution* but his heart pounding with a resurgence of anger and urgency. He wanted the satisfaction of telling her, to her face, what she was. A fraud. The lowest sort of human being, one who would hurt others with no remorse to get what she wanted. He wanted to watch her face crumble when he told her what he would do; that her life—and her parents' lives—were over in this city. An image of her *servicing* that sorry old excuse for a doctor rose in front of him and blinded him with revulsion and rage.

The house was dark, save for one flickering lantern hung at the foot of the spiral staircase. "Caroline?" he called, his voice tight and thick with fury. "I need to talk to you! Get down here!"

Silence.

He made his way through the foyer and searched the ground floor: parlors, sitting rooms, conservatory, library, ballroom, even the kitchens. There was not a soul to be found. *Where had everyone gone?*

He peered into the back yard, noting that the lanterns around the pool were lit, the light reflecting like a thousand glimmering diamonds. But the pool, too, was abandoned.

So she was upstairs; either that, or the entire household had been emptied. Maybe she knew what was coming, had confessed to her mother, had the servants pack up, and made for the train station. Was that possible? He frowned as he realized that he had no idea what Caroline was capable of. He didn't know her at all.

He mounted the stairs and took them two at a time, but after a thorough search, realized that the second floor, which included all of the bedroom suites, were empty. Clothes and furnishings were still there, but they could send for those later, perhaps when Mr. Vogler returned from his business trip. What an unpleasant surprise for him, to have to pack up the house in disgrace and start business elsewhere, probably in Boston or New York or Philadelphia. It was beginning to look more and more plausible that the women had made a run for it. No doubt Caroline had been wide awake the entire time he had been at Montgomery's, and upon overhearing Alice's revelations, had snuck out, guessing Jacob would run to find Bailey first and give Caroline enough time to make her departure without a furious and ugly scene.

He heaved a disappointed sigh, anger still coiled inside of him like poison. Maybe it was all for the best, her sneaking out, but since she had chosen to be a coward, he thought he'd go ahead and leak the story to Hedelga Jones anyway. The consequences of her deceit would hunt her down, wherever she ran. She'd be a social pariah for the rest of her life, and she deserved that and a hundred times more.

He closed his eyes and Bailey's face came to him. What would she say to that plan? *Let it go, Jake. Let her be. Come find me.* A wave of joy rolled over him and he smiled in spite of the pain in his hand and the shock of the day. With a little luck, she'd be in his arms yet today.

"Well, that's the Jacob I know and love. Look at that dimple and those blue eyes that just *sparkle*. Such a face. Such a pity."

Her voice was icy and razor-sharp. She had materialized down the hall twenty feet away, stepping from a room as he made his way down the hall and towards the stairs. He froze, startled, and then his lips drew back in a snarl.

"I'm glad you're here, believe it or not," he said, his words quiet and hard.

"Oh, is that so? Have you finally realized that we belong together, you and I? It took you long enough! I was beginning to think you were a nancy, the way you've been running from me." Her blond hair was still in a braid drawn over her shoulder, and she was wearing a long, white, loose gown of some sort. She looked like a ghost.

He felt a surge of fury unlike one he'd ever known, and it took all of his willpower to keep from hurtling toward her and knocking her down.

"I think you're more Montgomery's type."

She laughed, her head tipping back to reveal her delicate white throat. "Or more Anton's, perhaps."

He stared at her, his breath sucked away.

"Yes, that's right, Jacob. You might have a problem with sex, but I assure you, your brother does *not*. Ask him sometime, why don't you. We had quite a night at the Gaslight, in the very room where your girlfriend blew a hole in poor Adam Hawk's chest all those years ago. Anton is *very* familiar with the bed they hauled into court last week."

He swallowed, tasting bile. "You're lying. You're a sick, twisted, demented liar, and I can't believe I almost fell into your trap. Get out of town tonight, Caroline. Tomorrow it's all over for you here. I've already seen to it."

She chuckled and shook her head. "Oh, Jacob, that's sweet of you to go to so much trouble over little old me. But I've already made plans to leave town; tonight, in fact. And you're coming with me. We'll be married and live happily ever after, my love, in Moravia, where we belong. We sail from Boston in one week; I've already purchased the tickets. We'll have six days of rail travel, but don't worry; you'll be very comfortable and I'll see to your every need. I've sent Mama and the entire staff ahead of me. But I waited here for you."

He gaped at her. "My God, you really are crazy," he whispered. "You need help, Caroline. You need to be in an asylum. You're going to hurt someone."

She smiled brightly and nodded, and just as the warning bell in his head began to clang in desperate earnest, she pulled from the folds of her gown a slim whistle. At least he thought it was a whistle.

His last thought before he fell to the floor in a cacophony of pain was *why is Caroline playing a whistle?*

CHAPTER THREE

After the foreman uttered the words *not guilty*, everything was a blur in super-speed motion. She was instantly surrounded by her team; Cunningham lifted her from her chair and swung her into a bear hug, Lincoln leaned over and patted her awkwardly on the top of the head as though she were a small child, and Mooreland swabbed away tears, too overcome by emotion to speak. She turned to look for Jacob, and amongst the wall of people surging forward she caught a glimpse of him, his head sunk into his hands, shoulders heaving, his brothers pounding his back, and she beamed with happiness. He was *crying* for her! She barely had time to register that wondrous fact when she was pulled into a fierce hug by Hope, who had literally shoved her way through three rows to get to her sister. When Bailey could finally come up for air, she stood on her tip-toes to see him.

"Come on," Hope said, gripping her hand and beginning to push. "I'll get you to him. I'm quite a good plow!" But it wasn't to be: reporters and well-wishers blocked their way, grasping to touch Bailey, shout questions at her, congratulate her, or just gawk as though she were a monkey in a zoo. She felt a first prickle of panic as she realized she absolutely could not move, and somehow a reporter had wedged himself between her and Hope, whose grip on Bailey's hand was weakening. Hope finally kicked the errant man in the shin, and as he howled in pain, she took the opportunity to shove him aside and clutch Bailey's arm.

"We've got to get you out of here now," Hope gasped. "Move back, move back. Look; Cordy and Howard are waiting up by the judge's chamber door with Cunningham."

Bailey gave one last effort to spot Jacob, and was rewarded to get a glimpse of him in the aisle. But he wasn't working his way toward her; he was being yanked down the aisle in the opposite direction by a woman in a maid's uniform. *It must be Caroline's maid. Something is wrong with Caroline, maybe with the baby.* The thoughts occurred to her in rapid succession, and she balled her hands in frustration as she realized there was nothing she could do to get to him.

At that moment she felt the lace rip from her cuff: a desperate-looking man with wild eyes and greasy hair had procured for himself a souvenir, and he held it up triumphantly, cackling.

Bailey stood frozen to the spot, overwhelmed all at once with an onslaught of emotion. In the space of a few moments she had been exonerated for a deed that had haunted her since childhood, she had been freed from the Shrimp Hotel—she would sleep in a bed tonight, and have a bath!—something was dreadfully wrong with Caroline to make Jacob leave without speaking to her, and a lunatic had just ripped the lace from her dress as a keepsake. Her eyes filled with tears, but before she could fall completely apart, Hope grasped her around the waist and picked her up bodily, carrying her through the thick crowd, kicking anyone who got in the way. "Make way, the lot of you! Or I'll move you myself!" And after a few moments of struggle they arrived at the judge's door; the bailiff produced a key and unlocked it, and as Abe Lincoln and Mooreland formed a blockade, Bailey, Hope, Cordelia, and Howard slipped through.

Bailey's tears had turned to hysterical laughter. "P—put me d-down," she gasped, laughing so hard that tears were coursing down her face. Hope set her on the floor and Bailey bent over, clutching her stomach and shrieking with laughter. "Y-you k-kicked a ci-city councilman," she gasped. "An-And his wi-wife, that hor-horrible Glenda God-Godfrey!"

Her laugh had always been terribly contagious, and soon Hope was hooting just as loudly, the girls holding on to each other for support. Cordelia looked on fondly, a wave of happiness building within her. "Ladies," she finally said softly. "We must go before those horrible reporters catch on. Quickly now! Mr. Cunningham will lead us out."

It was not until they were safely packed away in the carriage that Bailey was able to draw a breath and stop the mania that had seized her. "Hope. Thank you for the rescue. I'm afraid I was— overcome back there. I guess the greasy man with a piece of my dress was the last straw."

"Anything for my little sister," Hope beamed, slinging her arm around Bailey's neck.

Bailey leaned forward and spoke in a low voice so only Hope could hear, grateful that Cordelia and Howard were engaged in a quiet conversation of their own, no doubt about the fact that no fewer than five carriages were currently tailing them through the city. "What do you suppose—did you see Jacob—" Bailey stopped, not knowing how to continue.

"What was he doing running after a maid, you mean?" Hope said gently.

Bailey nodded meekly. "Yes. I suppose Caroline is ill and he went to her. I know the Naplavas don't have a maid. I can't think of any other reason."

"You're worried about the baby, I presume? Lordy, I hope you're not worried about Caroline."

Bailey nodded miserably. "Yes, of course I'm worried about the baby."

"You want me to tell the driver to go to her doctor? Or her house? Are you up for some doctoring?"

She thought for a moment in silence, but finally shook her head. "No, I better not. I'm sure she's in good hands, and he ran *out* of the room with the maid, not to me to ask for help!" Her voice tightened and she realized for the first time how truly disappointed she was.

Hope murmured and squeezed her shoulder, pulling her closer. "I'm sorry, sis."

"Well, I don't know what I expected! For the future mayor to lunge forward, part the crowd, and lift me valiantly into his arms?" She ended on a sharp, empty laugh.

"Actually, that's likely just what he would have done, and was fixing to do, before that maid came in," Hope mused. "So it must have been something awfully serious."

Bailey shrugged miserably and made an effort to brighten her expression. "Look, it doesn't matter. I don't even know why I brought it up. Nothing has changed; it never does! He's going to marry her, and Hope, I think I need to move to Pennsylvania with you! And after a few months, you and I will need to go abroad—somewhere remote—we'll be undercover for awhile, okay?"

Hope's eyes were as round as saucers and lit with excitement. "Damn straight," she breathed. "But why? Are we going to be spies?"

Bailey giggled. "No, not exactly. But Jacob already promised to search the ends of the earth if I tried to run away, so we have to hide ourselves well."

Hope continued to stare at her sister, finally shaking her head and smiling ruefully. "Oh, Bailey, you are fated to be with him, silly girl. You might as well stay put in the city and save yourself the time and trouble trying to get away."

Howard instructed the driver to let him off in front of the Menger and circle back around in ten minutes, and ten minutes later they picked him up again along with two trunks and several bags. "I checked us out," he explained as he was met with a flurry of questions from Hope. "Those damned newspapermen are everywhere! Look there! They're following us still!" He gestured, irritated, to the line of rigs following them through the city. One of the men was hanging off the side of his wagon, trying to get a photograph.

"Where are we going, Howard?" asked Cordelia gently. "We can't drive around all day."

"We have to lose them!" announced Hope excitedly.

Her uncle grimaced. "Easier said than done, I'm afraid."

"I have a plan!" Hope was bouncing in her seat with excitement. "I chummed up to a girl at the Menger this last week, you know that lovely thing, Patricia Brownleigh; the one with the soft brown hair and just a little on the chubby side? She told me all about a dress shop she and a few of her friends have opened up, much to their parents' horror. It's on Lamar, right on the north corner. Three Peas in a Pod, it's called, because her friends' names are Penelope and Pricilla! Isn't that hilarious?"

They all stared at her for a moment, trying to catch up. "So your plan is to go shopping, dear?" Cordelia finally asked.

"No. Yes. We all go in and leave the cabriolet outside. And once we're in, we'll switch clothes with the girls, and if there's a man in there we'll get him to play you, Howie, or one of the taller girls can. And they all come out as us and drive away in the cab, the press following them. Then we can sneak out back and use one of their rigs to go wherever we want!"

There was a brief moment of silence. Bailey felt another jag of laughter building within her. "Darling, that is a—well, that's an ambitious plan," murmured Cordelia with a smile on her face.

"That's crazy," Howard elaborated. "That's what Cordy means. That's just crazy."

"You got any better ideas?" grumbled Hope, gesturing behind them. Bailey peered through the window behind them and groaned.

"There's at least six rigs following us now," she reported, struggling to keep her voice light and unconcerned. Truth be told, the newsmen terrified her. Now that the trial was over, they would be focusing on one thing: her relationship with Jacob. *When did you meet him? Did anything happen when you were kids? You spent a lot of time alone together, is that right? How did you become reacquainted? He's engaged to Caroline Vogler but he seems awfully interested in your wellbeing. How do you explain that?* Nothing about her time with Jacob riding the range and doctoring the Hill Country folks had been explored in the trial: nothing about her time at the Naplava ranch during the quarantine. They had been extraordinarily lucky, but she understood the tenacity of these newsmen: she was truly flabbergasted at how effortlessly they seemed to root out information. Anyone at that barn dance could provide a story about the two of them dancing or riding unchaperoned for days on end; perhaps a *pastore* looking to make a few bucks or a jealous girl who had been rejected by Jacob at some point. *Anyone.*

"I like your idea," she announced suddenly, turning to Hope. "Let's do it. I can't talk to the press. *I can't.*"

Something in her tone convinced Howard to direct the driver to Three Peas in a Pod, and in a few moments they were all disembarking from the cab and making their way inside the spacious, well-appointed store. Patricia squealed when she saw Hope, and after a flurry of whispers, Patricia locked the door and pulled the shades down, effectively stymying the newsmen who had just about reached the entrance. They knocked on the door furiously for several minutes, even going so far as to bang on the big display windows with enough force that Bailey was sure they would shatter.

"Come in back, everybody," Patricia announced. She pointed at a young gentlemen who was seated behind the counter, sorting through boxes of bows. "You too, Kent. I need you for a role."

Kent leaped up and clapped his hands enthusiastically. "Oh, that's fine! That's grand! Finally, some work in drama!" The girls giggled.

Kent and Howard disappeared into one room and the girls in another. In a few moments the clothing change was complete.

"I can't thank you enough," Hope exclaimed, hugging Patricia, who was now clothed in Hope's expensive blue silk. "I'll send a boy back with your carriage to exchange our clothing later today as soon we're settled. Is that agreeable?"

"Of course! Keep the rig as long as you need it, though. We can send Sammy for a cab later on—he's our runner."

Bailey thanked Penelope for her dress, which was a rather ugly gingham and much too large. She looked wistfully at her own beautiful tea gown, which was stretched across the curvier girl's much more generous bust. Fortunately, the girl's hair was copper; a different shade than Bailey's, but she had hastily arranged it to look similar enough. If Patricia, Penelope, Pricilla and Kent ran at a dead sprint to the waiting cab with newspapers over their heads, the pack of vicious hounds would be utterly fooled.

And that is just what happened: the girls and Kent ran out, boarded the cab, and drove away at a breakneck speed, followed by every single one of the newsmen.

Just a half an hour later they found themselves safely ensconced at Patricia's aunt's beautiful Spanish-style home which sat right on the San Antonio River, a lovely hacienda with a maze of charming courtyards and gardens. After a few seconds chatting with the charismatic Hope, the gracious woman welcomed them inside with delight. "To think of it! I'm housing The Red Rose!" she kept proclaiming until Bailey's face matched the embarrassing sobriquet. They were seated for tea and Bailey was peppered with questions for the next hour, until she finally excused herself with an excuse of fatigue and made her way to the room she would share with her sister.

She sank into the window seat and pressed her nose against the glass, longing for Jake; always, for Jake. He would never find her here, of course. But then again, he wasn't looking for her, was he? He was tending to his fiancé, to the mother of his unborn child. The peach tree outside her window blurred, and she bowed her head and gave into the grief, just this one last time.

By half past six the restlessness had almost driven her completely batty. She had thought she would be exhausted and would perhaps lie down for the night after the early dinner of delicious salmon, but she was so keyed up she could not sit still. She finally excused herself from the parlor and pulled Hope with her as the older ladies sat chatting about drapery fabric.

"Hope! I can't stand it for moment longer! I have to get out of here!" she hissed, making her way through the foyer.

"You're leaving? You can't leave! What about the press? Can I come with you?" They looked at each other and giggled.

"We're too much alike," Bailey said, bumping Hope off-balance with a friendly nudge. "That was a test; you were supposed to talk me out of it!"

Hope shrugged. "You should go if you need to some time alone. Or I could go with you."

Bailey sighed and slipped through the front door, heading for the stable. "I want to visit my clinic. I miss it so much, Hope! I doubt anyone's there now, but I just want to see it again, you know what I mean? It's been so long since I've laid eyes on it! I want to get my hands on my patients' files and see how they've been doing."

"Hasn't your—what is Karl, anyway, your uncle?"

"You could say that. My dad was adopted, but yes, they were brothers."

"Hasn't he been updating you?"

Bailey shook her head. "He's only visited me once, but it's not his fault: Gabby said he's been incredibly busy."

They arrived at the stable and Hope gave her a little push. "Go. I'll tell Cordy and Howard you went out for a little drive to clear your head. They'll be worried sick, but they'll get over it. Nobody'll be looking for you dressed like that driving a rig; or better yet, riding a horse. And sister, you're not fooling me, by the way. I know why you're going out; how will Jacob find you hidden away here?"

"That is *not* why I want to go!" Bailey blurted indignantly, her face flaming as usual. "He won't be looking for me anyway."

Hope ignored the outburst. "Better take a horse. Those little shitty newsmen won't be looking for a woman on a horse. And here; take my hat. Tuck that hair up into it. That red hair is a dead giveaway."

Bailey stared at the stable doubtfully. "I'm not a pretty rider."

"What? A Texan who can't sit her horse? That's a disgrace!"

They bantered for a few more minutes until the stable boy

had the horse ready to go, and then Hope gave Bailey a leg up. "Be home in a few hours, okay? By dark, you promise?"

"I promise, Mom." Bailey smiled, but the grin died on her lips as an image of Adele rose before them both.

"She'd be so proud of you. She *is* proud of you, I'm sure of it," Hope murmured.

Bailey leaned down to squeeze her sister's hand. "I'm so happy you're in my life."

Hope brushed a rare tear away. "Get out of here," she growled, and slapped the horse's rump.

The ride across town was uneventful: Bailey blended right into the busy city streets, congested with vendors, farmers, soldiers, and travelers. To ride in the open air with the sun on her face was invigorating! She almost gave in to an urge to go to San Pedro Springs Park to kick off her shoes and dunk her feet in the cool water, but in the end her desire to be back in her clinic won out.

She tied her horse out front and found the door unlocked, thankfully, realizing tardily that the clinic key was not on a chain around her neck, and had not been since before the quarantine. How she had missed the routine! The bell rang cheerfully and startled the sweet older woman sitting in her usual spot.

"Rachel!" shouted Bailey, and the two of them clung together for several long seconds.

"I heard they finally let you go," quavered Rachel, wiping tears away. "It was awful, just awful, what they did to you. Why, it's all over the papers how brave you were when you were nothing but a little girl. I hope you know everyone thinks you're a hero!"

"Thank you, Rachel," Bailey said shyly. "I was no hero. But it's so good to be home! This is home for me, you know! This is the first place I wanted to come!"

"Don't I know it, girlie. I've kept it nice for you, just like you like it. Dr. Schwartz is a kind man, but your girls miss you, doc.

When will you come back to work? You'll need some time, I suppose, to rest. You deserve it!"

Bailey didn't have the heart to tell her she was leaving for good, and the prospect of it made her breath catch in her throat. Leaving this clinic and the women and children she had dedicated her life to would be one of the most difficult things she had done in her life.

They chatted for a few more moments, then Rachel shooed her away. "I know you're dying to look through the charts, aren't you? Here, take these first." She turned and grabbed a huge stack of file folders and plopped them in Bailey's arms. "I've got these all nice and organized for you. Dr. Schwartz is a gem, but he's so sloppy about keeping the charts. I'm going to finish up the rest now; I wanted to get them done before you came back."

"Oh, Rachel! You don't have to stay late to do that!"

"Yes, I do! I want to! I care about these women too, you know! And Gerald's coming to fetch me at eight o'clock; I just got here a few moments ago, as a matter of fact. So you go ahead back to your office and get started."

"Thank you, so much, for everything."

Rachel waved her hand. "Oh, go on," she muttered. I'll pass the files through our peek-a-boo window as I get them done. My hip is acting up today or I'd walk them back."

Bailey meandered to the back, pausing to stroke the exam table, to touch the vials of medicine and rolls of bandages. She spent a few moments cleaning with her beloved carbolic acid for the sheer joy of it. She settled herself in her office to read through files, but found the space confining and too quiet, so she moved back into the exam room and spread out the files on the counter, calling questions to Rachel. She soon was absorbed in her work, so much so that her ever-present thoughts of Jacob were pushed momentarily to the side as she delved into the records. She discovered with a sharp pang that two of her patients had died since she'd been in jail: one from advanced cancer of the breast and the other quite suddenly from multiple stab wounds. That poor young woman had worked in a cathouse and occasionally on the street; no doubt her pimp had found out about her side jobs and used her as an example to his other girls. She found what she was sure were three misdiagnoses: not through any outright negligence on the part of Dr. Schwartz, but she had a gift for internal medicine and had learned to follow her gut. She made careful notes on the charts to re-examine these patients at the first opportunity. She mused over the multiple referrals to Harding House and wondered how many women were living there now. Perhaps she could stay just long enough to get the program she and Jacob had discussed off the ground in order to ensure city funding for the clinic. Karl was a fine doctor, but she wasn't sure she could see him in the role of reformist! Why, she couldn't leave just yet, could she?

She stopped for a moment and closed her eyes, letting her mind wander where it inevitably did whenever she wasn't keeping it fully occupied. Jacob. He would be looking for her: he might be seeking her out right now! What would she say, what would she *do* when she saw him? Would she be able to be his friend? Would he be able to suppress his feelings? It seemed impossible after what had been said between them. *We'll find a way;* that was his conviction now, but she knew there was no way to be found. The sacrifice would be hers to make: would she stay here and be his mistress? Is that the life she wanted for herself, for him? He would grow to resent her; if not her, then the situation. She had been over it all a hundred times before, and she suddenly found herself unwilling to think about it one moment more.

She would leave for Philadelphia at the first opportunity; she would vanish shortly after that, Hope in tow, ready for a wild adventure. An adventure of escape, of trying to forget that which could never be forgotten. It was a deeply-flawed plan, but it was the only plan she had, and she'd stick to it.

Her ruminations were suddenly interrupted by the jangling of the front door. "We're closed right now," she heard Rachel say sweetly, and then, "Oh! I beg your pardon, sir!"

Bailey's heart leapt into her throat; her face was instantly aflame. He had come! He had found her! She whipped around and launched herself through the exam room door and into the waiting area in five seconds flat.

There stood Wenzel Naplava, an impossibly large bouquet of bluebonnets in one hand and an envelope in the other. There was a delighted smile on his face, and his normally-placid eyes were snapping with excitement. "I found you!" he announced triumphantly. "And at the first place I looked!"

"Wenzel!" she cried gladly, and hugged him tightly, hiding the fact that she was somewhat deflated. His arms came around her awkwardly, his hands full of flowers.

"Hi, Bailey." He stepped back and beamed at her. He opened his mouth to speak but found that he needed a few more seconds to think, and she let him have it, grinning in return. "Jacob wrote a letter," he finally got out, much to his relief. He thrust the envelope at her. "And these are from him, too."

Bailey's disappointment evaporated and she accepted the flowers and envelope with shaking hands. "Thank you, Wenzel. But where *is* Jacob?"

Wenzel gazed at her for a few seconds and then finally spoke, drawing a deep breath. "He's hunting down Caroline. She's bad, Bailey."

Bailey stared at him, the blood draining from her face. "What? What do you mean? Is she doing badly? Is she ill? Is the baby okay?"

Wenzel shook his head, unable to process the words necessary to explain the bizarre situation. "Read the note. I have to go back to Anton's now, but tell me where you're staying, Bailey, in case Jacob comes back tonight."

She stood rooted to the spot, confused, and then turned to Rachel, who was already holding out a paper and a fountain pen. Bailey scribbled the address and handed it to Wenzel, who was smiling again. "It'll be all right," he reassured her with a pat, and then turned and ambled back out again without another word.

Bailey, her dark eyes huge and haunted, stared after him, wanting to ask a thousand questions but sensing that Wenzel was ill-equipped to explain. She turned back to Rachel. "I wonder what he meant, 'Caroline is bad'?" she whispered.

Rachel cleared her throat, realizing that she had overheard some very sensitive, personal information. "Dr. Rose, why don't you go on back to your office for some privacy?" she suggested gently.

Bailey nodded dumbly and stumbled back to the exam room, pausing to tenderly lay the flowers on the counter before she went to her office, closed the door, and opened the envelope with shaking hands.

A moment later the letter fell to the floor and Bailey very nearly followed it. She lowered herself into her chair carefully, as though any jarring motion would cause her to shatter. The world had shifted. Everything, *everything* was different, in just an instant; in the five seconds it had taken her to read his note. She found to her dismay that she felt numb, so she picked up the letter again and read it aloud, her voice tremulous. She read it again. And again. And finally began to feel the shock dissolve.

She'll be leaving the city forever...she's not pregnant...it was all a lie...we'll be together forever...I love you more than anything...Wait for me...

Her breath came in short gasps, and it wasn't until she reached up to touch her face that she realized her cheeks were wet. The laughter began as a whimper—a strangled sound in the back of her throat—and then it began to build and build and build. She sank to the floor on her knees, laughing, sobbing, praying, giving thanks to God, her mind a tangle of confusion. Why had Jacob left with the maid? Had it been a ruse? How did he find out about Caroline? And what did he mean, she would be leaving, forever? God in Heaven! Was he going to kill her? She took a deep breath and ordered herself to pull it together. She had to get to him!

She stood and mopped her face and nose, giving her ugly calico dress a few firm yanks and sternly ordering herself to think clearly. Think, dammit! Where would he be? Caroline's house? It seemed too simple, but it was a place to start. She could make it there in twenty minutes on horseback.

"Rachel! I'm about to leave," she called as she scurried into the exam room and began to put files away.

"Okay, dearie. I'll be finished in a bit," the older woman said kindly.

Bailey paused as her eye caught on the beautiful bluebonnets. What better way for him to send his love to her? She should put them in water, and they'd be here waiting for her. For her and Jake. She allowed herself to think of that, just one quick glance into an impossibly blissful future of *them*. And so it was with an ecstatic smile on her face that she found an empty pitcher and headed out the back door to the pump.

She didn't notice until she had pumped vigorously for a minute or so. Her arm was beginning to tire and the water was just beginning to flow. She knelt down to grab the pitcher and the hair on the back of her neck rose; hot ribbons of dread took root in her skull and spiraled through her body.

Someone, something was behind her, watching. *Waiting.* Breathing with just a whisper of a growl at the end of each exhalation. She could smell it now; a suffocating scent that was wild and sour and hot and evil filled her nostrils.

She contemplated running but fear had turned her limbs to jelly. So instead she turned, straightened, and pivoted slowly until she was looking directly into the eyes that had been tracking her every movement so stealthily.

Her fingers went limp and the pitcher fell to the ground, smashing against the wooden planks beneath her feet. Shards of glass flew around her ankles, but still, she did not move. Her mouth opened to scream, to release a surge of unspeakable fear, but no sound emerged. She stood, frozen like a statue, her mouth agape, her eyes bulging in horror.

CHAPTER FOUR

It was the wolf. The wolf from her childhood, the *thing* that tracked her from the wagon at Jacob's ranch. It wanted to slaughter her those many years ago, only to be foiled by the unexpected appearance of the Naplava family in the sheep pit. And now it had come back to finish the task. She knew it just as surely as she knew her own name. There was something thick and red in its mouth coating its tongue and teeth as it opened its jaws to pant. A brown leather bundle it had gripped in its jaws fell to the ground, followed by a few more thick crimson drops. Blood. *It was blood.* Fresh blood; she could smell it, sharp and coppery. The thing's fur was as white as snow, its eyes green. Penetrating. Deliberative.

Pale green.

The beast raised on its hind legs, front legs pawing the air, and as Bailey watched aghast, it began to change. *To shift*, she thought numbly. There were no other words for it. Everything was shifting. Her eyes were riveted to its face, for that was what was morphing first: the snout seemed to sink back into the skull, followed by the jaw; the horrific canines replaced one-by-one with perfect, straight white teeth. Human teeth concealed by pretty, pouting lips. The eyes, large and feral and almond-shaped, rotated and moved closer together, shrinking and rounding out. For one horrible instant, Bailey was looking at a wolf with a woman's face: sweet, smiling lips, an adorable pert nose, soft green eyes. She felt bile rise in her throat. A horrible stench invaded her senses: fear and death, rotting animal, the vilest reek of decomposing flesh. She closed her eyes and only then noticed the squelching, sucking sounds; the panting that grew less and less until it culminated in a great feminine groan and sigh. She opened her eyes and pinched herself savagely, but no, the beast was still before her.

Smooth white skin began to spread in patches over the coarse white fur, and for the space of five seconds, a truly incomprehensible creature stood before her, dropping to all fours and staring at her, its lips curling grotesquely in a human smile: a fiend with pale white skin and the face of a woman but the powerful body of a wolf.

"No. No," Bailey whimpered, her whole body shaking and her teeth chattering. There was no way to rationalize this. Either it was happening, which it could not be, or she had lost her sanity.

She closed her eyes again, pressing her fists to them savagely, willing herself to awaken, her brain to heal.

When she dared to look again, Caroline Vogler stood before her, naked, wiping blood from her mouth. She only gave Bailey the briefest of glances before moving toward her, pushing her aside, and pumping the handle of the well vigorously. Bailey sank to the ground, all strength gone from her legs, covering her mouth in horror with two shaking hands to stop herself from screaming. Her brain seemed to be immobilized. *Caroline's a wolf. She's a wolf. She's the wolf.* The words played over and over again in her mind, her own voice screaming. What did it mean? What could this mean? Was this really happening? It occurred to her that after the trauma of the last few months—not to mention that she had undergone a life-altering shock just a few moments ago when she read that note—that perhaps she was having a psychotic break from reality. Or perhaps the note from Jacob had caused her to swoon, and she was now lying in a dead faint on the cold, clean floor, her deepest anxieties and fears playing themselves out in the worst nightmare ever.

The thing at the well—she could no longer think of it as Caroline—splashed water over its face, cleaning the last bits of blood and fur from its smooth, bare skin—and laughed a short, sharp bark. "No, my dear one, you're not dreaming, just like you weren't dreaming fifteen years ago when I followed you through that wretched sheep pit. You were wide awake then and you're wide awake now."

Bailey remained frozen as Caroline scooped water into her mouth, swished, and spit out blood, over and over, until the water ran clear.

"That's the worst part, really. I have to eat right away when I alter. I *have* to; I don't have a choice. So all of the meat and gore is still stuck in my teeth when I change back; you know what I mean?" She turned to face Bailey then, full-on, and laughed again; this time her laugh was charming and girlish, as though they were having tea together on the terrace. Bailey stared at her still, clutching her hands over her mouth. The young woman in front of her was completely nude, her skin shining white in the sunlight, lovely and glowing. Some part of Bailey's brain registered the fact that Caroline was much heavier than she remembered her: had she gained weight on purpose so she would look pregnant? Yes, of course that must be it. Her white hair hung in a straight sheet to the middle of her back, flecks of bramble and leaves caught here and there.

Caroline regarded her silently for a moment. "Yes, I know," she finally sighed, wry humor in her strange, pistachio-colored eyes. "I'm a whale at the moment. Not to worry, though: the weight will slide right off now that I don't have to eat five times as much as I want."

Bailey lowered her hands and ordered herself to stand. She rose to her feet cautiously, still in shock, her brain still resisting what her eyes had reported to be true. She tried to control her breathing enough to speak.

"What do you want?" she finally managed, her voice tremulous despite her efforts to make it strong. That's not exactly what she had wanted to say. She wanted to say, *what are you? How can this be happening? How can you be a wolf? Am I dreaming? Did I die somehow?*

Caroline laughed again; the sound was a pick stabbing at ice. "No questions quite yet, Dr. Rose. First, I think I'll dress. Don't you think that would be appropriate?" She turned and picked up the leather bundle she had dropped, and it occurred to Bailey that she should run; that she was in incomprehensible danger. But with that same thought she understood that she wouldn't be able to escape Caroline by running, and a dreadful feeling of helplessness and impending doom began to descend, binding her feet to the ground.

Caroline dressed swiftly, pulling on underthings, dungarees, a simple cotton shirt, and boots. She tied up her long hair with a string and stuffed it under a decrepit old beret. She turned to Bailey again, and she looked like a short, sweet, chubby boy.

In her hand was a pistol.

She cocked it and aimed it at Bailey's head.

Well, I'm a goner. Goodbye, Jake. I love you.

Bailey closed her eyes and said her last prayer, offering herself up to her Savior.

Nothing happened.

Several seconds ticked by, and she opened her eyes, wondering if this perhaps after all *was* a dream.

Caroline stood smirking, the gun still leveled at Bailey's head. "Not yet, I won't. Get back in there, please." She waved the pistol toward the office door, and Bailey moved woodenly, her mind obeying dumbly, shock making her feet slow and clumsy. Caroline pushed her impatiently through the small office into the exam area. "I need something that will keep someone asleep for days. I have something, but I think it's too strong. I may have used too much on him already. What do you have, doc? Find something, quick." She shoved the barrel of the pistol into Bailey's back, but instead of the intended effect of spurring the girl forward, Bailey froze in her tracks.

Her hands tightened into fists and she felt adrenaline, sweet adrenaline, begin to course through her body in liberating waves.

I may have used too much on him already.

She had Jake. Caroline had Jake, and she had drugged him with something, maybe fatally. Bailey had one chance.

She spun and struck out with her arm as hard as she could, ducking as she did so to avoid a bullet in case Caroline got a shot off. The gun flew from Caroline's hand and clattered to the ground, discharging into the wall. The sound was deafening. The weapon slid across the floor and Bailey lunged for it, but her legs were snarled in the stiff calico skirt. Caroline moved easily in her trousers and retrieved the gun.

The last thing Bailey remembered was the image of Caroline raising her hand, a maniacal look in her eyes, and the butt of the pistol descending toward her head.

It only took Caroline a moment to bind Bailey's hands and fix a gag to her mouth; the exam room was chock full of every supply she could want. She perused the shelves, found a few bottles of ether and shoved them into her pockets. Those would work fine for Jacob: he would have a pleasant trip across the great United States of America on the SA&AP, fast asleep in his berth. She would care for him tenderly: she would bathe him and brush his hair, turn him so he didn't get sores, allow him to surface just long enough to give him water and food. It was all for the best, and eventually he would forget the unpleasantness and relish his life with his new bride.

She was just finishing up Bailey's gag and contemplating how best to drag her into a rig—she had seen one stabled outside and perhaps she could back it up to the rear door, if the horse would behave—when she heard a sound. It was the barest of noises; hardly more than a rustle of a paper, so slight she wasn't sure she had really heard it. Her head snapped up and her eyes darted, and for the first time she noticed a square cut out of the wall, fitted with a small wooden door with a knob. A peek-through window! Dr. Montgomery had something similar in his office for his receptionist.

And this one was open.

She let go of Bailey, who slumped to the floor, her head hitting against the tile with a sickening thud. Caroline made her way to the tiny window and peeked through. If it was Thomas Eckles, she was sunk. She'd have to kill him, and everything would be ruined. Or that Gabriella woman. She'd kill her, too, and not feel too badly about it.

But it was neither of them: it was a little old lady, shrinking in her chair, her face a mask of terror.

Caroline smiled, and after glancing to make sure Bailey was still unconscious, made her way through the adjoining door to the waiting room. "Why, hello! Who might you be?" she said brightly, deepening her voice to sound like a boy and waving her gun in greeting. The old woman gaped at it, her mouth working uselessly.

"Ah, it doesn't matter. This is your lucky day! I don't have to kill you! I don't think you know who I am, do you?"

Rachel stared at the young boy and shook her head, her body shaking from head to toe with fright.

"Well, that's good news for you. Let's just get you tied up, and if I have time, I'll come back and give you a little sweet drink to make you forget your troubles. I don't know, though: I'm running horribly low, and I have to save enough for someone else. No matter."

She pulled the woman to her feet and shoved her through the exam room door, and in a matter of moments had her tied up to a chair, her mouth taped shut.

"Now don't you go telling anybody nothin', you hear?" Caroline's voice was remarkably spot-on; she congratulated herself on sounding just exactly like her stable boy.

Rachel shook her head, her eyes shifting to Bailey and tearing up. Bailey lay lifeless on the floor.

"Don't worry, she ain't dead. Not yet!"

The boy cheerfully tipped his cap and began to drag Bailey from the room, and soon Rachel sat alone, weeping.

Wenzel was pulling into Anton's stable before he remembered the necklace. The necklace! How could he have forgotten? His mother had stopped him before he had left and tucked a pendant into his pocket. He had seen it before, of course: it was Mama's pendant: she never took it off! It was a strange, simple brown stone clutched by a silver claw. She never talked it about it, but she was never without it, and Wenzel had observed through the years how she touched it for comfort. She had shoved that very pendant in his pocket and whispered in his ear so the others couldn't hear. *Take it to her, Wenzel. Make her wear it. Tell her to wear it always, to never take it off. Promise?* The exchange had happened so quickly that he hadn't even had time to respond, and dammit, he had forgotten to give it to Bailey! He had been so excited to find her and so focused on getting back to Jacob to tell him that it had completely slipped his mind. Would he ever be able to do anything right?

He sighed and nudged the horse with his feet, clicking his tongue to tell her to back out of the stable, and she tossed her head, annoyed, resisting. She was hot and thirsty.

"Okay, girl," he said gently, sliding from her back. "Just a few minutes. Get a drink and I'll give you a good brushing." He would have taken another horse but Anton only kept three horses, and Wenzel felt he must leave the other two for the carriage in case someone needed transport this evening.

And so it was twenty minutes before he was on his way again, wondering if she would still even be there, but secure with her address in his pocket. He would find her, regardless. He rode quickly, an odd feeling beginning to build in his chest.

Something was wrong. He felt the certainty settle into his bones, like an inevitability. Something was wrong, and yet he felt a curious sense of rightness, as though he had been shown a path with a clear, bright lantern and he was following it as dictated. He spurred the horse on faster, his heart pounding.

When he arrived at the clinic the birds fairly screamed at him. *Danger! Danger! Danger!* And something about a wolf, if he was understanding them correctly, but that couldn't be, could it? He vaulted from the horse, pausing only long enough to throw the reins to the hitching post, hoping the horse would stay put. The door was unlocked and he threw it back with force, facing an empty, silent waiting room. The older lady was gone from her spot.

"Bailey! Bailey!" he shouted, lumbering for the exam room, a stone lodged in the pit of his stomach. Was she dead already? And why did that thought pop into his head? It made no sense!

He burst through the exam room and found Rachel moaning in the chair, tears making a watery path down her cheeks, surgical tape across her mouth and long bandages binding her hands and feet to the chair. He froze for an instant, staring, and then untied her gently, peeling back the tape as she winced in pain.

"He got her!" she gasped. "He took her! He knocked her out with a gun and tied her up and took her! Oh, Mr. Naplava, you have to find her!" She was gasping with panic.

Wenzel knelt before her. "Who took her?"

"I don't know! A boy!"

Wenzel stared again, his mind churning. Should he go for help? Was there time? He didn't even know where to look!

"Where did he take her, do you know?"

Rachel shook her head miserably. "No. He only said 'She ain't dead yet,' so I think he means to kill her! Oh, why? I don't understand! Maybe it was someone who didn't like the outcome of the trial? I don't know!" She gave in to a sob.

Wenzel gripped her arms. "Please. You have to tell me what he looked like. The boy."

Rachel nodded and took a few deep breaths. "He was strange. Soft. Looked like he had whitish-blond hair under his cap. Kind of plump, girly-looking, not like a criminal at all! And his eyes! They were green, like lime sherbet!"

Wenzel froze in place, his hands gripping her arms, his faded blue eyes wide with astonishment. "Like dew on new spring grass," he whispered.

Rachel nodded again. "Why, yes! That's exactly it!"

Wenzel leapt to his feet. "I know her. It wasn't a boy. I know her. I have to go get Bailey away from her. Where can I take you? I don't want to leave you here."

The frail woman shuddered. "No, don't leave me here. I think that horrible boy—or girl, or whatever it was—what if he comes back? He said he might. I don't know—" She looked around wildly, panic clouding her mind.

But there was no time for that. Wenzel bent down and picked her up easily, making for the door. "You'll have to come with me on my horse. I have to get her."

Rachel gasped and clung to him, confused and frightened. He set her on the back of the saddle, jumped on, and ordered her to hang onto his waist.

Caroline. That woman who was not quite just a woman; he had felt it, known it instinctively all this time, but had never said a word because he didn't trust himself. He didn't entirely inhabit this world—or *just* this world—and he knew people thought he was crazy. Never Jacob, but he didn't want to ruin any happiness for his brother based on a weird feeling. Now he understood the consequences of not heeding that inner dialogue that was always present, and never wrong.

"My sister's house!" Rachel suddenly called, her voice barely discernible and jumping wildly as she was jostled in the saddle. "It's just a block down this street, the next one on the left! Can you take me there? Oh, please? I don't feel so well."

Wenzel grunted a reluctant yes—surely he couldn't put this nice old lady in danger—and steered the horse down the cobblestone street, tore into the tidy yard with a white picket fence, slid from his horse and lifted her down, and mounted again, kicking his horse into action and leaving her in a cloud of dust without another word. Rachel stared after him in wonder and then sunk to the ground, her legs finally giving way, weeping into her shaking hands.

CHAPTER FIVE

The first sensation was pain. It seemed to be everywhere—a white-hot, nauseating throbbing in her entire body, controlling it, mastering it. She longed to slip back into the darkness but fought against it, trying to force her eyes open. The pain, she finally realized, was localized in her temple. *The gun. Caroline—or whatever that* thing *was—had struck her with the butt of the gun.*

She finally convinced her eyelids to part and groaned as an even sharper pain stabbed her tender head. She was looking directly into a lantern of some sort, fixed at some point above her, and she squeezed her eyes shut again, a fresh wave of nausea rolling through her. She moaned again and heard the laughter of a woman answer in return.

It was a few moments before she was able to open her eyes again, and when she did, she was acutely sorry she had gone to the trouble. Caroline stood before her. She was naked again, her pale skin glowing in the light cast by the gas lanterns.

"Don't you ever wear clothes?" Bailey croaked. She managed to look down, a thousand daggers driving themselves into her skull, and realized that Caroline had bound her to a wooden lounge chair; she was tied so tightly that her hands and feet were tingling. She was secured in a semi-reclined position, making her feel even more vulnerable.

Caroline smiled serenely. "Well. Sleeping Beauty awakens. And just in time for the show!"

"Untie me, Caroline. Or whatever you are."

Caroline frowned, flustered. "I *am* Caroline, my dear. I am a *who*, not a *what*. But I wouldn't expect you to understand that just yet. You will, in time."

"Let me *go*!" Bailey shouted, surprising herself with the volume she managed to produce. Caroline, startled, jumped to her feet, leaned down to grab a roll of thick tape she had procured from the clinic, and strode quickly to Bailey's side.

Bailey twisted her face away at just the last possible moment and let forth with a scream, but it was just the barest start of one, and Caroline silenced her with two pieces of the sticky, painful tape.

"Oh, no. You must be quiet. You must die *quietly*." Caroline clucked her tongue and shook her head reproachfully. "Let's agree not to attract attention. This show is for you alone, my dear."

Bailey glared at her, her chin thrust up defiantly. Her eyes darted, fresh shards of pain piercing her temple. Where *was* she? At last she caught sight of the edge of something glimmering and fluid: the pool, of course! Caroline had brought her to her home and tied her to one of the lounge chairs that surrounded the opulent pool. But why? It made absolutely no sense. If she meant to kill her, why not just do it at the clinic? Why go to all of this trouble?

Caroline offered no explanation; instead, she gave one last disdainful look at the disheveled girl and rose without another word, padding smoothly to the edge of the pool. She dove in and was gone from Bailey's sight.

Bailey immediately tugged at her restraints, pulling with all of her might, but to no avail. She looked around wildly; had anyone heard her yelling at Caroline? The air was utterly still, the evening calm and peaceful in this posh, out-of-the way neighborhood. No one was likely to come upon the scene, and Caroline meant to kill her, she was sure of it. She had to get out, now, while

Caroline was swimming! She thought for an instant and then began to rock from side to side as best as she could. She would try to knock the chair over and roll to the street, chair and all, to attract attention. Maybe she could even gain her balance and manage to hop. It was a ridiculous plan, but if she must die, she would do so fighting. The seconds ticked by as she rocked the chair, finally gaining enough momentum to teeter precariously on two legs, and then with the next thrust, she landed on the grass, the chair on its side. She held her breath and listened for sounds of Caroline surfacing: surely it wouldn't be much longer! She heaved her shoulders and head to the right a few more times and managed to roll the chair again: now she was face down, the chair on top of her. With her arms and legs bound, her middle sagged toward the ground, arching her back painfully. She tasted grass and her head screamed with agony. Breathing became a struggle.

Still no sound from the pool! She began the process again but was dismayed to find that it was quite impossible to move the chair from her hopeless position. She groaned in frustration and gave a sharp yank on the bindings. Her arm! She froze in surprise, then tugged again and was amazed to find that her left arm had come loose! She fumbled with the binding on her right arm, but it was tied much more tightly and she couldn't budge it. She couldn't reach the bindings on her ankles. So she pushed with all of her might against the ground with her left hand, starting with her elbow bent and then thrusting up onto her fingertips, and after five attempts was rewarded: the chair flipped to its other side with a creak.

She was facing the pool now and had to stop, her heart pounding and her muscles quivering with exhaustion and fear. *Where was Caroline?* She had been under the water for at least three or four minutes now! Had she drowned? Wild hope speared through her and she flipped the chair again, right-side-up, and again, onto its right side, and again, finding herself face-down once more. She was drenched in sweat and a dagger seemed to be jabbing itself into her temple, over and over; her free arm ached and trembled, but try as she might, she could not loosen the bindings on her right arm. She wondered briefly if she should attempt to drag herself across the yard by pulling on the grass with her free hand but dismissed that plan: her arm was too weak now. She pushed against the ground and flipped the chair once again.

She was lying on her side facing the pool again, and though she strained to see into it, she could not from her low vantage point. Caroline had now been under the water for at least ten minutes. She was certain she had not heard her surface; there was no possible way that she was alive. Bailey allowed herself a moment's reprieve as the truth washed over her. What did it all mean? Had Caroline drowned herself? Surely the woman was dangerously insane. Not a woman. A *thing*.

Maybe I'm the insane one. Maybe I'm still in that nightmare, laid out on my clinic floor, Jacob's letter in my hand.

She was jolted from her reverie with thoughts of Jacob. If this was really happening, then Jacob was in danger. Caroline had him—she was using some sort of drug on him; Bailey was sure of it. She had to get help!

And just as she braced herself for the next flip of the chair, Caroline emerged from the water.

Only it wasn't Caroline.

The thing that emerged from the water was impossibly, fantastically, dazzlingly exquisite. It was the form of a woman, retaining Caroline's features, but instead of skin there were iridescent, glistening scales. *Scales!*

Bailey gasped, the sound muffled by the tape. The scales were green, now blue, now silver, sparkling with such fierce luminosity that Bailey had to close her eyes for a brief moment. When she dared to look again, Caroline stood a mere five feet away, stock still, like a magnificent, tiny sun. Her white hair flowed down her back and her pale green eyes glowed in the deepening dusk. She was the most beautiful thing Bailey had ever seen. Bailey caught her breath as her eyes trailed to Caroline's hands and feet: there was webbed, scaled skin stretching between each finger and toe like the wings of a bat. The scientist in her marveled in awe:

Caroline was not breathing, but gills under her ear on the side of her neck were frantically working, opening and closing in vain, seeking water. As Bailey watched, the scales seemed to sink into Caroline's body, absorbed by layers of pale white skin. The gills closed, began to shrink, and disappeared altogether; the webbed skin pulled taut and then disappeared into the digits, drawing the fingers and toes closer together as if pulled by a magic string.

Caroline gasped once, pulling in a great lungful of air, her body giving a final great shudder. The transformation was complete. She stared at Bailey in her incongruous position on the ground, the chair sticking out behind her as she lay on her side like a beached whale, and Caroline's sharp, cracking laugh split the air.

"Oh, Miss Rose, the predicaments you get yourself into!" She shook her head as if laughing at the antics of a small, dumb child. "Now just let me get dressed, and I'll explain all of this to you, poor, confused, stupid girl. You must think you've lost your mind!" She waved her hand in a shooing motion. "Go on and keep rolling across my lawn, dearie, if it makes you feel useful. I'll only be a minute." She turned and began to dig in the leather bag on her lounge chair, pulling on the same boy's clothing she had worn before.

Bailey stared at her, heart pounding out of control. She knew two things for sure now. One, she was going to die, probably soon. She was utterly at Caroline's mercy at this point.

Two, Caroline was a Vodnik. *The Vodnik.* The one that had haunted her dreams from the age of twelve. It wasn't Adam Hawk, God rest his soul. It was Caroline! The woman who was to have married Jacob. *It's Caroline. Caroline. It was Caroline all along.*

Every bit of strength and ounce of determination left her body, and she lay limp on her side, staring into the glittering pool, shock rendering her numb and weak.

Caroline finished dressing and wrestled Bailey's chair back to a sitting position, noting but not bothering to re-bind the errant hand. "Miss Rose, I have a story to tell you, and then you're going to write a little something for me. Then it'll all be over, all right?"

Bailey stared at her, her eyes sliding slowly out of focus. That last flip onto her face had bloodied her nose, and it was becoming more and more difficult to draw in enough oxygen. She would be unconscious soon; the black dots were already beginning to appear around the edges of her vision.

Caroline sighed. "You know, you're no fun when you're all *compliant* like this. I think I like you better when you're fighting a bit. But never mind; we're running short of time." She dragged her own lounge chair close to Bailey's and sat back, regarding the velvety purple sky and the immense vastness of the Milky Way.

"You have already guessed by now, I'm certain. You know what I am? Well, first and foremost, I'm a woman. A female with feelings just like yours." She glared at Bailey defiantly, but Bailey's stare was glazed and empty. "I come from a proud line of people, Miss Rose. We are from Moravia, just like Jacob's parents, only my mother grew up on the Morava River. An ancient body of water, the river. I belong to the *People*. To the *Vodicini*, do you understand?"

Bailey stared, struggling to hold onto consciousness, and Caroline grunted with frustration. "We were *first*. Before the Common Folk. We have always *been*."

Still not a flicker of emotion from Bailey's face.

Caroline rolled her eyes. "I guess you must be suffocating. How anti-climactic *that* would be." She reached forward to rip the tape savagely from Bailey's mouth. Bailey gasped and sucked in sweet lungsful of air, and for several long seconds, the only sound was her effort to breathe.

"Now. If you don't want the tape back on your mouth, you will not make any loud noises, do you understand?" Somehow the pistol had reappeared, and it was pointed at Bailey's head once again. Bailey nodded, wincing in pain at the motion.

"You're a Vodnik?" she asked, her voice cracking. "They're *real*?"

Caroline looked pleased at the question. "Yes, of course we

are real! The People live still!" There was a strange mix of fierce pride and wistfulness in her voice. "There aren't many of us left; so many have inbred with the Common Folk, but there's nothing to help it. We can only love once, and we must obey that love."

Bailey's mind whirled in confusion. "How can you *be*?" she finally asked, her voice small. It was too much to take in. Surely she must be in the throes of some psychotic break from reality. This simply could not be happening.

Caroline sighed. "I don't have time for this. I just can't explain it all. Suffice it to say that the Common Folk are blinded to the Others. Every last dumb animal on earth can see the Others except the idiot Common Folk. There are many Others, not just Vodnik. I think your precious idiot friend Wenzel must know about the Others, but he'd probably never be able to explain it."

Bailey felt tingles of wonder explode in her body and opened her mouth to ask more questions. Caroline raised her hand to silence her.

"I do *not* have time!" Caroline looked nervously toward the house. "I will tell you that a few exceedingly rare Vodnik can shift to animal form, and I am blessed—or perhaps cursed—with that ability. My form is a wolf, the first of the People to take such a form. I despise it, but it has been useful, I can't deny that. And this is where you come in." She was speaking rapidly now, digging around in her rucksack as she talked, and Bailey sensed that the end was near. "I was born in the Mother country, and my parents were—*compelled*—to migrate to America with my brother and me when we were just babies. Father was—he still is—a wildly shrewd businessman, and soon we were wealthy and established right here in this cow-poke city. We came here because there were so many Moravians, and Mother hoped that I would find one to marry. She dragged us to every wedding, funeral, christening, birthday party, church event, and dance she could find. And one day we went to a barn dance—a famous Naplava barn dance, no less! That was a fateful day, Miss Rose. I met Jacob Naplava that day. We were both seven years old, and we played hide and seek in a stinky old barn. It was so perfect, just the two of us alone, for hours! And then another girl came to play with us—some poor fat trashy farm girl with scabby knees and a soiled dress. She was homely with big buck teeth and crooked eyes, and Jacob felt sorry for her." Caroline shook her head in derision. "When it was Jacob's turn to hide, the ugly thing told me that she had a crush on him and she hoped to marry him someday. So I punched her in the face and knocked one of those buck teeth right out of her head!"

Caroline paused to laugh fondly as Bailey gawked at her in horror. "I told her take it back, but she wouldn't. So I punched her again, this time in the stomach, and she threw up all over the place. Blood, vomit pouring out of her mouth; *so attractive*. So clearly not worthy of the attentions of Jacob Naplava! Oh, Miss Rose. Even at seven years old he was a killer of a handsome boy. The teenage girls at that dance fawned over him and were terribly jealous of the younger girls who had a chance." She smiled and stroked her soft cheek with the barrel of the gun while Bailey swallowed thickly, only now understanding the depths of Caroline's sickness. She had beaten that poor little girl; had she done even worse?

Caroline emerged from her reverie and snapped back to attention. "Well, wouldn't you know it, Jacob saw the whole thing. He came running from the other side of the barn, and I'll never forget what he said. It tore my heart apart. 'You're a monster, Caroline.' He said it low and mean as he ran by me to find that scummy girl; *he ran right by me!*" Her eyes had fired with anger. "Without as much as a 'We'll talk about this later' or 'I'm sure you had your reasons.'" She shook her head disbelievingly.

There was a silence. Bailey was sick with dread. How could Jacob ever have been engaged to this—woman? How could he have forgotten that horrific act in the barn?

"Later that night, I made him forget," said Caroline, seemingly reading Bailey's mind. "I slipped the Forgetting drink into his cider when he wasn't looking. I hid and watched him drink it all down, and then he just kind of fell to the ground. I overheard Mother telling Father the next week that the Naplava boy had taken ill at the dance and slept for three days, and when he woke up, he didn't remember a thing from that day. It was the perfect dose: I'm really quite talented with dosages. Too little, and they only forget a few hours. Too much, and they die. His day had just been wiped clean." She smiled again, the anger gone. "Mother had no idea I had stolen some of her potion. Works every time."

The Forgetting drink. Is that what Caroline had drugged Jacob with today? "Where is he?" Bailey croaked. "Where is Jacob? What are you going to do to him?"

"Anyway, as I told you before, a member of the People can only love once." Caroline continued her story blithely as if Bailey hadn't spoken. "Oh, we can marry and mate with whomever, but true love can only happen once in a lifetime for us. That is a flaw, I'm afraid. The one thing I envy about Common Folk is that you can love and love again, over and over, in some cases. We cannot. I fell in love with Jacob at the barn dance when we were seven years old, so I knew that someday, somehow, we would be together. I didn't see him again for years, or I should say he didn't see me. I could shift whenever I wanted and travel to see him, to watch him covertly. My favorite activity for years and years was to settle myself into the creek, right there at his favorite swimming hole—you know where it is—and watch Jacob and his brothers swim. He would bathe there, too. I could get my fill, Bailey. What a beautiful boy he was."

Bailey felt her stomach heave and thought she might disgrace herself and be sick, but forced herself to breathe slowly and keep her face passive.

"And then one day, Miss Rose, there was an interloper. It was the worst day of my life. I was only fourteen years old and I almost killed myself in my grief. It all started when my friend Marta told me that a whore's daughter had wandered into that stupid German school wearing a red silk harlot's dress, and that Jacob Naplava had jumped to her rescue in the schoolyard. Rumor had it that Jacob had hitched up his rig and left town. It didn't take me long to track him down. Imagine my dismay when I came upon a quaint little picnic. There sat Jacob, laughing and eating and consorting with *you*, a filthy, scrabbly, disgusting little *thing!*" She spit out the last word and glared at Bailey, then leveled the gun at Bailey's head again. "Just thinking about it makes me want to pull this trigger."

Bailey held her breath and forced herself to maintain eye contact. Caroline's eyes were filled with angry tears and her hand was shaking. Slowly she lowered the gun. "I followed you all the way to the ranch, and when Jacob left you in the wagon, it was my chance." She sighed and shrugged mournfully. "You know what happened next. The whole horrible revolting family came to your rescue."

There was a silence as Bailey fit the pieces of those two days together. She had been watched—stalked—by a fourteen-year-old, jealous Vodnik! It was all so ludicrous that she felt the impending hysterical laugh begin to well up and she bit her lip to keep it from escaping.

"Well, say something!" Caroline snapped. "Don't you have questions?"

Bailey blinked at her. "Not really. It was you in the creek when I was washing my hair. You pulled me in and tried to drown me."

Caroline nodded eagerly. "Yes, that's right. And I would have succeeded if you hadn't screamed for Jacob. One of the worst moments of my life, watching the two of you all wrapped up in each other, *naked*, on the banks of that river! It was enough to make me want to kill you both. But I exercised self-control; I was patient. And after that day I realized that I would never have to worry about you again; Adam Hawk took care of that for me."

Bailey sucked in her breath. "Did you have anything to do with that?"

Caroline shook her head, and her reply sounded almost tender. "No, Bailey. My God. That man was depraved. And what happened to him and your mother as children was—it's the worst thing I can imagine."

Bailey stared at her. The irony of her denunciation—her inability to recognize her own depravity—seemed to escape Caroline.

Caroline's look hardened. "But then you popped back into our lives. The day I saw you on the stage at that debate—oh, Miss Rose—I couldn't believe my eyes."

"Why didn't you just kill me then?" It was probably not a smart thing to say, but at this point, Bailey was desperate to stall. If she could keep Caroline talking long enough, maybe, just maybe, someone would happen along. She knew that anyone walking along the boardwalk would be able to hear a scream.

"With age comes wisdom. I knew that the only way I could have him was to give him what he longed for—a child."

"So you faked a pregnancy," added Bailey, noticing that Caroline's hand tightened on the gun. She would need to be very careful now.

Caroline laughed, a cold, chilling bark. "Haven't you ever wondered how I tricked him into that? He's not a stupid man, you know. I'll tell you how. I brought him to this very spot, on my birthday, and gave him the Forgetting drink. It wasn't a terribly strong dose: just enough to forget five or six hours, I'd wager. I didn't want him to become too suspicious. And the next morning I convinced him that we had made love. Oh, Miss Rose! How I tried that night to get him to make love to me. I stripped us both down; I put him in the water to revive him! It didn't matter: I convinced him the next morning that we had made love, that he was my first—what a joke; you know, I'm a very desirable woman—and a few weeks later, I told him I was pregnant. It was so easy. Everything is easy with money. Doc Montgomery was an easy payoff, and that idiot whore Honey was more than eager to sell her baby."

Bailey felt the blood drain from her face. "Honey? Honey Lane? What do you mean, 'sell her baby'?"

Caroline shrugged and yawned. "I'm getting tired of this story. That was the old plan, anyway. The new plan is so much better, because it will get me out of this hellish town and back to

Morava River where I was born, and then, when it's time, to London, where *civilized* people live. With Jacob by my side." She smirked at Bailey, waiting for a reaction.

"How would that be possible? He hates you now." She knew as soon as the words left her mouth she had made a grave mistake. Caroline's fist was swift, and Bailey's head recoiled back against the chair, her nose spouting blood anew. She gasped in pain.

"He doesn't hate me, you vile wretch," she hissed, her lips drawn back to reveal her teeth. *I wonder if she turns into a wolf when she's angry. If she does, it's all over.* "He just doesn't know me yet."

Bailey wiped blood from her nose with her free hand. "But you can't keep him drugged forever. You said yourself the Forgetting drink only works to erase memory on the day it's used."

And then the beauty of the plan struck her full force. Her mouth dropped open and her eyes widened in shock. She stared at Caroline, comprehension dawning in terrible waves, and Caroline smiled back at her, nodding.

"That's right. You know, you are a smart little thing, aren't you?" She sat back in satisfaction, the gun still leveled at Bailey's head. "I think you've got it figured out. When Jacob came to confront me a few hours ago, I shot him with a dart. It was a *curare* poison dart. Do you know what that is?"

Bailey nodded, still in a horrified trance.

"Yes, of course you do. It was a mild dose: don't worry; he's still breathing. But he can't move a muscle. He's upstairs right now, all cozy in my bed. And when he comes out of it, he'll be agonizingly thirsty, did you know that? Terrible, all-consuming thirst; it's a side effect. There's a big frosty glass of lemonade on the stand beside his bed. He won't have a choice: he'll drink it all. It'll be enough to erase the whole day."

"You put the Forgetting drink in the lemonade," Bailey whispered.

Caroline smiled and nodded. "That's right. He'll sleep for two or three days, and when he wakes, I'll put him back under.

If I run low, I borrowed some of your ether; I hope you don't mind? I need him to sleep for a long time, Miss Rose; for the duration of the rail trip to Boston and the voyage to the Old Country. Oh, I'll let him wake enough to eat and drink and move around a bit each day. But I know my potion well. He'll be like a child in my care, completely helpless and disoriented. When I let him wake for good, he'll have no memory of today, or of any of the days he was ill. It will all be a lovely blank page." She leaned forward to stroke Bailey's painful, swollen temple with the barrel of the gun. "I'll tenderly explain to him that he took ill, and while he was unconscious for two weeks, the trial concluded with your conviction and your execution. I'll make him understand that I thought it best to get him out of the country, away from the horrible pain of what had happened, so we could start life anew, with our child."

Bailey felt a coldness in the center of her chest. "He won't know that you're not pregnant."

Caroline smiled angelically. "Right you are."

"But you won't have Honey's baby."

Caroline flipped her hand dismissively. "There's always a baby to be found, Miss Rose. Money buys anything. *Anything.*"

Bailey shook her head. "Jacob's family will never let you get away with it. They all know what you did! And Jacob will want to be near them; he'll never want to stay in Moravia."

Caroline didn't seem to hear her. She began rooting around in the bag again, looking up every few seconds to make sure Bailey stayed put, still squarely in the gun's sights. "I'll let you ask one more question." The finality of the statement raised gooseflesh on Bailey's arms.

Bailey felt panic begin to rise in her throat; not so much for herself, but for Jacob. Caroline's ridiculous plan was doomed to fail, and when it did, she would probably kill Jacob, and then herself. She was crazy, or evil, or both.

"Why were you compelled to leave?" she blurted.

Caroline's head snapped up. "What did you say?"

"Why did they make you leave? The—the People?" Bailey

repeated. "You said you had to come to America; you couldn't stay in Moravia. Why not?"

Caroline's pink bow lips had hardened into a thin line and her eyes turned to ice. "Of all the questions you could ask. My, my. But I guess it won't hurt to tell you, will it?" She put the bag aside and stared into Bailey's eyes. "You won't understand most of this, and I really don't have time to explain, but there are *Vodníci* with special—skills. We can shift, you know that. There have never been many of us; we are the chosen ones, although the rest of the People don't quite see it that way. My mother is one, as was her mother. They call us the *Duśe Jedlíci*. I rather like the moniker; Mother hates it. What do you think?"

Bailey dreaded asking, but she had to keep Caroline talking. "What does it mean?"

Caroline smiled, her lips soft and pretty again. "Why, it means *Soul Eaters.*"

Bailey swallowed thickly, attempting to be as brave as possible, but found that her courage was flagging. She had her answer now. Caroline wasn't necessarily crazy, but she was evil—supernaturally evil, as it turned out.

"Why do they call you that?"

Caroline stood and pushed her chair back, stretching quickly before leveling the gun once more. "I said you had one more question. But I'll answer you. We don't really eat souls, Bailey. We collect them. In porcelain cups."

Bailey closed her eyes and prayed for strength. Really, the story could not possibly get any more bizarre.

"Don't you believe me?" Caroline persisted, chuckling. "It sounds fantastic, doesn't it? I don't have any yet. My father doesn't have any and never will; he's not a *Duśe Jedlíci*. But my mother! She has dozens! Fifty-seven, I believe. She keeps them on a shelf in her boudoir, right beside her bed. Tiny little porcelain cups, each with a lid. Each with soul trapped inside."

"How does one go about acquiring a soul?" asked Bailey, her voice heavy with skepticism. She dared not let Caroline know that she believed her, every word of it.

"Oh, you think I'm a lunatic, don't you? If Mother were here, she'd set you straight. She knows more history than I ever will." Caroline waited for a reaction but didn't get one. "One collects a soul by drowning Common Folk, Miss Rose. For my mother, it was any Common Folk that happened to go swimming or boating in her three-mile stretch of the river. She gathered her first soul when she was but a girl, eight years old. A little boy her own age, from her very own school, went swimming with her. It was all over so quickly, she said, that she barely remembers it."

There was no sound save the wind in the trees at the edge of the vast lawn.

"You might wonder how we gather souls. I would think that would be of interest to a *scientist* such as yourself?"

Bailey shook her head. "Not really," she whispered. She was sick with dread.

"Any little piece of the person will do. Most take a hair; that's the dignified thing to do. Gather a hair and put it in a cup. But any part will do. Mother took a finger once from a fine society lady; it had a ruby ring on it. And I believe she has an eyeball from a particularly handsome fellow she gathered. A pretty golden eye."

"Stop it," choked Bailey, squeezing her eyes shut. *A golden eye. Gacenka had said her handsome father may have drowned in the Morava River. Oh, no. Please, don't let it be.*

Caroline giggled, delighted. "Oh, once you put them in the cup they dissolve in a cloud of green smoke. Not smoke, really; I'm actually not sure what it is. It's fascinating, really. It looks like there's nothing in the cups, but the souls are in there, all right. Then you just put the lid on and store them away. The more you gather, the higher your status. That's all they are for, really. I personally think it's a little ridiculous, but my mother and grandmother—oh, they lived by it. The *Duše Jedlíci* are supposed to hate the Common Folk, so that's reason enough, but I've never hated them, at least not all of them. Just you, actually, and I almost gathered your soul, didn't I? It was so close, and I already had a handful of your ugly red hair after pulling you into that river." She shook her head regretfully. "Oh, but Mother! Mother was one of the most highly-regarded *Duše Jedlíci,* but only by others of our own kind. The rest of the People just don't understand us. And that is why we were forced to go. We were one of the last, actually; I know of three, maybe four other families, and they've probably been disposed of. We got out just in time. A damn shame."

"And you're going back to that? Aren't you afraid?"

Caroline shook her head. "We'll make our own way. It's been twenty-five years since we've been home, and the Morava is hundreds of miles long, with many hidden banks. We'll do just fine. And I don't intend to stay there for long! Jacob and I will move to London, of course, once the baby is a bit older, and he'll begin his political life anew."

Yes, she was evil. But she was completely delusional, too. A horrible combination, really.

Bailey's mind worked furiously. Her only hope now was to distract Caroline long enough to lunge for the gun. She opened her mouth to ask another question, but Caroline held up her hand, and Bailey flinched, expecting another blow. Caroline laughed.

"No more questions. I have a job for you now. You're going to write a little note."

"A note?" asked Bailey desperately. *Stall. Stall!*

Caroline nodded, pulling a parchment and quill from her bag. "Yes, that's right. Every suicide deserves a proper note, don't you agree?"

Bailey found that her mouth had gone too dry to respond.

"Now, if you don't mind, I'd like your note to state that you could not continue to live a lie: that you did live a life as a prostitute, that Thomas Eckles was your true love, and you cannot bear to live now that he has chosen another."

Bailey was so startled that she let out a snort of a laugh. "What? Nobody's going to believe that, Caroline."

Caroline glared at her. "Well, write something. I don't care what you write. Just make it sound convincing."

"And why would I bother to do that?"

Caroline backed up a step and pointed the gun at Bailey' head. "Because I'll start killing your friends if you don't. I'll start with Eckles, that sanctimonious bastard. Then I'll move on to the Mexican Pearl, because she won't want to live without him, will she?"

Bailey stared at her, horror clotting her throat. "You wouldn't do that."

"I will."

"But you have to leave. You won't have time."

"I'll make time. You see, I don't want your blood on my hands. I don't want my name involved in any way. A note will take care of that for me, won't it? Why don't you just write the truth? You can't bear to live without your precious Jacob. Everyone will believe that."

Bailey flushed, a wave of anger washing the fear from her body. "I won't do it."

"Who do you want to die first? Eckles or his whore? I'll go do it right now, and bring back a piece of him—or her—to prove it. They'll be sitting on their porch right about now. A wolf is a very stealthy creature, Miss Rose. I can jump on him from behind and puncture his jugular before he knows what is happening. He'll be dead in less than a minute. Here—let me just tie you back up and tape your mouth, and then I'll run upstairs and make sure a certain person is—indisposed—and I'll be back in less than half an hour. Then we'll finish up with you and I'll still make the train. Did I mention I hired a man to come move a very heavy trunk this evening? Guess who will be in that trunk? That's right; it will be lover boy's mode of transportation to the train station, but don't worry, I'll unpack him when we're locked in the berth and take *very* good care of him."

She was talking so quickly that Bailey barely had time to react. Caroline was a step away from her, brandishing the tape, before she was able to bark out a response.

"No!" It was louder than she anticipated, and Caroline gasped and shushed her angrily.

"Please—don't. I'll write it. Give me the paper." Bailey thrust out her hand, angry tears coursing down her cheeks.

"Ah. How sweet. How very loyal of you." Caroline smiled and handed over the parchment and fountain pen.

Bailey sank her head into her hands, desperately stalling for time while she tried to think. Think! What could she write that would lead a trail to Caroline? How could she save Jacob, even if she herself was dead? *God, please. Tell me what to write.*

"Hurry up," Caroline hissed. "And make it convincing!"

Bailey thought for a moment longer and then finally began to write, certain that Caroline would see through the thinly-disguised code. She carefully drew a circle around the 8, hoping beyond hope that Caroline wouldn't question it.

8pm
I have come to realize Jacob and Caroline belong together. I know it now definitely is time for me to let him go. A pain lies upon my grieving, weak, shattered soul. I do not want to become a thief of hearts, so I shall depart. I took my own life so my love, my Jacob, can raise his baby and rightfully grow old with the love of his life. This country will be better for it.

Caroline watched her, frowning, tapping her fingers impatiently against the barrel of the gun. Bailey wrote as slowly as she could, certain that once she handed the letter over, Caroline would shoot her dead.

At last she could stall no longer. She signed the letter and Caroline snatched it from her hand, reading it quickly. "Well, you're not much of a writer, are you? But I must say, it sounds all right, Miss Rose. I like the last little part about this country being the better for it; you're referring to his political career, I'm assuming?"

Bailey nodded cautiously.

"Shame that he will never be a senator here—but he will rise in the ranks in Europe, or perhaps in England; we shall see." She paused for a moment, imagining herself on the arm of a handsome, powerful politician, taking audience with the queen, and she shivered with delight. She folded the letter and set it up like a little tent on one of the nearby lounge tables, dug in her satchel and turned back to Bailey, several lengths of rope in her hands. She grabbed Bailey's free arm and tied it securely to the other arm, then cut the binding from the chair, warning her in low tones that if Bailey screamed or struggled, her friends would pay dearly. Then she bound her legs together and cut her away from the chair altogether, pushing her roughly to the ground. Bailey was gratified to be freed from the chair but quickly realized that she was no better off.

"What now?" asked Bailey, struggling to keep the fear from her voice. This was it. She was going to die. Her only option was to scream; she couldn't move or fight at all. She was on her back with her hands and feet bound, utterly vulnerable.

"Now? Well now I kill you, of course!" Caroline smiled brightly, waving the gun.

"Are you going to shoot me?" *Keep her talking as long as you can.*

Caroline shook her head. "No, it's too noisy. And besides, as a *Duśe Jedlíci,* I need to gather a soul, Miss Rose. At least one soul or I will die young, and I'm only going to be 'young' for a few more years, let's not kid ourselves."

Bailey frowned at her. "That doesn't even make sense, Caroline. Why would you die if you don't gather a soul? Do you think the souls give you some kind of life energy or something? You're an intelligent woman. You can't believe that!"

"I don't believe *that!*" She shook her head disgustedly at Bailey's blank look. "Look, it's just something we have to do. It's our destiny. That's it."

"But how would you die if you didn't gather a soul?"

"Because they'll come for me!" Caroline was agitated now, punching the air with the pistol, which was still aimed at Bailey's head. "They visit me all the time. I almost didn't make it out alive today."

Bailey gaped at her, completely confused.

"The Black!" Caroline sighed, exasperated. "The Black has been coming since I was young. Every time it gets worse."

"What do you mean, 'the Black'?" Bailey's voice was trained and soothing, and she was relieved to see Caroline lower the gun and take a deep breath.

"Ever since I was a child, really. I have these black times, where my mind kind of just—it clouds over in a big, black fog. It's cold and horrible and it tells me to hurry up and gather, or to do bad things to myself. It's *them*. They are warning me to make haste." Caroline suddenly sounded more like a scared young girl than a deranged young woman.

Bailey swallowed thickly and tried to think of a reply. There was no doubt about what she had seen today: Caroline had transformed twice right in front of her eyes. Either Bailey herself was suffering from an extended hallucination—she was hanging onto this possibility with a certain brand of desperate hope—or this world contained wild inscrutabilities that she could not possibly have ever imagined, something that Wenzel had actually taught her years ago. But here was something rational to latch onto—maybe. Caroline seemed to be suffering from delusions, perhaps a form of *dementia praecox* that she had read about recently in a textbook written by a German asylum doctor Heinrich Schüle. This would make sense with the timeline, since this kind of psychosis seemed to manifest in childhood. No matter what "the Black" was, it had to be some kind of a psychotic break from reality. *Just like the one I'm having now*, Bailey thought wildly. She could at least try to engage her about it.

"I've studied this, Caroline. It's quite common; lots of young people have these episodes. There are ways to treat it."

Caroline snorted. "I'm not sick. It's not a *disease*. There's nothing in your medical books for this, Dr. Rose!" It was the first time she had referred to Bailey as a doctor. "It's just who I am."

"But I can help you." Bailey's voice was calm, entreating, and she put every bit of caring she could into her expression.

Caroline jerked back, her demeanor suddenly shifting into one of angry derisiveness, and Bailey realized she had made a dreadful misstep.

"Oh yes, you will help me! One gathering, *just one gathering*, and the Black will go away forever. They already told me so. Just one will suffice, then I can be done with it. I have the cup right here in my bag." She knelt without taking her eyes from Bailey and fumbled around in the satchel until her fingers brushed against a smooth edge. She drew it out and brandished it at Bailey: a small, white porcelain cup, no larger than the teacups in Gacenka's corner cupboard, and similar in design. On top was a latched lid which opened with a press of the thumb and shut again when released, like a teapot lid. "You are so superior, aren't you? 'I can help you.' I don't want to be helped! I'm on the brink of having everything I want! I have more power and—and *majesty* than you could ever dream of in your pitiable Common state. All I need to make myself complete is your soul for my cup. I promise I'll look after it my whole life long. Do you know what that means? You will be trapped, Miss Rose. Unable to cross. But I might release you before I die, who knows?" She laughed a mirthless laugh, a sound full of rage and loathing. "When I am old and gray, Jacob and I shall take tea in the garden, and I shall open this cup and release your soul—it will just be my little secret; he won't know a thing—and then I shall pour a spot of raspberry tea and let Jacob drink the dregs of you."

Bailey closed her eyes, imagining it against her will; her young spirit, freed after sixty years in cold, dark, claustrophobic loneliness, hovering over a shriveled old man with faded blue eyes who was drinking, unaware, from the hellish receptacle that had imprisoned her.

Caroline rummaged quietly in her bag and then stood with the roll of tape: Bailey opened her eyes one second too late and was only able to let forth with one short, piercing scream before Caroline managed to silence her. And then Caroline bent down and began to drag Bailey along the ground by her hair.

Toward the pool.

CHAPTER SIX

Wenzel's mind was spinning in a panicked upheaval. In the very best of circumstances, this world moved much too quickly and could only be perceived through the senses in a very elementary manner. The veil was *always* drawn here; he had tried to explain it once to Jacob, and he thought Jacob almost understood, but it wasn't really something that could be explained with words. That was the whole problem. Language forced reality to a very limited construct here in this world. That was why his most authentic moments had been spent with babies, who still possessed *the sight* for that precious short window of time, and animals, and of course, the trees. In the worst circumstances, he could barely function here at all.

And this was one of those times.

He finally gave up trying to reason his way through it and just whittled it down to three imperatives: Caroline was bad. Bailey was in danger. Go to Caroline's. It really didn't make much sense at all to go to Caroline's, he suspected, in the logical order of things. But something had flashed into his mind as he had been sprinting through the clinic with that poor old lady slung over his shoulder. The Vogler Pool. He had heard about it from Caroline herself. She had bragged about it on more than one occasion, inviting the entire family to come for a swim with that tone in her voice that meant "Please don't come." And when the pool flashed into his mind, it was like a piece of a jigsaw puzzle slid into place. He never forgot anything, and he had remembered Bailey's encounter with a bad thing in the water when they were young all of those years ago. He had sat by her on the bank of Glory Creek, protecting her, vowing to protect her always. And now Caroline had come to get her, to kill her. Caroline with the pool. Caroline with the pale green Other eyes. She was not Common; he knew it beyond a shadow of a doubt, from the moment he laid eyes on her.

So running pell-mell to Caroline's house might make a bit of sense after all. He urged his horse forward, feeling the stallion's muscles gather and release in a burst of speed, and when they finally reached their destination, Wenzel once again vaulted from the poor beast while it was still attempting to reign in, not bothering to tie him, and tore toward the front door of the stately mansion. He noticed with a jolt that the front door was ajar and the house was dark; his stomach lurched.

"Bailey! Bailey!" He shouted, moving from room to room in a panic. How could the entire house be empty? And yet it was. He mounted the stairs and scoured the second floor, frantic, shouting her name. He must protect her for Jacob. He galloped down the hallways, pausing to pop his head into each room, his wide, frightened eyes darting for a glimpse of red hair. And that was how he almost missed him.

His brain didn't quite register the dark head until he had already passed by the last room on the right of the long hall and given it a quick scan. He had already backpedaled out of the room and turned to begin exploring the rooms on the north side of the hallway when he stopped stock-still, his whole body freezing, struggling to catch up to the message his brain was sending.

Jacob had been lying in that bed. Jacob!

Fear and confusion spiraled through him. Jacob. What was he doing here? What could it mean that he been stretched out in that bed? And his eyes! His eyes had been open, staring at Wenzel, but yet he hadn't called out!

Wenzel bent forward and clutched his head in his hands. It was too much, this world. He really didn't belong here, he knew. And yet he had something to do before he left; he was sure of it. That certainty propelled him forward, and he spun and bolted back to the room where he was sure he had seen his brother.

And there he was, now propped up weakly on his elbow, his mouth open in a silent plea, his eyes flashing.

"Jacob!" Wenzel managed in a hoarse cry. He reached his brother's side and pulled him into his arms. "What's wrong?"

Jacob shook his head and made a frantic gesture to his throat, then opened his mouth, indicating thirst. Wenzel looked around wildly and spotted a large pitcher of lemonade on the stand beside the bed, a glass beside it. He turned to pour it but Jacob clutched his arm and shook his head.

"No," he managed to croak. "She put it there. Find water." He seemed to lose strength and his hand went limp; he fell back onto his pillow and closed his eyes, his face twisting with pain.

Wenzel nodded numbly and rose again, running through the hallway to the water closet he had spied earlier at the end of the corridor. It was a small, tastefully decorated room with a toilet and a sink with a faucet: of course, they would have indoor plumbing in a place like this! A glass, a glass! Oh, why hadn't he thought to bring the one by the bed? But no, it might be poisoned, if he had understood Jacob correctly. He backtracked to an enormous, opulent bedroom—it must belong to Mr. and Mrs. Vogler—and grabbed a vase of fresh flowers from a table, dumping them unceremoniously onto the floor, water and all. He filled the pitcher with cool, clear water from the tap and bolted back down the hallway to Jacob's side.

Jacob drank and drank until the entire large vase was empty, Wenzel watching in an agony of worry and confusion. His brother finally handed the vase back to him, his hand shaking terribly.

"What happened, Jacob?" Wenzel ventured, his voice trembling.

Jacob cleared his throat and sat up straighter. "Caroline. She shot me with something, Wen." He paused to rest before he went on. "I couldn't move at all for the longest time. I really couldn't breathe at first, either, for the first few minutes. Now I can move my head and arms."

Wenzel stared at him, horrified. "Are you paralyzed?" he whispered.

Jacob shrugged. "Yes. I don't know! The feeling is coming back; my legs are starting to tingle now; I can feel them, but I can't move them."

They gaped at each other, trying to come to terms with what had happened.

"You've got to get me out of here before she comes back," Jacob whispered.

And then Wenzel remembered.

"Bailey!" he breathed.

Jacob's eyes pierced him with a renewed fire. "What? What do you mean? What about Bailey?"

"She has her. Caroline has her." And Wenzel told him, in his halting speech, about what Rachel had seen. "And Jacob, I think Caroline may be a Vodnik," he added, his voice thick with dread. "A shifter, even. A bad one."

Jacob shook his head. "I don't know what that means, Wen. What's a shifter?"

Wenzel was terrified that they would be ambushed by Caroline, and he wasn't really sure what that would mean. If she was Vodnik, she might be a shifter, too; his Mama had told him all about those Others a long time ago. He was pretty sure she had never told his brothers and sisters about them, though. She said he, Wenzel, was special and needed to know. Shifters gathered souls, he remembered. Drowned the Common Folk and kept a piece of them in a cup.

Drowned them.

Wenzel stood, realizing that he didn't have the time or wherewithal to explain it all. "We have to go, Jacob. To the pool."

Jacob nodded tersely, his eyes snapping with determination.

"You'll have to carry me until I can walk."

Wenzel leaned down and managed to push and pull Jacob into a seated position and heave him over his shoulder, the second time in the space of thirty minutes he had carried someone thus. Jacob's legs and pelvis—everything below his waist—were utterly useless, and his arms only barely so. It hurt terribly to draw a breath, and despite drinking a large vase of water, his throat was burning with thirst. Wenzel lumbered down the hallway and the grand staircase, reeling under his load, and made his way through the first floor to exit the house through the kitchen at Jacob's whispered instructions.

Just as Wenzel staggered into the yard, they heard a short, piercing scream, and Jacob answered with a hoarse croak. "Bailey! Wen, hurry!"

With five more steps they cleared the hedges by the house and saw a terrifying sight: a death scene poised to play out in just a few moments' time. Caroline had Bailey gagged and bound and was pulling her by the hair toward the pool, the gun in her other hand four inches away from Bailey's head.

A garbled sound emitted from Jacob's throat: an anguished, animalistic cry, and he willed his legs to move, to no avail.

Wenzel stood rooted to the spot for an instant. The strangest sensation had come over him. He felt adrenaline coursing through him. The veil lifted; the pieces of the puzzle clicked into exquisite place. Everything was right and good and crystal clear for the first time in his life. His muscles unlocked and he swiftly put Jacob on the ground, shaking off the hand that grasped his ankle, a brief look of apology at his brother. Jacob was worried about him; Jacob probably had a smart plan. But he didn't know what Wenzel knew. Wenzel knew the path.

He loped across the lawn, his feet silent in the thick grass. Caroline had not seen him yet: she was facing the pool, putting forth all effort into dragging Bailey.

Bailey, however, was facing Wenzel, and when she saw him, her eyes became huge and frantic. She was shaking her head, or at least trying to—Caroline had a deadly grip on her hair. She wanted him to go back. She was worried for him; of course she was. She was one of the most unselfish people Wenzel knew. She probably didn't see a need for Wenzel to die, too. But he knew something she didn't. He knew the path.

He drew closer, sprinting at his very limit, which he was knew was poor and slow, lungs bursting, heart pounding, sweat pouring from his brow. Caroline was ten feet from the pool now: if she threw Bailey in, Bailey would die. He'd never be able to fish her out of the pool before Caroline shot him, and then he and Bailey would die together, right before Jacob's eyes. Bailey went limp, not wanting to attract Caroline's attention, and tried to tell Wenzel with her eyes, *No! No! No! Don't do this!*

But on he came, his arms pumping at his sides, his own eyes wide, bulging with effort, his mouth wide open, gulping air. Bailey was eight feet away from the pool. Six feet. Four feet. Wenzel drew closer at an impossible rate, and before she could think of what to do next, he was upon her.

He looked down at her for what must have been the barest of a millisecond, his soft blue eyes locking with hers, and then he hurdled over the length of her with a mighty roar.

The gunshot was deafening. For a split second there was nothing else in the world except the sound of the report echoing inside her head, and then there was just a dull roar in her ears.

Caroline's painful grip on her hair vanished, and Bailey, once she realized she had not been shot, flipped over on her stomach and lifted her head. She didn't want to lift her head. She wanted to close her eyes and float away, for she knew what she would see.

Wenzel was lying on the ground, staring at her, blood pumping like a fountain from a hole in his chest, spreading a flowery stain over his shirt and soaking into the ground beneath him. Caroline lay on the ground at the very edge of the pool, the gun still in her hand. She stood slowly, her face frozen in stunned confusion, and when she saw Wenzel on the ground, she dropped the gun.

A cry—hoarse and full of terrible sorrow and rage, came from the far edge of the vast lawn by the house. Bailey did not look;

she knew it was Jake. But there was no time to comfort him; she had to get to Wenzel. To save him.

Caroline's head snapped up and her expression changed from numb shock to disbelief as she saw Jacob screaming.

Everything changed in that instant.

There would be no life with her one true love. It was too much to overcome now: that idiot brother had tackled her and was bleeding out on the ground at her feet, right beside his precious Bailey, who was bound, gagged, bruised and bloody. She would have to somehow get him back upstairs and drug him again, maybe with ether this time, because another curare dart would kill him. And then she would have to come back out here and finish off Bailey.

She didn't have it in her. She thought she would do anything to keep the atrocious Black at bay, and anything, *anything* in the world to possess Jacob. She gazed at him, her one true love. He was dragging himself now, grabbing tufts of grass and dragging himself across the lawn, his useless legs trailing behind him. She could hear him gasping for air from where she stood; he must be in incredible pain. But the effort was not to reach her. He drug himself to reach his brother, and most of all, to reach Bailey.

Her one true love. It was sacrosanct, this feeling. For the very first time in her life, she understood what love really meant. It was unconditional and absolute. She fell in love with him for real in that instant, watching him at the lowest point in his life. This love—my God—it was vast and all-encompassing. She gasped with the pureness and power of it, feeling it wash over her in a wave, completing her. She would do anything, *anything* to make him happy.

She would let him go.

She tipped back her head and screamed at the moon, the veins in her neck standing out in cords, tears streaking down her cheeks. As Bailey watched, horrified, Caroline's smooth features began to shift again, flesh giving way to fur, and she turned and loped away into the gloaming.

Bailey managed to roll herself toward Wenzel, struggling

mightily against her bindings but unable to budge them. Not knowing what else to do, she lay across his chest, trying to stem the flow of blood with the pressure of her own body.

"Bailey." His voice was faint but utterly calm. She raised her head with effort, and his hand came up to gently peel the tape from her mouth.

"Oh, Wen. I'm sorry. I'm sorry." She was weeping; he was dying, and there was nothing she could do.

"Shhh. It's okay. Look, Bailey. In my pocket is a necklace. It's from Mama. It'll protect you from them. Never take it off, okay?"

"Okay," she sobbed, her body shaking uncontrollably. She was so cold.

She felt his arm come around her and stroke her hair. "Don't cry, Bailey. It's not sad. I'm going to cross, but it's okay. I've been there lots of times before already, and you'll come, too, someday. You and Jake. You've been there before, you just didn't know it. It's so beautiful. It's the real world."

She wept even harder, lifting her head again to look into his eyes while she had the chance.

"Thank you for saving my life," she managed, and kissed him tenderly on the lips.

He gazed at her tranquilly, joy emanating in waves that Bailey could tangibly perceive. All at once she was warm and calm.

"It's what I was born for."

"I love you."

He nodded. "I'll take that with me. That's all that matters; the love."

She held him as he took his last breath; she could feel his chest rise and fall, and then he was still. Her tears flowed again; she would miss him terribly until they would meet again, this enigmatic, otherworldly angel.

Long moments passed before she became aware of the sound. It was a grunting, swishing sound. Groan, swish. Groan, swish. She tensed: was Caroline back to gather her soul? Perhaps she would be joining Wenzel much sooner than she had thought.

She was about to roll off of Wenzel to go rescue Jake when a hand slid up her back and cupped the back of her neck, squeezing lovingly, an achingly familiar feeling.

Jake. She knew before she moved an inch. Somehow, miraculously, he was here; how had he crossed that lawn?

She turned and he gasped, his beloved eyes filled with horror. "Oh, God. Not you, too, Rosie. Are you shot?"

Bailey looked down and realized she was soaked in Wenzel's blood from her throat to her waist. She shook her head, not able to speak for a few seconds. "No. I'm fine. But Wenzel—"

He put a finger to her lips. "I know. He's gone. I couldn't stop him; he came for me, and when we got outside and he heard you scream, he just dropped me and ran. He wanted to save you."

"I didn't want him to," she wailed, her grief descending at last. "I tried to tell him to go back, but my mouth was taped."

Jacob pushed her back and looked into her eyes with the most tender of expressions. "Rosie. Listen to me. Wenzel—he—he was *meant* to save you. I just know it. You know, he wasn't—he *isn't*—a Common Folk."

She stared at him. "You know about that? And you saw— you know about Caroline?"

He nodded numbly, still not fully able to process what he had seen. "She's a shifter; Wenzel tried to tell me. I don't know much at all. It's—it's crazy! Ma can tell us more." He shook his head, unable to make sense of it. "But I knew Wenzel better than anyone. And I know that as confused as he was sometimes, he absolutely knew tonight what he was supposed to do." He squeezed his eyes shut, and it was a few seconds before he could look at her again. "And I've never seen him as happy as he was when he dumped me on the ground and started sprinting across this damn yard like a big, lumbering bear."

They laughed together, desperate to feel normal.

"I got to tell him I love him," she said, feeling the warmth of it all over again.

He nodded. "You know, I told him today, too."

She smiled and cupped his face. "He took it with him; all that love. He said that's all that matters."

He gave into it then, sobbing, and gathered her close, bloody shirt and all. He held her as tightly as he could, rocking her, kissing her head, her cheeks, her lips. Their tears mixed together and began to heal them.

CHAPTER SEVEN

Jacob managed to extract a knife from his pocket and cut through Bailey's bindings, and when she was freed, her wrists and ankles raw and bloody, she wrapped her legs around his hips and her arms around his neck, holding on for dear life. She sobbed as he held her; she was completely undone, not believing that she was in Jacob's arms at last and that his beloved brother was dead. Perhaps only moments had passed, but time stood still as they lay entwined next to Wenzel. Bailey remembered the necklace and reached into Wenzel's pocket, putting it around her neck and gazing at the brown stone. It was glowing and warm, held in place by a claw of some sort.

"Mama's necklace," Jacob breathed. "Wen brought it to you."

She nodded, too emotional to speak.

And then everything seemed to happen at once. First it was only a few men, alarmed by the sound of gunfire and screams on the quiet street; and before they knew it, they were surrounded by a horde of people, all talking at once, lighting lanterns against the twilight, shouting instructions, aghast at the blood covering Bailey, checking Wenzel for signs of life.

Bailey stood and tried to pull Jacob with her, but his legs would not obey; they were like rubber, and he collapsed back to the ground with a painful gasp, trying to draw air into his lungs.

Bailey sat with him, supporting him with her arm, worry etched on her face.

"Here now, what's this?" shouted a man; Jacob recognized him as a neighbor of the Voglers. As the man searched his face in the deepening dusk, his expression changed to one of shock. "Jacob Naplava? My God! Is that you? What happened here, my good man?"

Jacob cleared his throat painfully. "I think we better wait to talk to the police," he rasped. Bailey felt herself go cold: the police! She had just this day been released from jail; what if she were to be imprisoned again? Jacob had cut her bindings: could the police make a case that she had killed Wenzel?

Finally the police arrived on the scene and parted the crowd. Jacob was assisted to a chair and tended to by a doctor, and Bailey, after insisting that she was not grievously injured, was led to another chair for questioning.

The story she told Officer Grady was the truth, but it wasn't the whole truth. Who would ever believe what had transpired that evening? No one! She wasn't sure *she* believed it. So instead, she explained how Caroline had come to the clinic disguised as a boy, knocked her unconscious with a gun, tied up Rachel, and brought her to her home and bound and gagged her with the intention of killing her. Bailey explained Caroline's fake pregnancy and the crumbling of that far-fetched plan, and Caroline's subsequent poisoning of Jacob and her plans to kidnap him. She described the note she was forced to write, and the officer recovered it, his eyes growing wider by the minute. She did not explain her poor attempt to devise a code: she had circled the "8" in the time with the hope that someone would read every eighth word: *Caroline is a soul thief. Took Jacob old country.* She would never be able to explain that one away! She recounted Wenzel's rescue of Jacob and his heroic action of tackling Caroline, whose gun had fired into his chest. She described how Caroline spotted Jacob and then had fled the scene, a detail that resulted in a barked order from Officer Grady, dispatching four deputies to find Caroline Vogler. *You'll never find her*, thought Bailey. *Never in a million years.*

The officer questioning Jacob came to her then, Officer Grady moved to Jacob, and she told the story all over again. Men scoured the house for clues and discovered the pitcher of lemonade, which Jacob reported had been drugged, as well as the empty vase on the floor of the bedroom and the pile of flowers in a puddle of water in the master suite. Not to mention the fact that most of the women's personal belongings and clothing were missing, verifying Jacob's and Bailey's stories that Caroline and her mother were planning to travel by rail that night and had released the entire staff earlier that day. More deputies were dispatched to Rachel's home to question her, more to find Cordelia, Howard, and Hope; still others to question Thomas and Gabby. The doctor, having finished with Jacob, insisted on examining Bailey, peering at the knot on her temple, her broken nose, and pointing out the bloody welts left by her bindings to Chief Sellers, who scribbled in his notebook, brow furrowed.

And then came the horrible moment when the coroner's wagon arrived. A sheet was drawn over the body, and Wenzel was reverently lifted onto a board and placed inside. Bailey went to Jacob then, not caring about the policemen's protocol, and sank onto the chair beside him, gripping his hand silently. The crowd looked on, hushed, as the wagon pulled away.

"Dr. Rose? Mr. Naplava? Your families are here now. We'd be happy to transport you to the hospital if you like, or your families can take you home." Officer Grady was kneeling beside them, his creased face kind and filled with concern. "Stay in the city for a few days, all right? We may have more questions, but my guess is that you've told us everything we need to know."

They both looked up, startled, and saw Johann, Anton, and Franticek striding toward them, their faces masks of shock and grief. Hope and her uncle Howard were just disembarking from their wagon.

"Is it true?" Anton cried when he reached Jacob. "Is Wen gone?"

All three men knelt by Jacob's chair, pulling Jacob and Bailey into a mighty hug, heads together, hearts breaking.

With assurances and hugs, she had gently declined the Millers' offer to accompany them and was warmly gathered in by the Naplavas. The ride to Anton's had been one of the darkest moments of Bailey's life: Jacob breathed in raspy, wheezing gulps, too exhausted to speak and still suffering paralysis, possibly permanent, and great pain from the effects of the *curare* dart; Anton wept silently, his face buried in his hands; Franticek and Johann murmured in hushed tones, making plans for delivering the devastating news to the women and collecting Wenzel to take him home.

When they arrived, Gacenka, Lindy, Alice, and Marianna burst from the front door and ran to the stable to meet them. Johann vaulted from the wagon, making eye contact with Lindy, who understood immediately and moved to Gacenka's side. Bailey saw none of this, but a few seconds later she heard the wails of a mother who has lost her child, and before she could fall apart herself, Jacob pulled her to him, and they clung together until Johann came to fetch them a short time later.

As soon as Gacenka saw Jacob carried from the wagon, followed by a blood-soaked, beaten Bailey, she dragged her apron across her face and lifted her chin, her spine straightening and eyes snapping. "Boys! Carry him upstairs straight to bed. Freddie, fetch Karl Schwartz, and make haste, boy!" The stable boy threw himself onto a horse and flew away without another word. "Lindy, Marianna, Alice: I need hot tea, hot water, and whisky."

"Ma, you know you can't hold your liquor," Jacob rasped, and everyone laughed, even Gacenka.

It took Lindy and Gacenka twenty minutes to convince Bailey to leave Jacob's side: after the boys had carried out Gacenka's orders, Bailey had immediately planted herself in a chair next to him, bemoaning the fact that she didn't have her medical bags with her. She took his pulse and laid her head on his chest to listen to his heart, Jacob stroking her hair and smiling as she laid there, an intent, anxious expression on her face.

"Bailey! *Please!* Let us clean you up, my dear. Your nose is all crusty, the lump on your head is getting bigger, and your poor wrists and ankles! It will take thirty minutes at the most, and we'll deliver you right back here." Marianna scolded her and tried to pry Bailey's hand from Jacob's. Gacenka fussed over her, her kind eyes swollen and red. She desperately needed something to do, someone to tend to.

Bailey stared at them all, stubborn, her dark eyes bleary and dull with trauma. Lindy leaned down to whisper in her ear. "Mama can hardly stand to look at you; you're covered in Wenzel's blood, my girl. Karl will be here any minute. Come on now."

"It's okay. Please go take care of yourself," croaked Jacob, tugging on her hair, ordering her away even though the heavy, warm weight of her head on his chest was what he needed more than anything.

And so she allowed herself to be led away. A hot bath was drawn and she scrubbed every bit of Wenzel's blood away, her wrists and ankles stinging, her nose horribly swollen and painful, and the knot on her head throbbing. After she dressed in a soft, white cotton shift, she was led to a room at the end of Jacob's hallway and fussed over by Libby, who had brought a rag soaked in ice and lavender for her temple. Alice knocked timidly on her door to ask if Bailey might let her brush her hair, but she was uncharacteristically quiet and subdued as she pulled the bristles gently through Bailey's wet, tangled mane.

"It's not your fault," Bailey finally said after moments of strained silence, reading the younger girl's mind.

"Wh--what?" stuttered Alice, lowering the brush.

"You think that your detective work started a chain of events in motion that led to Wenzel's death."

Alice flushed and nodded, miserable. "I really loved that goofy fellow. If it wasn't for my meddling, he'd still be alive."

Bailey smiled and turned to her. "You know what he told me before   he   died?"

Alice shook her head, her eyes haunted.

"He told me that he was born for that moment—to save me. He was *happy*, Alice." She paused, struggling to put her thoughts in order. "Look, I'm not sure I believe that things are preordained. I still think we have the power to change the course of our lives with every decision we make. That's free will, right? But I'm coming to understand that our decisions, when they're the right ones, lead us down a path that has already been laid."

Alice stared at her, struggling to understand. "But how do you know your decisions are right?"

Bailey shrugged. "You have faith. I have faith in God to lead me in the right direction. Others have faith in their ability to do what feels right. I think you go with your heart, whether you think it's guided by your own wisdom or something that transcends—well—*everything*."

The young girl nodded, allowing a small smile. "I felt it was right, every step of the way, when I was trying to find out what Caroline was doing."

Bailey returned her smile, but she was suddenly weary beyond measure.

"Will you brush my hair again, Alice? It felt so wonderful. And maybe sing to me?"

And so Alice brushed and sang the lullabies that Lindy sang to her children, and Bailey drifted away for a few lovely moments.

In spite of everyone's efforts to convince her to sleep in a spare bedroom, Bailey spent the night by Jacob's side, a chair drawn up beside the bed, holding his hand. He wasn't out of the woods yet: she and Karl had decided that while it was probable Jacob would make a complete recovery, his breathing and paralysis needed to be monitored closely for the next twenty-four hours to make sure there was no permanent or fatal damage. All of the Naplavas had offered to do that, and in fact had been quietly taking turns checking on Jacob throughout the night, but Bailey still adamantly refused to budge, even at Jacob's bidding.

"Honestly, you're the most contrary person I've ever met," he had croaked, exasperated, finally giving in to her insistence on staying.

"No, I'm not either," she quipped, sticking her tongue out.

He shifted in his bed, testing his legs once again, pleased to discover he could move them even farther than he could the last time he had checked, which was a scant five minutes ago. His knees bent slightly and his toes wiggled with ease. Although he hadn't shared his fears with Bailey, he had been anxious that he would be permanently paralyzed. And what then? After all of this time, he was finally with *her* again—*Bailey Rose*, the ephemeral girl he had almost decided was just a divine dream from his childhood; would she want him as a cripple? And if his legs were paralyzed, did that mean—did that mean that *nothing* was functional below his waist?

He looked at her then. She was staring back at him, her dark eyes full of humor and love; her hand squeezing his almost painfully tightly. Her nose was swollen and the skin under both eyes was a sickly gray-green; the knot on her temple made her head look misshapen; her clean, shining hair was coming loose from a hasty braid and was flying here and there, frizzy and ablaze. He had never seen her more beautiful, and as her thumb began to stroke his, he felt a surge of desire.

His question about functionality was answered.

He cleared his throat, hoping she hadn't noticed anything unusual. "Well then, wench, if you insist on serving me, then go fetch me a draught, and don't take yer time doin' it."

She pulled her hand from his and gave his hair a painful tug. "How do you ask nicely?"

He swallowed with effort. He knew how he'd *like* to ask her nicely.

"Please?" he finally managed.

How does he do that? Bailey wondered. *He says "please,"and I melt like an ice cube in the sun and turn into a red-faced, babbling fool.* Sure enough, she felt the usual horrible red stain flush up from her neck to her cheeks, and she spun away quickly before something monumentally stupid emerged from her mouth.

And just at that moment Lindy waltzed in with two frosty mugs of iced peppermint tea, much to Bailey's relief.

"I'm going to step out for just a moment," Bailey stuttered, pointing inanely at the door. She had nothing to do now that Lindy had brought drinks, but she needed an escape. Jacob studied her as she walked from the bed to the door, his eyes glittering.

Lindy smirked, helping him to a sitting position, plumping his pillows and handing him the glass. "Down boy," she murmured. "Plenty of time later for that. Let's get you well first."

He looked at her innocently. "What? I don't know what you're talking about."

She snorted. "What I want to know is who is going to be chaperoning the two of you tonight?"

He looked at her balefully. "I don't think you need to worry about *that*. I'm a cripple, remember?"

"Somehow the two of you always seem to find a way. Now, I don't want to come in here in the middle of the night to make sure you're breathing and whatnot—and interrupt some *heavy* breathing." She wiggled her eyebrows comically at him and he laughed out loud. It felt wonderful to laugh after the misery of the past several weeks.

He shrugged. "I can't promise anything. She might not be able to control herself. I guess I have that effect on women."

"You think you're kidding, but it's actually true, you rat." She shook her finger at him. "She is completely and utterly in love with you, as I'm sure you are well aware. *So be good.*" She winked at him as she left the room.

She had meant her words lightly, but Jacob sobered, staring at the door long after Lindy had left. She was right: Bailey was his for the taking—and he was hers—and *oh*, how he wanted to take, more than anything he had ever wanted or needed in his whole life. And so perhaps it was up to him to wait to see what became of his legs. He would never want to burden her with taking care of a crippled man her entire life long. She deserved so much better than that.

When she returned, chattering mindlessly as she did when she was nervous, her gaze averted in embarrassment from their previous conversation, he had an overwhelming urge to grab her and swing her onto the bed; to kiss her and tell her how much he loved her and how ready he was to spend his life with her. But he resisted, feeling tethered to the bed by his useless legs.

Useless. Helpless.

Instead, they sat and drank tea together, talking easily about the clinic, the ranch, the mayoral position; and then onto the more painful topics of Wenzel and the still unbelievable story of Caroline. They agreed that they must sit Gacenka down so they could begin to come to some kind of understanding about the fantastical, terrible things they had witnessed.

"Do you think people would think we're crazy?" she ventured. "I mean, if we tried to explain?"

He raised an eyebrow. "You mean people outside of the family?"

She nodded.

"Yes!" he laughed. "Would you have believed it without seeing it with your own eyes?"

She shook her head, eyes wide, remembering the horrible squelching noise of Caroline's flesh dissolving into fur; the sight of her small, pretty white teeth elongating into vicious fangs. She closed her eyes and forced a different image into her mind. "But Jake, you didn't see her when she came out of the water as a Vodnik. She was—beautiful is not even the right word. She was exquisite! Like an angel! All shimmery and lit from within." She opened her eyes and found a skeptical look on his face.

"I will never be able to think of her as beautiful, no matter what she looked like in that form. She was—is—evil. In ways we don't understand. I just hope she's gone, forever." He frowned down at his hands, and Bailey noticed his thumbs were circling furiously in the forward direction: his thinking mode.

"And I'm going to make sure of it, somehow. I promise you that."

They were silent then, bound together by a phenomenon they had no facility to comprehend, still experiencing a fair amount of shock and disbelief. Finally he broke the silence.

"You know though, I'm going to miss Mrs. Vogler's shortcake. They grew the strawberries right in their greenhouse, and she made the pastry herself. She may have drowned the occasional poor sap and—you know—trapped their souls in a teacup or what have you—but she made a damned good shortcake."

Bailey let forth with a peal of hilarity, and soon they were laughing like a couple of maniacs, perilously close to hysteria, but finding relief in acknowledging the absurdity of it all.

The next hour before bedtime passed pleasantly, but there was no talk about the two of them, even when they finished their tea and Bailey found his hand again, seeking comfort in the warmth and pressure. It was the elephant in the room, standing between them, incongruous and demanding to be addressed, but he just could not bring himself to talk about a future that may tie her to a man in a wheeled chair.

And so they sat, Bailey's stomach in a terrible knot. From the moment he had crawled across Caroline's yard to her and pulled her into his arms, they had been *together*; why, he had just been *flirting* with her before Lindy came in just a bit ago! And now she seemed to have become nothing more than a good friend. Had Lindy warned him away from her? She couldn't imagine that. What, then? What could have changed so suddenly?

Dawn came after a long, anxious, fitful night for Bailey. She had awakened every twenty minutes or so to take his pulse, to lay her head on his chest or put her cheek next to his mouth, making sure his breathing was even and deep. Then she would sink back into her chair and instantly fall into an exhausted slumber, only to wake again twenty minutes later to repeat the process.

Had she known that she awakened him every time she did this, she would have been appalled, but the object of her ministrations sincerely enjoyed every moment of it. He craved the feel of her hands on him and the smell of her skin when she bent close. Each time she sank back into her chair, her head nodding heavily, he would carefully move his legs, and he was delighted to find that with every passing moment the feeling and function was returning. By daybreak he seemed to have almost a full range of motion: he could bend his legs completely, lift them straight up and to the side, and flex all of his muscles. It was painful, to be sure, but everything worked. From what he could tell, his breathing had returned to normal as the effects of the paralyzing drug ran its course, just as Karl and Bailey had predicted.

Dare he hope? Was this it, then?

When the sun filtered gold through the lace curtains and cast delicate patterns across the wall, he knew it was time. He took a deep breath and sat up, sliding as silently as he could to the edge of the bed, glancing anxiously behind him to be sure he didn't wake his sleeping beauty. He reached for his trousers on the bedside table and was encouraged to find he could pull them on with a minimum amount of effort, pulling them up to his thighs and then lying back on the bed and arching his back to get them over his hips. Well, hot damn, at least he could dress himself! He looked over his shoulder at her again: she was sitting remarkably straight in her Hepplewhite arm chair, her chin on her chest, her hair unbraided and spilling wildly over her shoulders, snoring softly. He felt an upwelling of love so intense and complete that he had to stifle a gasp. *Please. Let my legs work. Let me be able to walk over to the dresser and reach into the pocket of my jacket. Please, Lord. Let it be so.*

He closed his eyes. If he crumpled to the floor, he would wake her, and she would find him sprawled, stranded by the bed. She would put her arms around him and heave him back into bed; he would be helpless, dependent. He knew that he should be able to walk this morning if he was ever going to be able to walk again: any permanent damage would make itself known by now. Karl had said as much, and he should know, with all of his experience in the war with paralysis. Everything was riding on this moment, on his ability to rise from this bed and walk over to that dresser. He was more nervous than he had ever been in his life. He hadn't even been this nervous waiting for the jury's verdict: he had already hatched a meticulous, quite brilliant plan with his brothers and a mysterious stranger who had approached them earlier that week—he'd have to tell her that story someday; it was a doozie—to break her out of her prison and hide her away if she was found guilty. But this was different: there was no back-up plan this morning. *This was it.*

He forced himself up without another thought, focusing all of his strength into his legs. He gained his balance and felt a surge of hope. He could feel his legs holding him up; it felt perfectly normal, albeit painful, so far. He took a tentative step, and though his muscles quivered and telegraphed ripples of pain as though they had been asleep, they bore his weight and obeyed his command. He took another step; there, that one was easier! Another cautious step, another, and another, and he was halfway to the dresser! He straightened, his confidence soaring, and his stride became more natural and assured. By the time he reached the dresser, he had his answer. He was whole again! He was!

He glanced at Bailey again, a huge grin wreathing his face, barely managing to suppress an elated laugh. He reached into his jacket pocket and there it was: the thing he had been carrying around since he had bribed a courthouse clerk to give it to him. The ring. Her ring. *Their ring.* It was smooth and warm in his hand, and he gripped it, tears pricking his eyes, and turned toward her. He froze.

She was looking right at him, her mouth open in shock. She began to rise from her chair.

"Don't move," he whispered, putting a hand up to stay her.

She sank back down slowly, and he made his way to her, moving stiffly but sure-footed, the smile never dying from his lips. She sat frozen, dumbfounded, watching him walk to her. Walking!

He reached her and very stiffly, very slowly, knelt down on one knee, and Bailey gasped, her shaking hand rising to cover her mouth, as she realized what was about to happen. Her whole world compressed into a moment, this moment, and every detail of it was inscribed into her brain. His rumpled blue cotton shirt that he had slept in stuffed hastily into soft, faded brown trousers—how had managed to put those on? His thick, tousled black hair, a hank of it escaping over one eye, just as it had always done. His lips, smiling, about to speak the words that would make her whole. His body, tall and strong and so perfectly fitted to her own. And those eyes, encompassing all of the bright blue heaven, piercing right into the heart of her.

He gazed at her, smiling, and then finally began to speak.

"Rosie. You are my life. I love you." He had to stop for a few seconds, his voice choked with emotion. "I've loved you since the day you walked into that classroom with that sorry bunch of magnolias. You hadn't even seen me yet, and you already had me. And you had me from that day on, even when I thought I'd lost you forever. Which happened more than a few times." They laughed together again.

"I can't lose you again. I can't. Marry me, Rosie."

The words hadn't left his mouth before she launched herself into his arms. He held her to him, feeling her lips on his neck, his cheek, and then finally, at last, on his own lips, answering "Yes, yes, Jake!" and trying to kiss him at the same time.

They were greedy, reveling, cherishing, halting the regular flow of time as it crystalized into a perfect, timeless moment. Neither of them knew how much later it was when he guided her back into the chair and slipped the ring onto her finger. He touched her heart, put his fingers to his lips, and touched his own heart. "Now you've done it. You're stuck with me forever."

She nodded, laughing and crying at the same time. He stood and pulled her up. "Let me hold you on my own two feet."

She lunged into his arms—exuberant, with a bit too much force—and they tumbled onto the bed, laughing, until they became still, lost in each other.

"What took you so long?" she whispered, touching his face, not believing.

"I'm sorry," he breathed. "I wanted to make sure I—you know—could walk. And put on my pants."

They laughed softly, foreheads pressed together. "I wouldn't have minded," she scolded.

"What? Me not wearing pants?"

She pulled his hair. "Well, that's true. But I meant I wouldn't have minded if you couldn't walk, Jake." She grasped his shoulders and gave him a shake, her expression turning grave. "I mean it. We've got to stop—running away from each other. If we belong to each other, it's for better or worse, remember? In sickness and in health?"

He nodded, lost in her.

"Do you promise?" She gave him another shake.

He nodded again, feeling lighter than he had since he was fourteen years old, in the back of a wool wagon with his hands buried in a girl's warm hair. "I promise."

"Even if you—get kicked in the head by a sheep and go blind? Even if I eat too many of Gacenka's pastries and get fat? Even if you go bald and lose all your teeth? Even if I decide I'm tired of combing this mess and cut off all my hair?"

He frowned. "Don't cut your hair."

"Jake!"

He ducked a punch and caught her hand. "I promise!" He laughed and hugged her to him. "I don't care if you cut off your hair and weigh three hundred pounds. I want you. I'll always love you."

She returned the embrace and then withdrew, cupping his jaws and forcing him to look at her. "Well, then have some faith that I feel the same way, okay? I thought you—I thought you had changed your mind about me, and it was worse than anything I've gone through yet. Prison, being kidnapped: that was a breeze compared to last night. I felt you pulling away and I wanted to die."

He groaned and pulled her to him again. "I'm sorry. I'm so

sorry, Rosie. Never again, I promise. No matter how bad it is, we're in it together."

"Kiss your fiancé," she breathed, and he obliged, feeling both of them ignite like a flash fire.

And that was precisely how Lindy found them.

CHAPTER EIGHT

For two more days, time stood blessedly still at Anton's as they recovered. Chief Sellers paid a short, formal visit and announced that no charges would be filed against either of them. He also regretted to inform them that there was no trace of Caroline Vogler: it was as if she had vanished. The Chief seemed distracted and red-faced, and Bailey couldn't help but notice that he couldn't look them in the eye when he spoke Caroline's name. She was too weary to wonder about it for too long, especially when Jacob leaned closed and muttered in Bailey's ear, "They're looking for the wrong species, I reckon," to which she had just managed to stifle a nervous giggle, causing the family to shoot curious looks their way. Mrs. Vogler had been detained for questioning while attempting to change trains in Austin: but as she was being held at police headquarters in the state capital, somehow they seemed to have lost track of her. She was gone, just like that. Bailey wondered what had become of her fifty-seven porcelain cups that Caroline had claimed had been shipped ahead. Mr. Vogler was still traveling abroad, conveniently out of reach of any law enforcement; Mrs. Vogler apparently had wired him to warn him.

The family enjoyed a joyous, elaborate engagement feast prepared by Libby and Gacenka. Jacob could not seem to keep himself from touching Bailey: a hand on her arm, on the back of her neck, entwined in her own hand. He had pulled Bailey's chair so close to his that Marianna had teased that Bailey may as well sit in his lap, to which Bailey had responded by rising and doing just that, much to Jacob's delight. He pulled her down for a lingering kiss, causing everyone to hoot and holler.

There was much laughter that night, and Johann raised a toast to Wenzel. "Wen would be furious—well, in his own quiet, circumspect way—if any of you were sad tonight. Raise your glass to our brother, our son, and our hero. Knowing Wen, he's probably here with us in some sort of weird, alternate universe or some such thing." They all laughed. "To Wen!" Everyone raised their glass and repeated it, and Bailey felt a wonderful sense of peace.

Gacenka made a great fuss to shoo Bailey out of Jacob's room and tuck her into a guest bed that night, much to everyone's amusement, and early the next morning the entire family packed up and departed, headed for the train station and Bluebonnet Ranch, to the somber task of laying Wenzel to rest. Hope, Cordelia and Howard saw them off, Bailey and Hope embracing tearfully.

"We didn't have much time together," Bailey whispered to her sister, clinging to her.

Hope's eyes sparkled. "Then you'll be happy to know that I'm staying for a good while longer, little sister. Maybe forever! I'm to help at the Harding House; I've just fallen in love with your best friend Gabriella, and she talked me into it. She would have come today, but Jelly—you know, the girl from China—is in labor."

Bailey gave a bit of an uncharacteristic squeal, gripping her sister's shoulders in a tight vise. "Really? Oh, really, Hope? You're moving here?"

The older girl shrugged. "Well, you know me. Always up for an adventure. But yes, I'm seeing Cordy and Howie off in a few days and I'm staying behind."

"You'll be so close to me! St. Ursuline's isn't far from Harding House, you know! And you can spend time at the clinic!"

Hope quirked an eyebrow, glancing at the young man with dark hair who could not seem to pull his eyes away from Bailey for more than two seconds at a time. He caught Hope's eye and gave a sheepish grin.

"Something tells me you won't be living at St. Ursuline's for long."

Bailey stretched her left hand shyly, revealing the ring, and Hope nodded without a hint of surprise. "I figured as much. Marry that boy before something else cataclysmic happens, okay? Maybe, say, tomorrow."

"Okay. Well, not tomorrow. That's Wenzel's funeral. And I want you in my wedding."

"I wouldn't miss it. You know, Gabby and Thomas are marrying in three days. Are you coming back? She wanted me to ask you, but to let you know that you should not feel obligated, after all you've been through and what's still ahead for you in the next few days."

Bailey smiled at the news. Life moved on, after all. "Of course. Jacob and I will be here. Are they to marry in St. Mark's? Or has he been..." She couldn't quite bring herself to say it: the thought of him being forced from the church that he loved was a painful one.

"Kicked to the curb? Well, no. But he did leave; Paine Church has been seeking a pastor and they were thrilled that he accepted the position. And they are very accepting of Gabby."

Bailey's shoulders slumped in relief. "I'm so happy for them. Please tell them we will be there."

"That's good, because you are her maiden of honor, of course, if you're up for that." She reached up and traced the angry bruises and swollen flesh on Bailey's face, her face full of concern. They turned and walked arm-in-arm toward the platform as the final whistle blew. "And you promised me a cowboy, don't forget."

The short train journey to Boerne was a blur: it was back to the grim reality of saying goodbye to Wenzel, and the buoyancy of the past twenty-four hours began to leave the small party. Wenzel's body had been collected from the morgue and was somewhere on the train, Bailey knew, in a plain pine casket. The thought of it made her mute with sorrow. Gacenka and Franticek retired to a Pullman car, Gacenka looking ten years older than she did a few days prior. Johann and Lindy shared a facing seat with Anton and Alice, playing a listless, mostly silent game of Faro with a shabby deck of cards Anton had procured. Marianna and Miguel had excused themselves to the dining car, leaving Bailey and Jacob alone, huddled together; he had seated her and was pressed up next to her just as close as he could be, his arm around her, her head on his shoulder.

"I'm not crowding you, am I?" he finally asked, a hint of irony in his voice. "Marianna tells me that I've been on you like flies on a cow."

"That's a lovely sentiment," smiled Bailey. "Marianna is a poet, isn't she?"

He returned her grin, though his eyes were clouded with grief. "Seriously, though. I think I may have some separation anxiety going on when it comes to you; you just have a way of slipping away. Let me know if I'm too close, all right? I don't want to be one of those clingy fellows whose wives are always trying to get away from."

Bailey lifted her head and gazed at him, a look of wonder on her face. "*Wives*. Wife! I am to be your wife!"

"Damn straight." He traced her lower lip with his finger, stopping at the dent.

"You cannot possibly get too close to me. You're not close enough, as a matter of fact. What's wrong with you? Come closer, please."

He didn't waste any time; he kissed her tenderly, briefly, and then sat back to look at her.

"Is it wrong," he whispered, "for me to be grieving Wenzel at the same time I'm—I'm *wanting* you?"

She pulled him closer and the spark ignited again, only to be interrupted a short time later by loud snickers.

"Honestly, you two. Jacob, get *off* of Bailey. You appear to be swallowing her face," remarked Johann, and Lindy and Alice snickered.

"You know, we could all pitch in for a Pullman. There's a few empty ones in back," added Anton helpfully, reaching for his wallet and placing a few bills on the table.

"Right you are," answered Johann, a thoughtful tone to his voice. He pulled out his own wallet and slapped down some bills. "An early wedding gift; think of it that way."

Jacob sat back to respond hotly, but then shrugged and leaned forward to kiss Bailey again without a hint of self-consciousness, to the amazement of his brothers. Jacob had always been acutely embarrassed by the teasing of his two oldest brothers when it came to Bailey, but the bashfulness seemed to be a thing of the past. After a long moment he eased back against the seat and let forth with a long sigh, running his fingers through his hair, staring at Bailey with a look that made her stomach explode into a million butterflies. Johann and Anton hooted and hollered; Alice and Lindy fanned themselves comically, and for a moment, everything felt good.

All too soon, the short journey was complete, and as they traveled to Bluebonnet in two wagons, a heaviness of heart descended on them. The rest of the family had already been notified, but there would be many embraces and tears today. Jacob dreaded the look on Ginny's face; Wenzel had been so dear to her.

As it turned out, Ginny greeted them with a bright smile, bursting from the house and flinging herself into Gacenka's arms. The rest of the family waited on the porch, hanging back, faces long and sorrowful: Franz, who sat glumly on the porch swing, refusing to meet anyone's eyes; Eveline, who stood composed by the stairs, ready to fetch Ginny if need be; Joseph, Clarissa and the baby; Amalie, her husband and their brood; Annie and her family; even Rosalie and her family was there: Bailey hadn't seen her for fifteen years. Kube and a few of the senior ranch hands stood respectfully back by the stables, hats in hand. Everyone avoided looking in the back of the second wagon, where Wenzel lay in his casket.

Ginny gave her mama another hug and kiss, wiping away her mother's tears, and made a beeline for Jacob and Bailey. She pointed at Bailey. "You're to be my sister. I *told* Eveline that Jacob was going to marry you, the way you two moon over each other, and she just kept hushing me!" Her voice piped across the yard and porch loud and clear, and Bailey just couldn't help herself: she burst into laughter and knelt to squeeze Ginny to her.

"You were right, so stick it to her!" she whispered.

"Let me have some of that," growled Jacob, and leaned down to spin his sister in wide arcs. When he finally put her down, she was shrieking with glee.

"Really, Ginny, hush!" called Eveline, trotting down the steps toward her irrepressible sister. "This is a solemn occasion."

Both Jacob and Bailey opened their mouths to reply, but Ginny beat them to it. "No, it's not, either, Evie! Jacob and Bailey are *finally* gonna get married. And if you're talking about Wenzel, you know he's in his other place now. He's happier there, he told me so lots of times." She turned to address her entire family, who seemed to have frozen into place. "So quit your moping, everyone! Wen is probably around here somewhere watching, and who wants to see a bunch of old, grouchy faces?"

Ginny's impromptu speech seemed to release a floodgate of emotion. Gacenka ran to Rosalie, exclaiming over the children who had grown so much since their last reunion; Joseph trotted down the stairs and clapped his brothers on the back; Kube and the farmhands gathered around Franticek to report on the goings-on at the ranch; and soon, everyone was gathered around Jacob and Bailey, offering congratulations, handshakes, and hugs.

"You're a sight for sore eyes. And I do mean sore eyes," Kube snorted, peering closely at Bailey's still-battered face. "Lordy, girl! What does the other guy look like?"

Bailey barked a laugh and rolled her eyes. "You wouldn't even believe me, Kube!"

He tipped his hat back and shook his head. "Well, you've been through the wringer. You deserve some rest and relaxation. A honeymoon, maybe!"

Jacob cleared his throat and Bailey could have sworn that she detected a flush rising up his neck.

"'Course, a honeymoon for the two of you ain't likely to be much rest."

"Kube!" exploded Jacob.

The cowboy grinned and held his hands up, palms out defensively. "All right, all right!"

"Oh! Kube!" Bailey piped, desperate to change the subject. "I almost forgot! I know a girl from Philadelphia who wants to meet a cowboy!"

Jacob threw back his head and bellowed as Kube frowned, his dark eyes narrowed.

"A *what*?"

Bailey bit her lips, looking from one man to the other. "Did I say something wrong?"

Jacob, still laughing, punched Kube on the arm. "You tell her, *cowboy*."

Kube straightened and puffed out his chest. "All right. I will! A cowboy is a cow wrangler, Dr. Rose. He hustles cows for a rich old asshole rancher on the back of his sad-sack nag. He steals our water and grass and cuts our fences, in case I didn't mention it before. I am a *mayordomo*, which I believe we established quite some time ago. I live on the range, free and unencumbered."

Bailey nodded, pulling a regretful face. "Oh, that's too bad. What a shame. Did I mention this person is my sister? Oh well; she's quite lovely, so I'm sure I won't have any trouble finding some cowboy or sheepboy or horseboy or what have you, to give her a ride. On his horse, I mean."

Jacob bent over and held his gut, he was laughing so hard. Kube's eyes bugged out of his head: he had no idea this smart-as-a-whip little woman doctor was so ornery and—well—*earthy*.

He cleared his throat officiously and offered a formal bow. "I would be most honored to accompany your sister around Bluebonnet Ranch," he declared.

Bailey smiled and clapped her hands. "That's wonderful! I shall be happy to make the introduction."

Jacob stood up and draped an arm around Bailey's shoulder. "Now that we have that worked out, come see Rosalie, Bailey. She's dying to see you."

And so, thanks to Ginny, the homecoming wasn't quite as gut-wrenching as it very well could have been. Gacenka gathered them inside for a big, noisy feast, and while they were dining, the ranch hands carried the casket into the back parlor. As per custom, the mirrors and windows in the house were covered with heavy drapes. After dinner they all gathered in the dark room, and Bailey's heart swelled with love as Jacob consulted with his parents, and after they nodded tearfully, he blew out the candles, flung open the heavy drapes, and opened the windows, letting in an invigorating breeze and the light and sounds and smells of the outdoors. The casket was closed and many family members paid his or her respects by murmuring a few private words, hands lingering on the pine. Bailey hung back, not wanting to say her goodbyes until tomorrow.

Afterwards they gravitated to the porch once again, the boys finding fiddles and guitars, the children scampering through the gloom to catch fireflies, the women passing around babies and dancing with their lovers. Bottles of chokeberry wine were uncorked and the music and dancing became louder and merrier, and Bailey believed she had never been so happy and so sad, the joy and grief mingling to produce an emotion so complex there were simply no words for it. Everything was so real, so *genuine*, for the first time in her life. So much of her life had been spent in a sort of fog, a purgatory of waiting, waiting, for what she knew not. Now she knew: she had been waiting for this, to be by Jacob's side again, with this family, on this land in these beautiful hills, where she had learned the trees could talk and her heart could love. It was almost too much, all at once, and she handed a baby back to Rosalie and sought out Jacob, who was roaring a song with his brothers. He stopped at once when he saw her face.

"What's wrong, Rosie?" he murmured, leading her to the end of the porch, out of the light of the lantern. A line of concern appeared between his brows.

"Just needed my Jake fix," she whispered sheepishly, wrapping her arms around his waist and pulling him near. "Wanna go to the hen house?"

"Hell yes." His grip tightened and he ducked his head to capture her lips.

"I was speaking metaphorically," she laughed, as soon as she could speak. "I don't want to leave your family just now. But I sure do—well—you look..." She trailed off, embarrassed, as he stood there and smiled at her.

"I look what? Handsome? Dashing? Irresistible? Impossibly manly?" He held out an arm, crooked it, and made a muscle, admiring it with a dopey grin.

"I was going to say you look half drunk!"

He pouted. "Aw, that's what you were going to say? Really?"

She pushed him back and he stumbled, laughing. "No, not really. I was going to say that you look like you did when I knew you back then. When you were fourteen. Seeing you up there horsing around with your brothers—it reminds me of the days I spent out here with you, and what a terrible crush I had on you."

"I was crushing on you pretty hard, too. 'Specially after you seeing you bare-skinned by the creek."

"Jake! You are drunk, you big turd!" She swung at him but he ducked in time, then stood and captured her hands. "You didn't have a crush on me. I was a skinny, messed-up twelve-year-old with two black eyes. You just felt sorry for me."

The smile died from his lips and his grip tightened. "You're right. I didn't have a crush on you. I *loved* you. Before you fell in the creek. Before I almost kissed you when we were fishing with Wenzel. Before I *did* kiss you in the wagon. I told you, remember? You had me from the moment you stepped into that school room."

She stared at him, entranced, wondering if the sensation of her head lifting from her shoulders was a result of the wine or of something much more magical.

"Is this real?"

"Sometimes I think it's the only real thing in my life," he answered.

They stood and stared at each other, dumbstruck again by the twisting, divergent paths that had brought them together.

"I hope I don't spend the rest of my life waiting for the other shoe to drop. You know what I mean? I almost can't believe it's real, even though you're standing right in front of me."

He nodded gravely. "Yes. I mean, I know what you mean." He plopped down on the edge of the porch, pulling her with him, and they sat dangling their legs as if they were two kids again. He leaned back on two elbows and regarded the bright starry sky, brow furrowed. "After I lost you, I spent a lot of time—well— mad at you. After that passed, I grieved for you; I was probably impossible to live with."

Bailey nodded. "Yes, Marianna told me so."

He shrugged and grinned ruefully. "Well, I spent a lot of time by myself for a while. I never wanted to step out with any girls. I danced with them and kissed them in the barn, but it never felt right. Like I was cheating on you."

She felt a surge of love and empathy—how many times had she felt that way when she was with Ben and Thomas?—but she remained quiet, sensing he had something to tell her that had been weighing heavily.

He was quiet for a moment, and when he spoke again, his voice was strained. "But the worst was when I turned sixteen. You see, Blanche told us that you were my age, so in my head I thought you'd be sixteen, too." He sat up and turned toward her. "On my birthday, I went to the meadow—Feather Hill—and I sat for hours. I thought that maybe if there were a God, He would deliver you to me, and you'd come walking over that hill."

"Oh, Jake." She felt the tears begin to build.

He shrugged. "You have to understand, Rosie. If you would have stayed, I would've asked you to marry me just as soon as you turned sixteen. That's pretty much the earliest allowable marrying age up here in the Hills. So that day, I pretended you were turning sixteen, too—I didn't know when your birthday was—and that I was on one knee, giving you the biggest diamond I could afford. Which at that time would have been a little speck of dust." He chuckled and glanced at her shyly.

"Yes," she breathed.

He lifted an eyebrow. "Yes, what?"

"I would've said yes. My fourteen-year-old self says yes to your sixteen-year-old self's proposal."

He groaned and pulled her close, breathing in the scent of her, imagining what could have been and allowing himself just a moment to mourn the tragically wasted years.

"I started having the dreams then. Before, I just dreamed of the things we had done at the ranch: the shearing, the river, the wagon. Fragments of those moments played over and over in my brain, all night, every night. Once in a while I dreamed I caught a glimpse of you in a crowd, usually in Military Plaza, and I'd chase you for what seemed like hours, but you were always just out of reach. I'd reach out to touch your hair or your hand, and you'd vanish like a ghost. That's what you were becoming to me: a ghost. My ghost, the girl I loved, just a ghost in a rotten dream." He pushed her away then to look into her eyes. "But when I turned sixteen, the dreams changed. You began showing up—in my bedroom."

Bailey felt her face flame but looked at him steadily, nodding. "Oh, Jake. I had those dreams, too."

"You did?"

She nodded, swallowing thickly. "And remember, I was living in a convent school!"

They laughed then, relieving the tension a bit. "In my dreams, I'd come in the house and find your lace collar. A few steps more, and I'd see your shoes, then your dress, then your unmentionables, all laid out like a trail leading right to my bedroom. I'd be sure I'd get there and you wouldn't be there; you'd just be a ghost, but you were always there, waiting, sitting by the window, your skin glowing in the moonlight. You always stood up when I walked in and held out your arms to me, and—well—." He chuckled again and rubbed the back of his neck vigorously, at a loss for words.

"We'd light the fire," she finished.

"Yes! Oh, mercy. Bailey. I had to ask Ma for my own room because the dreams were so—so real, and, well, *productive*, if you know what I mean."

Bailey blushed again and nodded, nervous laughter bubbling up. Talking about sex had always been difficult and painful after the trauma of her childhood years, but she found that she was enjoying this conversation immensely. "Did Gacenka know?"

"She never said a word, but I'm sure she figured it out when I started offering to do the laundry. Every morning."

Bailey had a good belly laugh then, and Jacob joined her, wiping away tears of mirth. She settled against him and they looked at the stars together for a long silent moment before he spoke again.

"I guess it's a normal part of every boy's life, so Ma wasn't scandalized; heck, it was probably worse with Johann and Anton. But for me, it wasn't just dreams about sex. It was dreams about making love to a girl who felt like my *wife*. And every time I woke up, my arms felt empty and everything felt wrong and pointless."

She felt a great bubble of grief well up. "Me too. All the same for me, too, Jake. We were dreaming the same dreams and feeling the same emotions at the same time, all those years ago." She reached up to touch his jaw, turning his face to her. "And I'm so sorry, *so* sorry that I didn't come back. I was a killer and my mother was a dead prostitute. I just didn't want to hurt you and your family. Please know that I didn't come back because I loved you too much for you to be touched by all of that filth."

"I know. I know all of that, and I don't blame you. I would've done the same thing if the situation were reversed. There's nothing to forgive."

She regarded him somberly. "So we need to let go of those fifteen years, don't we?"

He smiled and she touched his dimple, her heart pounding, incredulous at her fortune in having this man as her very own. "Yes, I think we need to put it to rest. I think our paths were the ones that we were supposed to take. I don't know if you would have become a doctor if you would've stayed here."

"I wouldn't have. I wouldn't have wanted to leave your side. And you wouldn't have gone off to law school or become the mayor. We would have a dozen kids running around and I'd still be trying to learn how to make proper *svickova na smetane*."

He shook his head wonderingly. "*I* don't even know what that is!"

"Sirloin beef with thick cream sauce."

They both laughed, and then they gazed at each other, marveling at how different their lives would have been.

"It would have been good, though, Rosie. So good. There's no use saying it isn't so. I curse every minute of those fifteen years I didn't have you. But I'll let it go now; I promise."

"Me too."

They smiled at each other again, still not quite believing they were about to belong to each other, forever this time.

Jacob folded his arms across his chest. "But about this doctoring gig. You'll be a rancher's wife now, and babies won't be far off. Time to trade in that doctor's bag for an apron, don't you think? Oh!" He snapped his fingers, as if just remembering. "Not to mention the fact that you'll be a mayor's wife! You'll need some fancy clothes befitting the wife of a public official—and yes, that means a corset!" He waggled a finger at her. "You'll be holding teas and luncheons, so this—" he paused to tug her hair, which she had worn down for him tonight, tied back in a simple bow, "this will have to be all smoothed out and tied up, or whatever you call it."

For a second she simply gaped at him, not quite believing

what she was hearing, then stared at her hands, abashed. She had imagined having this conversation with Thomas, and had dreaded having to face the possibility of giving up her clinic and the vocation she had worked so hard to achieve. But Jacob? Never in a million years had she thought he would ask her to do so! Yes, they would need to plan, but for him to assume she would give up her clinic, her profession that had saved so many lives! She felt a rush of anger.

Until she was able to look up at him and see his huge, ornery grin, that damned dimple flashing, eyes sparkling. She swung at him and he ducked away just in time, bellowing. "Oh, Rosie! You should have seen your face, girl!"

She gave a little scream and lunged at him, but he slipped off the porch and hobbled through the yard, still hindered by the final lingering effects of the curare dart. She caught him easily by the sprawling live oak and commenced to poke him in the ribs, an area she knew to be exquisitely sensitive. He gasped and twisted away, laughing. "No fair! No tickling!"

"Stand still, you rat, and take what you deserve!"

"I love you, Rosie!" he yelled at the top of his lungs, causing his entire family to cheer and whistle.

"You get him, Bailey!" called Marianna.

He finally captured her hands, pinning them to her side. "Kiss me," he ordered, and she complied, pecking him on the cheek and eliciting boos from his brothers.

He suddenly ducked, and before she knew it, she was flung over his shoulder like a bag of wool. He carried her back to the dark corner of the porch, pumping his fist in victory while the family cheered on.

He deposited her with a thump and plopped down beside her, still laughing. "Sorry about that. Really, I couldn't resist. I guessed that you and Thomas may have had that kind of conversation, am I right?"

She nodded, marveling at his acuity.

His bearing became solemn, and he took her hands in his, turning them over to look at her palms and stroke her fingers for a long moment. She felt tingles reach to every part of her body and found she suddenly needed to remind herself to breathe. If he affected her this way just by holding her hand, how would she ever survive her wedding night? She would *swoon*, she was sure of it!

"Bailey, these hands are miracles. You save lives; I've witnessed it with my own eyes. These hands saved Clarissa and her baby and my little Ginny." He shook his head, struggling for words. "You have a rare and wonderful gift. I would never, *I will never*, ask you to give it up. It would be like giving up a part of who you are, and I love that person more than anything in this world."

She nodded and gulped and blinked furiously to keep the tears at bay. "But Jake, I *do* want to be a rancher's wife and a mayor's wife, and I *do* want to have your babies. And I want to be a doctor, too." She shrugged glumly. "I don't see how that's all possible."

"Of course it is. All we need is a plan, Rosie, and we need to trust each other."

She nodded again, relieved but uncertain. "Do you have a plan?"

He smiled and leaned back against a wide, white post, turning her around to settle her in the lee of his legs. She felt herself relax as she leaned back against his chest, his arms coming around her to find her hands again. They looked at the stars together for a quiet spell.

"Do I have a plan?" There was deep irony in his voice. "Maybe that's one thing you still need to learn about me. I *always* have a plan, just like my old man. Drives my brothers crazy."

"Then let's hear it," she encouraged him.

"Now this is just an idea," he cautioned. "Just the start of one. So I need you to chime in, too."

"Get on with it," she ordered with a smile, pinching his leg.

"All right. For the next four years I'm going to be—well—busy! This whole mayor's gig is going to keep me in the city quite a bit." There was a pause. "I hate that," he confessed softly. "I

102

never would have pursued this election on my own. My family, my friends, the folks up here in the Hills; they all had such high hopes in me. Me! The kid who always knew he wanted to be a rancher. You know, I wish it would have been Johann or Joseph they would have sent off to law school."

"They don't have your brain," noted Bailey wryly. She felt him shrug behind her.

"This city is at a turning point, and there really is a lot I hope to accomplish. Nobody knows this but Johann, but I won't be seeking re-election. I'm bowing out after four years; I'll be lucky to make it that long."

She squeezed his hands, hard. "I already knew that. You're going to do great things, Jake. Bluebonnet will be here for you when you're finished being Mr. Big Shot Mayor. And you'll only be thirty-four. We have our whole lives ahead of us!"

He returned her squeeze and kissed her on the top of the head, burying his face in her hair for a moment. Breathing her in.

"So. I was thinking that we'd get a place in town and you'd continue on with your clinic. You and Thomas and Gabby—and Hope, too—can set up the mentor program for Harding House."

She nodded enthusiastically. "I have lots of ideas for that already!"

"And when we can, we'll come home for some short stretches to visit and I can check on Bluebonnet business." She heard the wistfulness in his voice and felt a pang in her own heart. She loved it in the Hills as much as he did; leaving would be so very hard.

After a beat she broached the question he had not. "And what about babies, Jake? Do you want to start a family soon?"

He pushed her forward gently and turned her around so they were face to face. "Rosie," he said earnestly, "I want your babies someday. I love thinking about it. But I want time with you, just us, making our way for a while. We've waited so long for this, you know?"

She felt the weight of the world lifted from her shoulders. "Yes! I feel the same way! I just didn't know how you'd feel about it."

He cleared his throat, looking discomfited for the first time they had begun this momentous conversation. "Can you—I mean, I know there are ways to—"

She held up a hand, nodding wisely. "Of course! I mean, we'll just have to be abstinent for a while. That's all right with you, isn't it? We've waited this long, what's another four years?"

His jaw dropped open and she barely managed to keep a straight face. She saw his Adam's apple bob a few times and a flush begin to crawl up his neck. "Oh! Well, Rosie, if that's what you think, I guess we can figure out a way..." He stopped, looking for all the world like a little boy who has received underpants for Christmas and is desperately trying to hide his crushing disappointment.

She reached up to stroke his face consolingly. "Aw, my poor Jake. Payback is hell after all, isn't it?"

It took him a few seconds to register her hijinks, but when he did, the relief on his face was so comical that Bailey burst into her infectious laughter.

"You should have seen *your* face!"

He yanked on her hair and pulled her forward roughly and kissed her hard, his hands rubbing her back possessively. "That was just about the meanest thing anyone's ever said to me," he admitted huskily. "I think I just about had heart failure."

"You're in the right hands, then," she said brightly, biting his neck. She scooted back and took his face in her hands. "Oh, Jake! Honestly! I'm going to be lucky to make it four more days, let alone four years!"

He stared at her, so very, very tempted, but tucked his hands under his armpits and sat back. "Okay. So we have the next four years figured out."

She laughed. "Isn't that enough? Four years at a time, maybe? And Jake, you have to remember, birth control is not foolproof. A baby may happen in spite of it. What then?"

"I am one hundred percent positive that Eveline would be beyond thrilled to move to the city and become a nanny," he smiled gently. "Or any number of my nieces. But the question is, after my stint is over, what will become of your clinic? We need to talk about this, Dr. Rose." The worry line reappeared between his brows. "I don't want you to give it up if you don't want to. But I'll be more than ready to move home and take over full operations of the ranch: Pa is ready for that, too. He's already making noise about retirement. He and Ma want to travel the country, he says!"

She smiled distractedly, imagining Franticek and Gacenka as tourists at Niagara Falls and the Grand Canyon. And then she nodded, equally serious. "I'll be ready to come home with you, Jake!"

His face flattened in surprise. "You will?"

She nodded again, feeling another wave of relief wash through her. She was about to give voice to an idea she had been brewing; she had told no one and had scarcely admitted it to herself. "I'm going to be brutally honest. Working at the clinic with that population is emotionally draining, especially for someone who grew up in that environment. And I see the same cases, day after day after day: sexually transmitted disease, unwanted pregnancy, injuries from violence. This is going to sound awful, I know, but I would have actually enjoyed treating Eveline, Franticek and Ginny for diphtheria had I not been deathly afraid for them. I mean, the time I spent riding around the Hills with you, treating the folks out here—that was probably the most rewarding doctoring I've ever done. If you think the people out here would want me, I would love—." She had to stop then, because Jacob had jumped up and was dancing a jig in front of her. "Hmmm, Jake, what are you doing?" she giggled.

He gave one last impressive kick of his heels, rubbed his still-sore muscles, and squatted in front of her. "I've been imagining how this conversation would go, hoping that you would want to make Bluebonnet your home, but realizing that I had some pretty stiff competition. Are you sure?" He grabbed her hands, not believing his luck.

She returned the pressure and nodded happily. "Yes! I just

need to staff the clinic before I leave with a doctor and nurse I trust. Karl's son may be interested, but I need a woman in there, too. But I have four years to find one, right?"

"Right! And Bailey, you can retain ownership. It needs to remain The Rose Clinic! You can visit periodically and make sure things are just as you want them. We can pay for everything, you and me, with profits from the ranch."

She stared at him. "You would do that?"

He laughed and sat back on his heels. "I may have forgotten to mention that Bluebonnet is pretty damned profitable. And we want to invest in the city, don't we? I mean, it's your decision, too. It won't be my money anymore. It'll be *our* money."

Bailey was speechless for a moment. She wondered if there was another man in Texas who had ever uttered that sentiment and really ascribed to it.

She tilted her head, an ornery glint in her eye. "So the money I make doctoring up here will belong to you, too?"

"Sure thing. Although I have to warn you, you're likely to get paid in honey, wool, and goats more times than you can count."

"You can share in my honey and wool. But the goats are all mine: I have always been partial to goats."

He nodded solemnly. "That settles it. Now that the matter of goats has been decided, we can move forward. I propose that we marry immediately, say, in the next five minutes."

She shrugged. "All right. Go fetch the preacher."

They gazed at each other, considering it seriously for a moment, powerfully tempted.

"Really?" he finally croaked, heart pounding.

She smiled tenderly. "Oh, Jake. If only. But let's wait a few more days. We have Wenzel to lay to rest tomorrow. And I have a few things I need to do in the city." Her gaze shifted back to the stars. "I need to fetch Hope and find where my Mama is resting so we can tell her we love her. I need to stand up with Thomas and Gabby; they've been waiting so long to be together."

"Not as long as a few other people I know," muttered Jacob, but he was returning her smile. "One question. Can I come with you? You know—with the forces of the universe working to keep us apart—I'm thinking of handcuffing us together."

She leaned forward and kissed him lingeringly. "The handcuffs are for later," she whispered, and he lost his balance and fell clean off the porch.

CHAPTER NINE

Wenzel was laid to rest the next morning at sunrise, his very favorite time of day, in the family cemetery. The women were dressed in black crepe gowns with long, netted veils that completely covered their faces. With no spare costume for Bailey, Marianna had lent her a somber, dark green dress with a hat and veil, helping her to smooth and twist her hair back severely, and then stood back and shook her head ruefully. "You look much too beautiful for a funeral. But Wen would have approved." Bailey's mouth twisted in pain and she turned away.

The men milled in the yard in their black Sunday best, waiting for the women and children to emerge. When they all exited together, holding hands and clutching children tightly, Jacob, Johann, Anton, Joseph, Miguel, and Franticek turned silently and walked past them into the house, emerging with the casket on their shoulders, faces drawn with grief. They were a solemn procession, treading silently from the ranch house over two gentle hills and around a bend, the path bordered with the ubiquitous bluebonnets and spiky green yucca plants, finally emerging onto the plateau of another hill. The small, peaceful family graveyard was guarded by a ring of trees: Texas mountain laurels, whose lavender-colored, grape candy-smelling blooms had faded in the waning days of autumn, replaced by brown, leathery pods that resembled necklaces as they dangled from almost every branch. Interspersed among the laurel were the tall cottonwoods with their thick, twisty trunks and bright golden fall leaves. Emerging from the thick green grass were half a dozen white marble tombstones, and Bailey wondered if Franticek's younger brothers who had perished in the war were laid to rest here.

The men laid the casket reverently by a freshly-dug grave and stepped back to stand next to their families, gathering them close. For several long moments they stood this way, heads bowed, silent save for soft weeping.

The minister stepped forward, and the women lifted their veils to receive his message. He delivered a quiet missive of eternal life, his voice soothing and certain. When he had finished, he asked if any of the family would like to speak, and one by one Wenzel's loved ones came forward to recall fond memories and say their farewells.

When everyone had spoken but Bailey and Jacob, their eyes met, his questioning, hers, tortured. How could she speak to this family? If it weren't for her, Wenzel would be alive! She had removed herself from Jacob's life all of those years ago to keep him and his family safe and untouched by her catastrophic childhood, and sure enough, within months of re-entering his life, his brother was dead because of her. Just a few days ago she had reassured Alice that Alice wasn't culpable, but somehow Bailey could not shake this cloak of guilt she herself wore. *If only I had turned away from the stage that day at the debate. I saw him first. I could have run away.* But that was ludicrous: Jacob had already been trapped by Caroline at that point. *If only I had stayed at the ranch fifteen years ago. Wenzel would be alive today.* She knew she was being irrational, and she and Jacob had already laid those regrets to rest. But grief was clotting her throat, making it hard to breathe, hard to think. She would never behold him again, that mystical boy with otherworldly eyes. Never again in this lifetime.

Jacob regarded her for a beat and then leaned forward to murmur in her ear. "It's not your fault. Remember what he said." She stared at him, ever amazed at the way he could read her mind.

She nodded and made her wooden legs move to the casket, touching it lightly, gazing down upon it, wondering where he really was. She tried to resist looking into the grave itself, into that yawning hole, out of equal parts personal dread and delicate respect for the family. But she could not resist. The earthy, fecund smell of the fresh soil consumed her senses with a dizzying aroma of decayed leaves, pungent roots, and—what was it? That familiar scent—then it struck her. Worms. It smelled of the worms that were always flushed out of their hidey-holes in a hard, sudden rain, sprawled across the cobblestones in town. She always diligently avoided stepping on the poor souls, and when she was a child, she had spent hours gathering them tenderly, pulling her skirt into a basket to give transport, carrying them back to the mounds of mud and dirt bordering the streets.

But that was not all; it wasn't just worms. It smelled of spring gardens with freshly-turned soil, ready to be sown. Not just of death, but of rebirth. His body would feed the trees, she supposed. *Would the trees know it was Wenzel who nourished them?*

She thought she might swoon after all.

They were going to put him down there, into that hole. She stared down into it, forcing herself to consider the stark truth. Wenzel was in the box, and the box would be put in the hole. She stared and stared, knowing that the family watched her do so, but needing to know it fully, this final resting place for Wenzel, for her mother, for Adam Hawk, and ultimately for herself, for Jacob, for their children, and their grandchildren someday, and on and on. She tried to come to terms with it, with this shared, ignoble end. She had never in her life attended a funeral, although she had attended countless deaths.

She found herself thinking instead of the many times she had been present at her patients' passing. It was always the start of something: they were traveling somewhere intensely beautiful. Not just traveling, but *returning*. Surely that place to which they traveled was not to a hole in the ground full of roots and worms and beetles; that destination was for the body that they shed like a superfluous coat on an early day in March that has suddenly turned from chilly to warm, from winter to spring. That's what the hole was for: a receptacle for the organic matter that would enter back into the cycle of life. The hole was for their bodies in this world, but there were other, more glorious worlds, and she had been there before and would be again, Wenzel said.

A light seemed to fill her, and suddenly she felt buoyant and fearless. She supposed she was having an epiphany! There was more than just *here*. So much more! She could sense it now, all around her, as though she was awakening slowly from a dream.

She turned to face the family—*her* family—her face shining. "Wenzel taught me to fish fifteen years ago, when we were just kids," she began. Gacenka beamed and nodded encouragement. "On that day," she continued quietly, "I told him a secret. He promised that he would protect me. He—he held my hand." She bowed her head and took several deep breaths, tears spilling to the grass. "A few days ago, he kept his promise." She gazed out at the family, her eyes resting on her beloved, who was smiling through tears of his own. Her eyes shifted to the trees, wondering if they were listening, if they could understand her words. "He died for me. I held him in my arms as he passed. He told me he was born for that moment, so I could live, and he was so *happy*. Happy!" Gacenka and her daughters were sobbing now, but Bailey felt strangely calm and tranquil, and wondered if Wenzel were standing right beside her. Yes, he was. She was sure of it. "I've been thinking about paths lately, and I really feel as though Wen walked the path he was meant to. He *chose* it, it didn't choose him, but he was meant for it. I hope you find comfort in that." She looked up and Jacob's arms were out, waiting, and she walked right into them, relieved.

At last, only Jacob remained. The bond he had shared with Wenzel had been extraordinary; she wondered how he would ever be able to let him go. He gave Bailey one last squeeze and moved forward to stand by Wenzel's casket, gazing at his family for such a long moment that Bailey wondered if he would be able to speak after all.

111

Then he put his finger to his lips. "You're all going to have to stop crying now," he said unexpectedly, and the family looked at him, taken aback. "They won't come unless you're quiet."

There was an absolute silence. Every last person looked dumbfounded, perhaps wondering if the traumatic events of the past week had finally pushed Jacob over the edge. Only Gacenka wore a look of understanding, and she was smiling broadly through her tears, hands clasped to her heart.

Bailey felt a vibration hum through her body as she began to understand what was going to happen next.

They came then, like a black cloud blotting out the sharp morning light. They came in wave after wave after wave, thousands of them, the beating of wings stirring the air. It seemed they would never stop: the trees were heavy with them, every branch sagging with bobwhites, woodpeckers, flycatchers, wrens, warblers, towhees, orioles, and goldfinches. Large black crows stood side-by-side with the tiny titmice. The last to arrive, a simple field sparrow, landed on Wenzel's casket and stood as still as a statue, and he and Jacob regarded each other for a moment.

Jacob turned back to the family and smiled. "We're all here now." He gazed around at the trees for another moment as he collected his thoughts. "Wen is here, too. I can't explain it. But he's here, just as surely as you and I are here. Wen could always be here *and* there. Not much has changed, except we forgot how to see him." He paused a long moment and seemed to be adrift in his own thoughts. "You know, I reckon we all could do that when we were little, see everything, until we got too busy and distracted and concerned with putting on labels like *real* and *imaginary*." He looked meaningfully at Annie's youngest, a toddler with wispy brown curls, who was sitting in the grass, waving her chubby arms and babbling happily with what seemed to be empty air.

"I think Wen would like you all to take time to just *be*. To drop our silly tasks and just live in the moment when we can. What did that fellow Thoreau say? Life is frittered away by detail. A man has to *live*. Count your fingers and toes and lump the rest."

Bailey stared at him, this magical man in his black Sunday best, hat clutched in his hand, professing peace and simplicity as he looked at the trees, his eyes full of things she couldn't quite see. He could see it—what she had sensed—at least some of it, she knew. *What have I done in my life to deserve this man?*

Jacob's gaze shifted to her, his ghost girl. She was unbearably exquisite in her borrowed green dress, the wind blowing her hair free from a carefully-twisted knot, her face shining with joy and a kind of dawning comprehension. *I don't know what I've done to deserve you, but I'm never letting you go.*

The birds lifted as one a short time later, silent and majestic, their wings beating against the azure, cloudless sky. In the space of a moment they were gone, and the small group craned their necks to watch the last traces of them vanish in the distance.

There was a heavy silence; no one wanted to be the one to break the magic of the moment.

Jacob jammed his hat back on his head and clapped his hands briskly, smiling broadly at the group. "Now it's time to eat and dance! Come on! You know the drill!"

Ginny gave a whoop, deciding not to be sad, and her cousins followed suit; soon the children were swarming over the grass, anxious to dig into the food laid out in the yard that the women had been preparing since the dark hours of early morning. Jacob's siblings and in-laws laughed and erupted into a low hum, sharing incredulous glances and shooting shy looks Jacob's way. *Did he talk to that bird? He has the* darovala *like Wenzel, doesn't he? He has the gift!* The murmurs were all around them, but he didn't notice: he made a beeline for Bailey and swung her into an exuberant hug.

"You get it, right?" he whispered.

"You and I are going to be spending a lot of time over the next fifty years walking very dreamily through these hills, counting our fingers and toes and talking to the birds and trees," she smiled.

He gave her a squeeze as they made their way to the festivities.

"That's my girl."

Much later in the day, as the men began to roast chicken and mutton over a huge spit and the women prepared *cibulačká*—traditional Moravian onion soup—in the most enormous cast-iron pot Bailey had ever seen, Gacenka took them aside. They strolled together in silence, Gacenka deep in thought. Bailey looked at Jacob nervously, clutching his hand, but he gave her an encouraging wink and bumped her hip, shoving her off-balance. She bumped back, giggling, but they quickly straightened as Gacenka turned to regard them sternly. "Over here. Sit." She pointed to a spot under one of the ranch's wondrous, sprawling live oak trees, and they all sat in the soft grass, facing each other.

"I suppose the two of you have many questions," she finally began with a weary smile. "I will try to answer them as best as I can."

She waited patiently as they stared at her, stared at each other, and stared at her again.

"Ma! I don't even know where to begin!" Jacob finally laughed.

Gacenka regarded Bailey. "Maybe you should begin, dear girl. Tell us what you needed Wenzel to protect you from those many years ago."

Jacob cleared his throat and shifted anxiously. He had never revealed the near-drowning incident to anyone, and he found, to his surprise, that even fifteen years later he still dreaded a scolding from his mother about leaving Bailey alone on the creek's bank to bathe. He carried a tremendous amount of guilt about that day.

"Ma'am, do you remember that day long ago, when you first saw me? I was sitting in the sheep pit? And I told you I had seen a wolf?"

Gacenka nodded silently, brow furrowed. Bailey couldn't bear to look at Jacob, but she felt him stiffen beside her. Only now was he beginning to understand the extraordinary reach of Caroline in their lives.

"And later, when Jacob and I got in a bit of a *tecolé* fight?"

Gacenka snorted. "Yes, of course I do! I almost laughed myself sick, and so did your father," she added, looking at Jacob. He offered a tepid smile in response.

Bailey twisted her hands in her lap. "Well, you sent us to the creek to bathe. When we got there, we separated so—I mean—Jacob wanted to give me privacy."

The older woman gazed at them both; her lips were stern, but her eyes were sparkling. "Yes. That was probably very wise." Bailey's face grew scarlet and Jacob squirmed.

"And—well—I laid on my back and put my head in the water. I almost had all of that goop out, and then..." She paused, closing her eyes, reliving the horror of the moment. "I heard a voice. It sounded like a man and a woman, or neither; I don't know! It called me by name and told me to come into the water. I thought someone was on shore, but then it pulled my hair—a vicious yank—and in I went. It pulled me under. I couldn't swim, so I started to drown." Jacob stared at her: she had never told him about the voice, only the sensation of being pulled into the water.

Gacenka's expression had changed from one of suppressed amusement to outright horror. The blood drained from her cheeks and she covered her mouth. "Oh no, Bailey, my child..."

"I screamed and Jacob heard me. He rescued me. He pulled me out of the water and squeezed the water right out of my lungs until I was breathing again."

The image of the two of them on the mossy bank of the creek, entwined, terrified, *awakening*, struck them both then, and as one they bowed their heads, unable to meet Gacenka's gaze. That moment in time was still so very bewildering: pain and panic and shock juxtaposed with arousal and a burgeoning love. Death, then life. Innocence, then longing.

"It was all my fault, Ma. I shouldn't have left her alone. I knew she couldn't swim. I should have stayed and turned my back."

Bailey reached for him and squeezed his hand.

"It wasn't your fault," she said quietly. "It was her fault. Caroline's."

He stared at her, his expression flat with shock, still not wanting to believe. "What?"

Gacenka moaned, shaking her head. "Oh, Bailey. Oh, my dear. How I wish you would have told me that day. I understand why you didn't—it must have seemed unbelievable. Now the pieces of the puzzle are coming together in my thick skull; what a shame that I've always been a little slow to understand things. So much pain could have been avoided."

"Bailey." Jacob's lips moved soundlessly for a beat as he tried to gain equilibrium. "Are you telling me that Caroline—all the way back then—tried to drown you? But how? Why?"

And so she finally lifted the burden from her heart, telling them everything Caroline had revealed to her as she had been bound by the pool just a few scant days ago: the incident with Jacob and the poor girl in the barn, when Caroline had been caught beating her. "She had to make you forget," explained Bailey, as Jacob gaped at her. "She gave you the Forgetting drink, and it worked."

"Yes," he breathed. "But I remember now, bits and pieces. I've always been uncomfortable in that spot of the feed barn and I never knew why; just that something bad must have happened."

Bailey nodded patiently, dreading every revelation. "She watched you, Jake. She spied on you over the next several years. And she followed the wagon when you brought me to the ranch." She just couldn't bring herself to say, *in her wolf form*. She was afraid she may burst into hysterical laughter. All of it was so far out of the realm of the believable that she didn't yet know how to talk about it, so she squeezed her eyes shut and finished as rapidly as she could. "She tried to—to *get* me—when we stopped and you went in to fetch your Ma, but she was foiled by the whole family coming out to see what I was squalling about. So she waited and watched, and then had her chance at the creek. Only she wasn't a wolf then."

"*Duśe Jedlíci*," murmured Gacenka. "Just like her horrible

mother, and her mother before her, God save us."

"You know about Aloisie Vogler?" breathed Bailey.

Gacenka nodded and wrung her hands. "I didn't make the connection until a few days ago when you were attacked. I just didn't realize that Aloisie Vogler was the Aloisie I knew as a girl; it was such a common name. Oh yes, we all knew about Aloise; those of us who lived in the woods, anyway, back in the Old Country. Nobody in the village believed it, but we knew it was true. Caroline's grandmother—Alzbeta Fiser—she was the first *Duśe Jedlíci* born in a thousand years, they say. The last name, "Fiser," it means "fisher," of course. Mama was five years old when Alzbeta was born. The river turned to blood for three days. An impenetrable fog encased the woods, and there were unbearable shrieks and screams for days; human sacrifices, she said it was. The birds all went away. She remembers her own mother, my grandmother, laying a stone circle around the cottage and chanting, burning sage and sweet grass in the ancient bone bowls she had inherited. Then after three days the fog lifted and the screaming stopped and the river flowed as water again. The birds began singing again, but nothing was the same, ever again. Alzbeta married her first cousin—his name was Fiser, too—and Aloisie was born, another soul eater, she was, even worse than Alzbeta. Mama always warned us children to stay away from the Morava River where that ancient stone bridge stood crumbling: it was their lair, only five miles' walk from our house, it was. Oh, Lord. Evil, evil women, they were. Folks began to disappear." Her eyes darted to Jacob, and Bailey felt him stiffen again.

"What? What else, Ma? I can tell there's more."

Gacenka shuddered, hugging herself, her pretty face looking the oldest Bailey had ever seen it. "I never knew for sure, but my Otec, my poor father, I think Aloisie drowned him. She was so beautiful; she could have easily seduced him to the river. I remember him mentioning a blond fairy, so beautiful, who lived by the river. He had helped her to haul fish to the village. He told me when he was drunk, and I ran away from him, my hands over my ears."

Bailey thought of Caroline's smug recall of her mother's acquisition of a particularly handsome man's golden eye, and she felt her face drain of blood and a wave of nausea roll over her.

"Ma, this is enough for now," Jacob said softly.

Bailey shook her head. "No. I need to understand. I want to know I'm not crazy!"

"It's all real, my sweet daughter," murmured Gacenka. "I know it cannot seem to be so, but there is more in this world than you could possibly imagine."

Bailey nodded numbly, clutching Jacob's hand.

"I haven't thought of Aloisie Fiser for decades. I never knew what happened to her. She married that Vogler man, obviously, and emigrated here, but for the life of me, I can't figure why."

"I can answer that," said Bailey. "Caroline told me that her parents were forced out of the *Vodicini* community. They were aberrations and were made to leave. So they came here because her mother knew there was a large population of Moravians here, and she wanted her daughter to marry a Moravian man, even if he wasn't a Vodnik." She paused uncertainly before continuing. "Caroline—she mentioned that she heard voices telling her to hurt herself, and she knew the only way to quiet them was to collect a soul. But she only wanted one."

"Yours," said Jacob softly.

Bailey closed her eyes briefly and then looked at him. She knew he wouldn't want to hear what she had to say next; that any defense of Caroline would be incomprehensible to him. "You should know that she didn't mean to shoot Wenzel, Jake. The gun went off when he tackled her. She could have shot me. And when she shifted, she could have killed me; she could have had my throat in an instant, but she didn't. I think her love for you stopped her. After all the horrible things she had done, her love for you let me live, because she saw your love for *me*. I just know it. So she ran away."

Jacob's jaw bulged and his hands gripped hers painfully. He wanted to refute Bailey's words loudly and forcefully: he felt downright murderous toward that—that *thing* that had destroyed

Wenzel, drugged and seduced Anton, and almost drowned Bailey. He found no clemency in his heart, and he suspected that Bailey's generous nature was giving credit where none was due.

"I don't believe that," he said stiffly. "I'm sorry. I know you see the good in everyone, but I just can't. Not yet anyway, and probably not ever."

They all sat in silence then, each trying to come to terms with something so nefarious that it remained just beyond the grasp of their understanding; so incomprehensible and evil that the temptation to just put it behind them and relinquish any attempt at understanding was tremendous. *Pretend it never happened. Don't let it become a part of our lives. She is gone. Caroline and her wicked mother are gone, probably fled back to the muddy river of their genesis, far across the ocean. Leave it. Leave it far behind.*

CHAPTER TEN

The very next day, Bailey and Jacob boarded the train back to the city, Anton and Alice riding with them. They were a quiet foursome, Alice asleep with her head on Anton's shoulder, Bailey and Jacob stuck together like glue, whispering and laughing quietly and just gazing, soaking each other in. The train was over-crowded; passengers stood in the aisle, and more than once Jacob and Anton stood to relinquish their seats to women. The last leg was particularly chaotic, and Bailey gave up her seat as well, urging a sweet old lady with red cheeks and a stooped, arthritic back into her seat. She stood in front of Jacob, and when the train began to roll, he let go of the handle and wrapped his arms around her waist, under cover of the mass of people pushing against them. She leaned back into him, letting the motion of the train sway her body in rhythm with his, at one point feeling his face in her hair, kissing the back of her neck. She relived the sensation of his goodbye embrace all of those years ago: he had hugged her and kissed her neck. She had thought she would die of happiness, and she felt just like that now, like a breathless twelve-year-old girl, falling in love hard and fast and forever. *Rosie, come back to me.*

They disembarked amidst the bustle, struggling with their luggage and shouting instructions to each other and Anton. They were to stay with Anton, all three of them, but Bailey had wired ahead and planned to spend the day with Gabby and Hope preparing for Gabby's wedding, which would take place the next day. Jacob rented a rig and lifted her up into it, insisting on driving her to Harding House and picking her up later.

"I can drive myself, you know. I don't need an escort," Bailey teased. "Are you to be a caveman who carries around his woman over his shoulder our whole married life?"

"Not if that whole three-hundred-pound prediction comes true," he said thoughtfully, and was unable to avoid a well-placed punch on his arm.

"Seriously, Jake. I can take care of myself."

He was quiet for a beat, then nodded and smiled, pulling the rig over and stopping a scant two hundred yards from the livery. He turned to her and tipped back his hat.

"I know it. I know you can." He sighed and stared at his hands clutching the reins. "To be honest with you, I'm scared, Rosie."

The vulnerability in his voice made her eyes sting.

"Scared of what?"

"Just like I told you before. Scared of losing you. Scared that you'll vanish, again."

She let that admission hang between them, giving it the due it deserved.

"Well, it takes a man to be able to admit that," she said softly.

He smiled at her sadly. "Yeah. Some man, letting Caroline almost kill you three times. Some big caveman protector I am."

She stared at him. "Is that what this is about? Caroline?"

"No. Yes. I don't know. I don't know where she is. I don't know what else is out there that might—take you away from me. There's a million things, aren't there? You could get sick. You could get thrown from this rig. You could die having our baby. You could get shot or stabbed in the District when you visit your patients."

She laughed in amazement. "Well, thank you, Jake, for that jolly rundown of plausible ways I could die!"

He laughed too, rueful and ashamed of himself. "I'm sorry, Bailey. I know I'm being ridiculous. I don't know how to control it, though, these things that could take you away from me."

She shrugged. "You can't. Just as I can't control what happens to you. And if we try, well, we would probably just meet our destiny on the way to prevent it, isn't that what they say?"

He nodded glumly.

She shoved him gently, then grabbed his chin and forced him to look at her. "What happened to the boy who told me to live in the moment? To count our fingers and toes and chuck the rest?"

"He's here," he said softly. "I just want to count them with *you*."

She regarded him for a moment longer, and decided that the separation anxiety he had joked about on the train was real, and overcoming it would be a process. "Tell you what. I want you to drive me to Harding House. In fact, you can be our escort today. Thomas is busy and we shall need a driver as we look for a gown and flowers and—oh, hell, I don't even know what we're shopping for today! Planning a wedding at the last minute is crazy! I thought that Gabby would have had it all sorted weeks ago."

"You are coddling me," he muttered, but he already looked much, much happier.

"Well, yes, but let's take baby steps. You cannot chain yourself to me, but if you need a fix, well, I'll be within reach."

His eyes glittered. "I need a fix *now*," he whispered, and before she could respond, he pulled her to him, sliding his hand into her hair, and kissed her so long and deep that she was breathless, heart pounding, her entire body turning to liquid fire, when he pulled away.

"Holy hellfire, Jake," she managed. "You can't do that to me in public."

He stared into her eyes and looked like he was about to start it up again, but to her surprise, he jumped out of the rig and jogged around to her side. "Scoot on over and drive," he ordered. "I'm walking back and getting my own damn horse. Just stay with Gabby and Hope tonight; have a girls' night. You all need each other. See ya' at the wedding tomorrow." He turned away and muttered loudly enough for her to hear. "Needy woman, always trying to hang on like a barnacle. Won't give me my damn space."

She laughed all the way to Harding House, admitting to herself how terribly much she missed him already, knowing how hard it had been for him to get out of that wagon. She sobered, remembering the feel of his mouth on hers, his hands in her hair, gripping her skull, and wondered who was suffering from separation pains after all.

Shopping, as painful as it had always been for Bailey, proved to be an exercise in hilarity with Gabby and Hope. Hope, with her east-coast flair and life of wealth, had just the gown in mind for her new friend, and she wanted to buy it for her. She found it immediately in Carson's Garments, one of the few upscale dress shops in town. It was a gown of ivory lace, satin, and tulle, inspired by a painting of Elizabeth of Austria by Franz Russ, the shopkeeper shared in a hushed, dramatic tone. The dress featured a triple layered lace skirt, scattered with mother-of-pearl sequins, worn over petticoats and a crinoline hoop. The velvet train was edged with appliquéd details in gold, and the corseted bodice was encrusted with intricate beaded patterns in crystals, sequins, pearls and facetted stones.

Hope oohed and ahhed, her face alight with excitement, while Gabby stood silent, arms crossed over her chest.

"Whatever is wrong?" Hope finally asked, interrupting her soliloquy over the gown long enough to notice that Gabby was not on board.

Gabby smiled thinly. "That looks exactly like something I would have worn at the Purple Pansy," she muttered. "You know, maybe during one of those nights when I dressed up as the blushing bride and the john was the altar boy."

Hope stared at her a beat and then burst into laughter. "Oh, Gabriella! You are *so* funny!"

Gabby shared a sidelong look with Bailey, who knew she absolutely was not kidding.

"What do you think of it, sis?" asked Hope innocently.

Bailey gulped and decided that this would have been the perfect time for a Jacob fix. "Well. Gee. I'm not much of a judge of fashion, as you both know. I mean, I'd wear britches every day if I could."

"But don't you think this is perfect for Gabriella? Oh, the way the crystals would set off her dark hair! We can pile it up real high on her head, like a queen. All curls and ribbons!"

"I don't know," she stuttered, her face reddening.

"Oh, come on now," insisted Hope, holding the dress up to Gabby. "What do you think?"

"Ummm..." Bailey waited for the *deus ex machina*, but nothing presented itself.

"You like it, don't you?" Hope smiled engagingly. Bailey felt Gabby droop a bit. For as outspoken as Gabby was, she apparently did not want to bruise a new friendship over something as frivolous as a gown. But this was her wedding!

"Look, Hope. Gabby is too nice to say so, but she wants something simple. You remember that Grecian gown she wore to court? Something like that, maybe. With a little less leg showing. And we won't be piling her hair up on her head with curls and bows. Maybe a simple low bun, with white pearls strung throughout it."

Both of the women stared at her. "Well, *damn*. Why didn't you say so before?" Hope laughed.

"Why didn't *you* say something?" Bailey accused Gabby, putting one finger on her chest and pushing.

"Because I really don't care what I wear," smiled Gabby. "I just want to marry Tommy. And I will be out of that dress as fast as I can, if you know what I mean. Probably in the carriage ride on the way to the train. So just find something without too many buttons."

Hope threw the dress up in the air and gave a mighty whoop, and the three of them found themselves holding onto each other, laughing until their sides ached.

"Bailey!" gasped Gabby. "You know you feel the same way."

Bailey nodded, barely able to speak, she was laughing so hard. "He—he kissed me in the wagon today and I thought we—we were going to have to find a dark corner!"

"You haven't found a dark corner either, then?" asked Gabby, once they had collected themselves a bit.

Bailey shook her head, her cheeks pink again. "I mean, we have, but every time, we get interrupted."

"*Coitus interruptus*," said Hope gravely, her face comically somber, and that set them all off again.

By the close of the afternoon they had found the perfect gown, made of layers and layers of very fine Indian muslin embroidered with an elaborate floral pattern. The fabric was unabashedly white and flowed like water over the lines of Gabriella's body, trailing the floor behind her. Bailey and Hope both cried when Gabby emerged from the dressing room, her face shining.

The rest of the evening was spent passing Baby T.J. around, eating Gabby's scrumptious *tamales* and sipping a sweet red wine that Hope had snuck in the voluminous folds of her skirts— Harding House had a no-alcohol policy. The girls pushed two beds together in Gabby's room and talked and laughed until midnight, hushing each other by turns when the baby whimpered, until Bailey finally insisted they turn off the light and let Gabby get rested up for her big day.

But Bailey found sleep to be elusive until almost dawn: every time she closed her eyes, she saw Wenzel sailing over her again, tackling Caroline and landing in a bloody heap on the ground; she heard him take his last breath and felt his body deflate in her arms; she saw Caroline's face bloat into a horrific, hairy, savage form. She finally rose to stand over the baby, touching his silky hair, leaning down to breathe in his scent.

"Bailey. Come here." It was Gabby's low whisper, and Bailey turned, startled.

"I'm sorry," she said. "I didn't mean to wake you. I can't sleep."

Gabby smiled and scooted over in her bed. *"Venir aquí."*

And only after Bailey had settled beside her lifelong friend, nestled in her arms, was she able to sleep.

Gabriella de Los Santos Canales Moran de Flores married Thomas James Eckles at two o'clock in the afternoon the next day in a quiet ceremony in the Paine Church chapel, a lovely limestone Methodist Episcopal church on the corner of Navarro and Travis, just a stone's throw from St. Mark's. The sanctuary was serenely beautiful, the walls whitewashed and the deep pews blonde pine, populated with parishioners eager to celebrate their new minister's marriage: modest, kind-faced middle and working class folks not quite as well-connected and wealthy as the St. Mark's congregation. They were sneaking surreptitious glances at the guests on the left side of the aisle: Harding House residents in various stages of pregnancy and bedecked in all manner of outrageous costumes: feathers and beads and brightly-colored silk gowns that showed a considerable amount of skin. Bailey smiled at them mistily, and several of them waved to her excitedly, the rustle of silk accompanying the flurry. Anton and Alice sat with them, as did Karl Schwartz, his wife Becky, and his son John.

Bailey had not laid eyes on Jacob until she was walking down the aisle on the arm of Josiah Johnson, the best man; she found Hope immediately, as her sister was wearing a bright red satin gown topped with an equally-shocking hat: she had purchased it the day before when the shop owner had assured her that it was "Western." The hat featured red ostrich feathers around the crown with red roses and red pearls in front, finished off with red English netting train down the back. Bailey felt a pang as she was reminded of the red dress she had made all of those years ago, wearing it to the German school with stars in her eyes. Somehow, the gown and hat looked perfect on Hope.

And then her eyes were drawn to the man sitting beside her sister. He sat straight, shoulders wide, his black hair combed carefully but looking to be mutinous. The organ struck up Brahms, signaling the attendants, and Bailey found she could barely breathe. Her eyes were riveted to the back of Jacob's head, and as the guests began to crane their necks to view the procession, his head turned as well. Their eyes locked, and for a second he forgot to breathe. Then he smiled slowly, taking her in, hungry for the sight of her after a day of separation. Bailey was wearing a simple Grecian-style dress to resemble Gabby's, only hers was a dusky pink. Pink! He grinned even wider, guessing that she was wearing that dress with much chagrin. There were large pink cabbage roses threaded throughout her hair, which Hope had artfully arranged in a series of braids and twists and curls. Bailey had let her have a free hand with her dress and face paint and hair, and the result had been—well— flamboyant. She had never worn pink as a rule; she felt that it made her hair look orange. And speaking of her hair, it was a bit *towering*. She had wanted to tell her sister to tone it down five inches or so, but couldn't bring herself to. Hope had powdered and rouged her face in an effort to hide the bruises, but the end result resembled a geisha girl. Self-conscious, she missed her footing and tripped, and the audience tittered quietly as Josiah steadied her. Her face flamed, and she wondered what Jacob thought of it: was he smirking on the inside, watching this pink-clad, orange-haired woman with a purple eye and swollen nose stumble down the aisle? Was he having second thoughts, or would he, after he got a look at the extraordinary beauty of Gabriella?

Jacob was *not* having second thoughts. He was aching, wishing with all of his heart that this was his wedding and that the girl walking down the aisle on the arm of Josiah Johnson was about to be his wife in a few short moments. He swallowed thickly, his Adam's apple bobbing, and winked at her, trying to quell his longing and lighten the moment. She offered a shaky smile and made herself look away before she fell flat on her face. Somehow, incredibly, he still had the power to make her feel shy.

Finally she and Josiah arrived at the front of the chapel and stood on each side of a euphoric Thomas, who was dressed to the hilt in a black tuxedo. Bailey noticed that his hands were still; there was no nervous pulling of the earlobe. He was happier and more at ease than Bailey had ever seen him, and as she caught his eye, they beamed at each other. And then there was a breathless moment before the wedding march commenced; when the organist struck the chords, the guests stood and turned, waiting for the bride.

Suddenly, there she was, floating down the aisle, eliciting gasps from the women and dumbstruck expressions from the men. She was a queen, nothing less, with the sculpted, flawless lines of her face, her head held high, her bright emerald eyes shining, her full lips smiling, her dark hair gathered low on her neck and strung with pearls. She did not wear a veil, and her unconventional dress seemed to be made of liquid silk. Every woman in the room imagined herself in it, then immediately dismissed the idea, for no one could wear it like Gabriella. She made her way down the aisle on her own: she had no one to give her away, and she had decided she belonged to herself, anyway. She and Thomas would give themselves to each other.

The young man officiating was a friend of Thomas's from the seminary; serving to partially fill the void left by Thomas's absent family. His parents did not approve of his marriage and had severed ties with him weeks ago. But his family was the furthest thing from his mind: his attention was riveted to the vision moving down the aisle, still unable to fully believe that she loved him and was to be his wife.

She arrived at Thomas's side, and after a complicated look shared between them, they faced the minister, who delivered a sweet sermon of forgiveness and love. The couple repeated their vows in low, emotion-filled tones. Bailey felt the tears trail down her cheeks and supposed that they were leaving tracks in the powder and rouge, but she didn't care a whit. Gabby's life had held even more tragedy and heartache than her own, and to see her transcend it to begin a life with a man she loved so deeply— one who had given up his family and church in his love for her— was a miracle to witness. *Look where we landed, Gabby*, she thought incredulously. *We finally found our lives.*

They saw the happy couple off in a grand carriage lent by a parishioner, Bailey and Hope huddled together and giggling behind their hands, wondering if Gabby's dress was being dispensed of as quickly as she had predicted.

"I can't imagine what you ladies are whispering about," came Jacob's voice from behind them, and Bailey spun around and reached for his hands.

"I missed you!" she gushed, gripping his hands just as hard as she could, and then suddenly released them, blushing madly. She must sound like a besotted schoolgirl, perhaps just like one of the tittering throng that was forever chasing after this man. She glanced at Hope, abashed, and found that her sister was smiling at her tenderly.

Jacob captured her hands and tugged her closer to him, leaning down to whisper in her ear. "I missed you too. You're beautiful, Rosie. I wish we were married right this minute." His breath was warm on her cheek and she felt a blush infuse her entire body. *Every inch of me must be red now*, she thought dazedly, and they stared at each other in silence.

"Hey, you two," broke in Hope with a broad smile. "Why don't you join Cordy and Howard and me for a bite to eat? We'd love to get to know this fellow better. I need to make sure he's good enough for my sister," she added sternly.

Bailey kept her gaze on Jacob, who was moving closer with every passing second and would soon be within kissing range, something that was certainly not proper for a mayor-elect to do in a church yard in broad daylight. "Oh, Hope. He's perfect."

Hope rolled her eyes and made a gagging sound. "How disgusting! As if I haven't suffered enough with Thomas and Gabby's sloppy lovies!"

Bailey finally looked at her sister with an apology in her eyes. "I'm sorry, Hope, but we were planning on traveling back to Boerne this evening, and I wanted to try to find Mother's grave before we went. Won't you come with us? I know the potter's field where she's buried; it's just a few miles out of town."

Hope's merry face drew down and a flicker of pain passed over her pretty features. "Of course, Bailey. Thank you for asking me."

Jacob cleared his throat nervously. "Actually," he interjected softly as the three of them made their way to his rig, "I have a bit of a surprise for you first."

"For me?" Bailey asked.

"Oh! Why, you can just fetch me at Harding House when you're done!" Hope hastened to add.

"This is for both of you," smiled Jacob, and took each of them by an elbow, steering them onward.

It was a short ride, and Jacob refused to tell them where they were going. But when they turned onto Hondo Street and into the National Cemetery, Bailey was thoroughly confused.

"Jake," she said gently, touching his arm. "Sweetheart, she wouldn't be buried here!"

He turned and grinned at her. "Did you just call me 'sweetheart'?"

Hope snorted and Bailey reddened again. "Maybe. Should I call you something else? I can think of a few other names."

He held up his hands in defense. "No, no! I love 'sweetheart,' honestly. Now, I want you to trust me, okay?"

She shared a look of confusion with Hope, who just shrugged and waved him on. He drove the rig between two large white columns and over to the ornate iron hitching posts cast in the image of military horses, and all the while, Bailey and Hope were speechless, worried frowns creasing their brows, sure that Jacob was wasting time here. He handed them down, and the three of them began to stroll through the cemetery in silence, gazing at the white stones placed amongst the oak and magnolia trees. American and Texan flags adorned each grave, and they paused often to read the inscriptions; but Jacob seemed to have a direction in mind and steered them gently toward the northeast corner of the four acres.

At last, they stood before a large monument—at least six feet tall and made of marble, no less, beautifully adorned with two doves perched on a branch, beaks touching, wings stretched for flight. When Bailey saw the engraving on the stone, she gasped, her hands covering her mouth, tears springing to her eyes. She moved forward and touched it, tracing her fingers over the letters etched in the exquisite marble, not daring to believe. She stared at Hope, who was struggling to understand, and Jacob, whose eyes were filled with such tender love that she couldn't bear to look at him for long. She returned her gaze to the monument, and then took a step forward and laid her forehead against it, hugging it to her.

Here lies Dr. John Alfred Bailey
First Regiment Calvary of New Orleans
Who gave his life for his brothers and his country,
And his wife,
Adele Olivia Rosemont,
Beloved mother, sister, and daughter,
Who gave her life for her children.
Rest in peace and heavenly immortality.

She felt a hand on her shoulder, and she spun into his arms, laughing and crying.

"You did this?" she choked.

"Yes," he whispered. "Karl helped. Is it okay? We wanted them to be together."

She nodded, unable to speak. The three of them stood silent for a good long while, and then Jacob guided Bailey to Hope's side and discreetly drifted back to the rig, giving them some time and space.

"It feels weird, you know," Hope said after a long while, her voice thin. "I didn't know them, of course." Hope tried to keep the jealousy at bay, but she was afraid that some of the bitterness may have seeped through.

"I'm so sorry," murmured Bailey. "I wish you could have known her. But I don't have any good memories of her, not really. By the time I was old enough to remember, she was already—well—gone, if you know what I mean. She was never *with* me."

Hope hung her head. "I'm the one who's sorry, Bailey. I lived a life of privilege with a mother and dad of sorts. And you—"

"I grew up in a whorehouse and a convent."

They glanced at each other and Hope was relieved to see a glimmer of humor in her sister's eyes.

"You know what? We both turned out okay, didn't we? And here she lies, together with him, someplace where we can put flowers and imagine them forever young, together." Bailey moved to the stone again, placing her lips on the cold marble, trying with all of her might to conjure memories of kissing her mother's cheek. She was rewarded with a flash of memory that was so strong and sudden that she sank to her knees.

She was rocking with her mother beside a fireplace. She felt the warmth from the flickering flames and the warmth from her mother's body: her mother was cradling her, kissing her forehead and her nose, and singing a lilting song, something about pretty ponies. She could smell her mother's skin when she leaned close: it smelled of vanilla and something else unnamable, just *mother*. She wore her hair in a thick brown braid over her shoulder; she could reach up and tug it, and her mother would close her eyes briefly, open them, and laugh. Oh, her smile! She had forgotten all about it. Her mother's smile was her *world*; how could she have forgotten?

"She loved me. She loved her baby," she whispered, and she sobbed then; great, heaving wails of grief, and felt both Hope and Jacob wrap their arms tightly around her.

CHAPTER ELEVEN

The journey to deliver Hope back to Harding House was surprisingly buoyant: Bailey felt as though a thousand pounds had been lifted from her shoulders. Hope was rambunctious, peppering Jacob with impertinent questions and waving at men passing by in wagons if she felt they warranted her attention.

"Now Jacob. I know you adore my sister, but Bailey is a *doctor*, in case you've forgotten. You won't be putting her on your mantle next to your other trophies, understand?"

"My wh--?"

"She's not a doll or a prize, my dear boy," Hope interrupted with a flip of her hand. She shook her finger at him, making the feathers on her red hat shake in indignation. "She's a woman, with needs."

Jacob's face turned an alarming hue and he was rendered speechless for a beat, a rare state of affairs for him.

"Hope! Honestly!" Bailey swatted at her sister, but Hope was not to be silenced.

"That's right. Someone has to say it. She may look delicate and precious, what with all of that—*bone structure*—and her pretty little puffy lip and those big puppy dog eyes…"

"Hope! Lord in Heaven!" shouted Bailey.

"But underneath all that lies the heart of a lion. Can you

satisfy her emotional, intellectual, and well, let's be frank, Jacob, her *womanly* needs?"

It was Bailey's turn to be flabbergasted. She knew Hope was outspoken and outrageous and unpredictable, but she never imagined she would cross *that* line.

Jacob had recovered by this time and straightened, tugging on his lapels and nodding gravely. "Yes, ma'am. I do solemnly swear to spend my life, right down to my last breath, satisfying her every need." He flashed a dimple and winked at Bailey and she felt herself go weak.

"Whew!" Hope produced a fan from the voluminous folds of her red gown and began to wave it in front of her face. "I think I just fell in love with you a tiny bit there, Mr. Naplava. When women finally do get the vote, you really should consider running for president."

He shook his head, still grinning. "No, ma'am. I'm a simple sheep farmer."

Hope pointed a finger at Bailey. "Will you be satisfied being the wife of a simple sheep farmer? What will you do stuck out there in the hills with all of those smelly sheep, anyway? Are you giving up your practice?"

Bailey regarded her sister with an exasperated look. "Don't hold back, Hope. Ask anything you want! Yes, I'll continue my medical practice and serve the families in Boerne; they are in desperate need of a doctor up there. I like the way the sheep smell. And yes, he will—*satisfy* me." She added this last part with her own wink at her fiancé, who responded by throwing the reins to Hope, grabbing the girl beside him, taking off his hat to block curious stares, and having a long, private moment.

"Three more days? Really? The two of you are going to make it three more days?"

There was no immediate answer, and Hope talked to herself the rest of the way home.

Later that afternoon as they made their way through Military

Plaza to the train station, Bailey laid a hand on Jacob's arm.

"Can you do something for me?" she asked.

"Anything."

"Can you let me off for a few moments? There's just—something—I need to do."

He smiled at her. "No problem. We have about thirty minutes before the 4:08 leaves. Of course, we could give up our seats and get a Pullman car on the 5:36…"

They regarded each other, both of them considering it, terribly tempted.

"Don't tease me, Jake."

"I'm sorry. No Pullman car just yet, young lady; what were you thinking?" He laughed and pulled the rig over. "I'll see you in about twenty minutes? Is that enough time?"

She nodded. "Aren't you going to ask me what I'm doing?"

"No," he said simply, tipped his hat, and pulled away.

Lucky, lucky, lucky me, she whispered to herself, thanking God—as she found herself doing quite frequently in the past few days—for the blessing of this man.

She allowed herself the luxury of wandering through the Plaza for a few moments, savoring the sights and sounds and smells of her city. She purchased a tamale, peeled it from the husk and ate it in three bites. Little had changed from her childhood: there was the same frenetic bustle of cattlemen, farmers, sheepmen, soldiers, and vendors; only now, there was a fair amount of the fine folk mixed in as well; women strolling about with brightly-colored parasols to shield their faces from the brutal sun with their dandy men in striped trousers and tall hats squiring them proudly. Nannies chased after toddlers; older children pestered the sidewalk vendors; courting couples lined the chili benches, gazing into each other's eyes. The whole area was definitely tidier than it had been twenty years ago, with its clean boardwalks and carefully landscaped gardens. The Plaza felt more like a respectable, proper town square, and she both loved it and mourned the loss of the rough-and-tumble place of her childhood, the place where she had said goodbye to Jacob those many years ago, where he had hugged her to him and kissed her neck and made her fall in love.

She made her way to the edge of the Plaza where the old Mexican woman in rags sat forlornly in the sun. Bailey was astonished to realize it was the same woman: she and Gabby used to call her *Morosa* because she looked so sad. She was still alive! And the mockingbirds; they were still here, suffering silently in their cages like their forbears, too traumatized to make a sound. *If only Wenzel were here.* She approached the woman carefully, kneeling down and murmuring to her in Spanish. Morosa listened, fearful at first, then incredulous as she understood what this young woman was proposing. She covered her mouth with a gnarled, trembling hand, her ancient eyes glimmering. Slowly she nodded, her mouth falling open as Bailey withdrew a roll of bills from the pockets of her dress, carefully shielding the transaction with her body. She showed the woman the number of bills and quickly folded them into the corn husk and brown paper; it looked like a simple tamale she was passing along. They put their heads together a bit longer, then the woman leaned forward and kissed Bailey's cheeks, one after the other, made the sign of the cross, and stood. She untied her tired old pony and mounted him and rode away without a look back.

Bailey gathered the cages as inconspicuously as possible, but there were five of them; one more than she could carry. Morosa's business had grown over the years! She chewed her lip, gazing at the birds, wishing she had asked Jacob to stay close.

"What do I do now?" she whispered to one of them. "Got any ideas?"

The bird, delicate gray with a white breast and bright, yellow eyes, cocked its head and looked at her suspiciously, but he didn't make a sound.

"I have an idea." The voice came from directly behind her, and she spun around, four cages clattering against each other, and laughed in astonishment when she saw him.

"I seem to be able to conjure you just by thinking, *I need Jake.*"

He shrugged. "Naw, that's not it. I just like to stay close."

"So you were spying on me?" She said it with a tease to her voice, but his expression was sober.

"Well, maybe. Kind of. Not really. Dammit!" He glared at the ground, jaw bulging. He finally sighed and looked at her.

"Remember this afternoon when you told Hope that I'm perfect?"

"Yes…"

"Well, I'm not. I'm not even close. I'm terrified of losing you again. It's turned me into this overprotective—I don't know—lurker."

"Jake, we've *talked* about this already. Yesterday, remember? We'll work through it."

"There's more."

"Oh?" She suppressed a grin and her heart swelled at the earnest look on his face. He looked like a six-year-old confessing the theft of a cookie.

"I'm grouchy in the morning. I take long baths; it drives my family crazy. I chew with my mouth open sometimes. Ma hates it. And girls—they follow me around, Bailey, and I don't know why; I don't encourage it like Anton! I swear. So you might hate that, I think. And I have a lucky pair of socks that I never want to throw away; they've been darned so much that they're five different colors."

"I see," she said gravely.

He stared at her. "What do you think? There's more horrible stuff, I'm sure. I just can't think of it now."

She nodded slowly and looked off into the middle distance, marveling at how her love for this man seemed to grow by the moment. "Well, I know you're grouchy in the morning. I make a good cup of coffee and I know how to bake your favorite muffins, so I imagine we'll get along fine. I've had the luxury of very few baths in my life, so I think I may join you in your long baths, if you don't mind."

He swallowed thickly and shook his head. "I don't mind."

"Good. I really couldn't care less if you chew with your mouth open. I shall guard the sanctity of your lucky socks, but when they need darned, you'll have to do it yourself."

"I already do it myself."

"Wonderful! Okay then! Can you help me carry these infernal cages?"

He reached for them and they began to make their way to his rig. "You know, Jake. I'm not perfect, either."

He nodded and flashed her an ornery grin. "Oh, I *know* that."

She kicked at him but he danced out of range, and by the time they pulled into the livery, they were entertaining each other with long lists of idiosyncrasies that were growing more ridiculous by the moment.

"I sometimes snore so loudly that I wake myself up," Jacob confessed gravely.

"I'm terrified of chipmunks. Nothing furry should be allowed to move that fast."

"Well, I'm scared of crickets! They make me scream like a little girl. Fine thing for a grown man, don't you think?"

"I have a tooth back by my molar that's turning brown."

"I have an extra toe on my right foot. It's small, but it's definitely extra."

"I refuse to believe that one." Bailey laughed breathlessly, jogging to keep up with him; they were so late that they were running through the depot to catch their train.

"All right, that one was a lie. But I do have an abnormally long toe, the one next to my big toe. I always have to buy a shoe one size too big to make room for it."

They reached their car and the porter grabbed their satchels and frowned at the five cages of birds. "You can't take those on board."

"These are a wedding gift, sir. Please, can you let us by? They don't make a sound." Jacob produced five bills out of thin air and pressed them into the porter's hand, Bailey's eyes widening as she saw that each bill was a ten.

The porter nodded, a bit dazed, and waved them through, and Jacob steered them to an unoccupied car, tucking Bailey and himself into one seat and setting the cages gently on the seat across from them. "Hopefully no one else will want these seats," he muttered. "This time of day is usually pretty sparse, so I think we'll be okay."

"Did you just give that man fifty dollars?"

"Maybe." He shrugged. "They're worth it, don't you think?"

They both looked at the birds; the poor things look terrified. Three birds were jammed into each cage with barely room to maneuver.

"And how much did you give to that old woman? Or should I say, how many tamales? Enough to set her up for a while, I suppose?"

"I hope enough to keep her from catching and selling any more birds. I told her Thomas and Gabby needed somebody to do light housekeeping for Harding House; I don't know if she'll do it. I think she thought I was crazy, honestly, caring about these birds so much."

"You *are* crazy. That's one of those things I love about you, along with, you know—your brown tooth and irrational fear of chipmunks."

A few hours later, after the hubbub of arriving home and greeting family members whose numbers seemed to be growing exponentially as they travelled in for the wedding, they walked among the hills in peaceful silence, carrying the five cages between them. The birds began to chirp and sing, and the two of them smiled at each other, delighted.

"What are they saying?" Bailey asked, striving to be nonchalant.

Jacob laughed. "How should I know?"

She sighed, exasperated. "There's no use pretending, Jake."

He quirked his eyebrow at her and turned his attention to the cages, holding one up to eye level and gazing at the birds intently. Finally he nodded sagely. "They're saying that we need to take a quick detour to the hen house."

"*Jake!*"

He shrugged. "Hey. I'm just translating, lady. Blame the birds."

"Keep moving, smartass."

"Really, Rosie, I don't think mayors' wives are supposed to refer to their husbands as *smartass*."

"Well, I have a few other terms, if you'd care to hear them."

He barked a laugh and trudged forward. "Never mind, then."

They walked on, Jacob's words echoing in her mind.

"You know, I had twelve years in a bordello and seven years in a convent. Sometimes I don't know whether to cuss you out or pray for you."

He flashed a smile at her, and then realized that her mood had changed from one of joyful buoyancy to one of self-doubt. "Aw, Rosie…"

"No, really; you were right. A mayor's wife shouldn't be using language like that."

"I was kidding!"

She thrust her chin up impatiently, unable to use her hands. "I know you were kidding. But who knows what will fly out of my mouth at any given time? Will it be 'Holy God We Praise thy Name' or 'Molly, Roll Your Leg Over'?" She stopped in her tracks and set down her cages, suddenly overwhelmed be a wave of doubt. In a few days she was to marry this fine man—this finest of men—and she would stand by his side for the next four years, expected to be the first lady of San Antonio, full of dignity and grace and sophistication. *Her!* Bailey Rose! Refined! She would rather be running barefoot through the grass chasing after sheep on these hills any day than attending fancy dinners and schmoozing with the city's movers and shakers. *Caroline.* She was the one who excelled at that kind of thing. Caroline had been the picture of cool refinement. Bailey would be the picture of blushing, stammering *faux pas*.

Jacob saw at a glance every destructive thought of his cherished; he saw it in her troubled dark eyes, the downturn of her expressive mouth, the clenching of her hands. He put his cages down and in five strides was in front of her, bracketing her face with his hands and forcing her to look at him.

"Don't. I don't ever want to see that look on your face again."

"Oh, Jake! I'm terrified! I don't know if I can be proper the way you need me to be."

"I don't care about any of that. Do you think *I'm* proper? Did you hear what happened when I gave my speech at the lawn party?"

She smiled in spite of herself, remembering descriptions of his hat sailing across the lawn. "Oh, yes. I remember. You stripped for the ladies."

"Yes. Exactly. Can we just agree to be awkward together? And not to care about it too awful much, and to remember what's important?" He remained in place, holding her face like a precious piece of fragile art.

She nodded, swallowing, and he lowered his face as if to kiss her, but stopped a fraction of an inch short. "Now let's forget about all that and set these fellows free," he whispered, raising gooseflesh on her arms. "This—what we're doing here with these infernal cages—this is about setting the past free, right?"

"Yes."

He stroked her lip once and backed away, and they picked up their cages and moved on through the glimmering sunlight that filtered through the trees like vaporous gold. When they reached the spot, they knew it—or at least Jacob did: the birds seemed to increase their excited chatter and she could have sworn that he cocked his head to listen carefully.

He set his cages down again and plopped himself down on the grass. "Here. Right here. You do it; you're their savior, m'lady."

She took a deep breath and put down one of her cages, carefully opening the latch of the door on the other. The three birds inside froze for an instant, and she thought maybe they wouldn't go after all. Maybe they had been caged too long and had forgotten how to be birds. But with a sudden soft whoosh of feathers they were gone, a blur of expanding wings, alighting on an uppermost branch of the magnolia tree, making joyful noises. The remaining birds began to flap madly in their cages, and it was all she could do to unlatch each cage before they trampled each other.

By the time she reached the final cage she was laughing and shrieking like a child, ducking to avoid flying birds, her heart full of an emotion she was sure she hadn't felt in a very, very long time; so long ago that she didn't have a word for it. When she had spun in a circle with Jacob and Wenzel by Glory Creek, after catching her first fish—the moment that she had held close to her heart for fifteen years as the moment that clarified what she wanted her life to be. What she had felt then was what she was feeling now.

She looked at Jacob and wondered how to share it with him.

"Happiness," he said, grinning at her.

She stared at him. "What?"

"It's just being *happy*. Like when we were kids. You know, by the creek. Or in the wagon. Those moments when everything is uncomplicated and good."

"How did you know—"

He laughed and jumped up from his position in the grass, grabbing three empty cages and handing the other two to her. "Just get used to that feeling. C'mon. We've got a wedding to plan."

CHAPTER TWELVE

"So, my dear, we have two days to plan this grand wedding! Two days, mercy. Can we ever do it?" Gacenka was standing behind Bailey, braiding her hair, and although she knew she should share Gacenka's anxiety about the wedding plans, her eyes were drifting shut with pleasure. The feel of Gacenka's gentle hands in her hair was just so lovely and soothing.

"Does it have to be a *grand* wedding?" Bailey finally murmured.

Gacenka sighed. "There will be well over five hundred guests, my dear!"

Bailey felt her first twinge of genuine alarm. "*What?* Why? Why so many?"

The older woman continued to smooth and plait Bailey's hair, coiling it and pinning it into intricate nests, unpinning and uncoiling and doing it all over again, practicing to get it just right for the wedding. She didn't miss a beat with her quick fingers even though her voice betrayed her distress. "We have over two hundred under our own employ here at Bluebonnet, when you count family members. Not to mention all of the surrounding ranches and the extended family and friends, and of course, our congregation. And Johann felt it necessary to invite the mayor and some of the other big wigs from the city, and your family:

the Millers, the Schwartzs, Thomas and Gabby, Sister Anna. Oh, the list goes on and on, my dear!"

Bailey slumped a bit in her chair. She was no good at any of this, no good at all. She opened her mouth to say something along the lines of *How about Jacob and I just sneak away tonight,* but Gacenka began to speak before she could manage it.

"Then there's the food to consider, the wedding feast. What would you like me to serve, my dear? I feel like I should consult you about this! Should it be roast pork? I know you love that. Certainly not mutton, I would think? It's too common. But we can do beef tips as well. I've started preparations for some of it already, of course, but I feel you'll have a preference. Would you prefer a more American meal? I thought maybe Jacob would admire a meal from the homeland; he loves my cooking so." Her voice wavered and Bailey felt a surge of sympathy.

"Of course he does, and so do I," she said softly, but she doubted that her future mother-in-law even heard her.

"The side dishes are no concern; we'll have roast potatoes, green beans with bacon; oh, I don't know, sweet yams, perhaps, and maybe a Mexican dish for Miguel and oh, gosh, most of our sheep herders. Miguel makes a delicious tamale. We can do onion soup and chicken pie, of course. But it's the main dishes I'm concerned about. I don't want to overstep or interfere with your ideas."

"Oh, I wouldn't worry about that," Bailey said faintly. She felt a sweat break out under her arms even though the room was quite cool.

"And the cake! My heavens, the wedding cake! What do you like, my sweet Bailey?" Gacenka finished her hair with one last quick jab of a pin and walked around to face Bailey. "Will it be chocolate? White? Lemon? Oh, Rosalie makes the most delectable strawberry cream, but I don't even know if you like strawberries! And the icing and decorations: shall I whip it? Or do you prefer a creamier frosting? Clarissa is a talent with cake decorating; maybe she'll help. It takes ever so long to make all of those tiny little roses and vines. She makes her own fondant, you know. Now, we'll serve several different cakes, of course, but I'd like to know what you'd like for the big wedding cake. Oh, don't fuss about your hair, Bailey dear; those braids just won't stay, but it doesn't matter. The head piece will cover all of your hair, anyway."

Gacenka began to pace. "And that's just the *food*!" she muttered. She was at full steam now. "However will we fit all of those guests into our church's sanctuary? They'll be standing in the aisles and sitting on the floor! I suppose we could have it in the big barn; we could clear it out and put up some ivy and flowers. It will be quite simple, since it's last minute, but I can get the girls started on gathering flowers. Oh, dear, would you mind terribly being married in a *barn?* That doesn't seem right." She paused for air, pressing her lips together in consternation, and Bailey opened and closed her mouth three times and felt like a like a fish gasping for air.

"What do you think?" Gacenka prodded. "After we settle the menu and where to have the ceremony, we need to get started on altering the dress, my dearie. You're a good deal thinner than Rosalie was when she married, and about four inches smaller in the bust area, if you don't mind me saying."

Bailey looked down at her chest forlornly. She was finally putting on some of the weight she had lost, but she was still scrawny in all of the wrong places. "I'm going to look like a boy in that dress," she said under her breath, but Gacenka didn't hear her. She had left the room, calling over her shoulder that she'd be back with the gown so they could begin pinning it.

Bailey moved to the mirror and stared at the woman reflected there. Yes, she was too thin, making her dark eyes appear too enormous. Her hair, however, was an impeccable wreath of braids of different widths and styles, so intricate that she touched them in awe. However had Gacenka made her hair behave that way? She stared and stared. She looked her age and maybe older with this sophisticated hair style and the ravages of the past six months. For the past several years people had mistaken her for a teenager, but she doubted that mistake would be made today.

Quarantine, jail, kidnapping: it was all right there on her face as apparent as a tragic story written on a page. She closed her eyes and imagined Jacob: he was so handsome. They were not evenly matched in looks, to be sure.

Gacenka burst back into the room with Rosalie on her heels, and before she quite knew what had happened, they had her stripped down and she was stepping into the gown. It was a traditional Moravian wedding gown, simple yet—*huge*! Yards and yards of white cotton layers lay over a huge crinoline, the sleeves equally as poufy and trimmed with lace with a wide green and red sash at the waist. An embroidered trim at the bust matched the sash at the waist. And the headdress! Bailey's mouth fell open as they brought it forth from a green box and prepared to place it on her head. The very front was a tight black band; the top was an elaborately-embroidered and beaded piece that covered her entire head—it took them fifteen minutes to stuff her hair into it. Cascading down from the headpiece were twelve wide ribbons on each side, all embroidered and beaded in reds and greens and yellows.

At last they were done with the pins, and after giving her a final going-over, they led her to the mirror, covering her eyes until she was standing before it.

When they moved their hands and she beheld her image, her mouth fell open in astonishment. She did not even recognize herself! She was certain that if she had a photograph made and looked at it later, she would not know this woman to be her. The dress concealed her thin frame, aided in strategic places, of course, by Rosalie's clever padding. She looked like a plump, well-endowed, proper Moravian maid from the neck down, and a thin waif with the last fading traces of a beating from the neck up. Rosalie's makeup job had served to add pink cheeks and even pinker lips.

She successfully quelled an awful urge to laugh, but found to her dismay that a great bubble of emotion was rising to the surface nevertheless. *Don't do it! Don't you do it! Since when did you become such a crybaby?* But there was nothing for it: she dropped her face into her hands and sobbed, much to the dismay of Rosalie and Gacenka.

"Oh, my dear! Whatever is wrong?"

"Are those tears of joy or—something else?" asked Rosalie. "You're just crying because you're so happy, am I right?"

Bailey managed to nod. "I *am* hap—happy," she wailed. "I love Jake so much."

She loved him so much that she wouldn't blame him one bit if he ran for his life when he saw her in this get-up.

Gacenka clapped her hands with pleasure. "And he loves you, too, my daughter. He'll be so happy when he sees you in this dress from the homeland."

"What in the *bloody hell* are you wearing, Bailey?"

The three women spun around: Marianna had wandered in and was gaping at Bailey, her hand over her mouth, aghast.

"Marianna!" scolded Gacenka. "I can't think what you mean! This is Rosalie's wedding gown! She is going to work so very hard to alter it today."

Marianna let forth with a peal of laughter. "Oh, Mama! Honestly!" She reached forward and squeezed the two spots where Bailey's breasts were rumored to be. "That's what I thought," she said. "Unusually soft and big!"

"Marianna! You are rotten, through and through!" chided Rosalie, but Bailey detected a glimmer of humor in her eyes. "Bailey loves this dress."

"Bailey does *not* love this dress. She may love it on *you*, but she doesn't love it on *her*."

"Why don't you let Bailey speak for herself?" said Gacenka sharply, now that she had recovered from the shock. "You were always such a know-it-all, Mari."

Marianna turned back to Bailey, her hands on her hips. "I don't need to ask her. She won't say, anyway, with the two of you deriving such pleasure dressing her up like a baby doll. She looks ridiculous. She looks like an over-stuffed doll who's been sucking on red lollipops. And the headpiece will never work, Ma. Look; her hair is already fighting its way out."

Bailey turned to look in the mirror, and sure enough, curlicues were springing forth. She took a deep breath, wondering how on earth to proceed, but her efforts to breathe dislodged a stocking, which chose that moment to pop up out of her bodice. Marianna howled with laughter and reached down the front of Bailey's dress to pluck out the offending padding, and Bailey was soon joining her, tears streaming down her face, laughing until she was weak in the knees.

Gacenka and Rosalie looked on, reluctant smiles on their faces, shaking their heads and throwing their hands in the air.

"Well, I don't know what's going to happen now. What will she wear?" The older woman sighed and sat down heavily on the high chair.

Marianna recovered and shooed her mother and older sister out of the room. "You two have enough to worry about. Let me handle the dress and hair."

"Fine, fine. I would be ever so grateful. But Bailey, what about the food? And the barn?"

Bailey looked at Marianna helplessly. "Go on with you now," ordered Marianna. "We'll talk it out and give you directions in a bit, won't we, Bailey? Go relax and have a glass of wine, my goodness, Ma. And let the bee out of your bonnet for good measure."

When all was quiet at last Marianna pulled Bailey to the bed. "Sit. Now honestly, Bailey. Are you happy in that dress?"

Bailey shrugged. "It's so beautiful, and I imagined myself in a traditional gown, but, I don't know. It seems—I feel—like a stuffed turkey, maybe. I don't quite feel myself." She heaved a sigh of relief; now that she had experienced it, she felt a pang of sympathy for Gabby, who had gone through the same ordeal just a few days before. It was so very difficult to disappoint those who meant well, especially when she was feeling un-beautiful to begin with. "I don't want to disappoint Jacob."

Mari rolled her eyes. "I have just come from the porch, Bailey. Jacob is *delirious* with happiness. He can't shut up about you, honestly. They've made a drinking game of it, I'm afraid.

Every time he says "My Bailey" or "My Rosie" all of the boys tip the mugs. They're all getting *soaked*."

Bailey giggled and felt a wave of relief.

Marianna clapped her hands briskly. "Look. I have an idea for your dress and hair. I'll be right back, all right? And if you like it, don't tell the others, promise? I want everyone to be surprised."

Bailey stared at her with big eyes. "Oh! Well—all right, Mari. But what about the rest of it all? I don't know what to tell your Mama about the food or barn or any of it. I feel so stupid about it all."

Mari narrowed her eyes and nodded her head. "I've got the location worked out, too. And do you really care about the food?"

"No," Bailey confessed sheepishly. "I'd skip the whole thing if I could and run away with Jake tonight. I mentioned that to Gacenka, but I think she ignored me."

Mari smiled and was quiet for a moment. "I'll order the food; Ma will think it all came from you. And do you trust me for the rest of it?"

"Of course!"

"Then I have an idea."

The next day was a quiet, blissful one. Gacenka ordered Jacob and Bailey from the house shortly after breakfast, corralling all of her daughters as well as nearby cousins, in-laws, and sheepherders' wives for the gargantuan task of preparing food for five hundred. Ginny was spared: Gacenka declared that the bride and groom-to-be required a chaperone, much to the amusement of everyone present at the table. Jacob responded by pulling Bailey's chair noisily toward his own and leaning forward for a kiss; Ginny squealed, whipped off her straw hat and stuck it between the two lovebirds, and everyone howled and whistled.

It was the best day Bailey remembered having for a long, long time; so reminiscent of her time at the ranch years before that she found herself looking for Wenzel more than once. They saddled up Frenzy, Estella, and Ginny's little mare, Josie, and rode the nearest thirty acres, stopping periodically to examine sheep and chat with the sheepherders. There was an unnaturally warm breeze for late fall and a flawless blue sky, and Bailey felt her whole life expand with each passing mile. The wild beauty of the hills seemed to be imprinted onto her heart: she could not keep the wide smile from her face, and many times she caught Jacob staring, his own face lit with happiness. When Ginny grew tired of riding, they grabbed a few cane poles and hiked down to Glory Creek, right to the very spot where Wenzel taught her to fish, and put their lines in the water, catching nothing but relishing Ginny's musical voice going on and on about foot-long rainbow trout and white bass she had snared with Wenzel. After an hour they pulled their lines and laid on their backs, hands linked, eyes closed. Ginny grew bored and wandered upstream to try a new spot, and as one, they opened their eyes and turned their heads.

Jacob reached out and traced her lip, stopping at the dent, and Bailey felt as though she had stepped through time. "Rosie," he whispered. "I fell in love with you on this bank. I wanted to tell you, that day so long ago, but I was scared."

"Stupid boy," she whispered.

"I'm so sorry for wasted time."

"No regrets, sir. Remember?"

He smiled and reached out to cup her cheek with his hand, and just as her eyes drifted shut, Ginny dumped a bucket of ice-cold creek on their heads.

She shrieked and jumped up, gasping and then laughing; Jacob roared and began the chase immediately, and Bailey could hear Ginny screaming with glee long after the two had disappeared from sight.

They picnicked on a hill overlooking the ranch, relishing cold mutton sandwiches, boiled eggs, and jujube fruit.

"You know, tomorrow, this will all be yours. Well, over half of it. Pa still owns a little less than half, but he's eager to give it up." Jacob leaned back on an elbow and grinned at her.

She just barely managed to swallow a bite of sandwich without choking. "What?" she finally got out. "What do you mean, it will all be mine? It's *yours*, you goon."

"Goon! Yes, Jacob, you're a goon!" added Ginny sleepily, but her steam was quickly running out as the day waned. She yawned hugely.

"What's mine is yours, Dr. Naplava. Or perhaps you prefer to keep your name."

She regarded him with an equal measure of amusement and astonishment. "Am I marrying a radical suffragist? I have no idea what you're referring to with 'what's mine is yours.' You must have forgotten your training as a barrister now that you are getting on in years! The wife owns nothing unless her husband leaves it to her upon his death. Everything I own, of course, becomes yours tomorrow. In case you're wondering, that consists of a shabby doctor's bag full of instruments that will need to be replaced within the next few years and a bank account of—oh, let's see now—twenty-four dollars and thirty-three cents, I believe."

Jacob waggled his eyebrows. "I didn't realize you were hiding money from me, you hussy." He glanced quickly at Ginny, but she appeared to have fallen asleep.

"And it's well-hidden; you'll never find it."

They smiled at each other for a beat. "Honestly, Rosie, I want to own the ranch with you. It's yours, just as much as it is mine. And I won't mind if you keep your name. Your patients know you as Dr. Rose."

She gazed out over the ranch. "Jake, I've wished my whole life to be your wife, to be Mrs. Jacob Naplava. I used to write it on the used parchment the nuns discarded after the last lessons on Fridays. I'd offer to wash the boards, and after everyone had gone, I'd go through the trash and pick out all the bits of paper. And all weekend I would write you letters."

"Letters?"

She shrugged and looked down at their linked hands. "I never sent them, of course. They were the pathetic letters of a lovelorn teenager, I'm ashamed to confess. Sometimes I would pretend we were betrothed, and I was away at boarding school. I would sign them 'The future Mrs. Naplava,' and I would rub geraniums on my lips and seal them with a kiss. It was a poor substitute for the real thing, let me tell you."

Something powerful happened to Jacob at that moment. He thought of her curled up in her cot, missing him, kissing the letter and pretending it was his lips she was kissing. He felt a tremendous pull, somewhere deep. His eyes stung.

"You know, I didn't think it was possible to love you any more than I already did, but I find every moment of every day that I'm wrong about that."

They shared a look that transcended words, and she reached for him, stroking his face, running her fingers through his thick hair, finding the base of his skull and pulling him toward her.

"I don't want to wait until tomorrow," she finally whispered. "Tomorrows are so slippery." She slipped a hand inside his shirt and felt the hard warmth of his chest, feeling her own body grow warm.

He let out a careful breath and glanced at Ginny, who seemed to be stirring. "Think we can sneak away?" He found his mouth had gone dry.

"*I* don't think you can sneak away. Johann said you'd say just that thing, Jacob. And he was right!" Ginny's eyes had popped open and she was shaking her head sternly. "Time to feed the chickens, anyway. Come on, you two."

At the mention of the hen house, the two in question burst into laughter, and Ginny pestered them the entire way there, wanting to know what the great joke was.

Bailey was ordered to bed directly after a light supper that night, having been scolded soundly by Gacenka and Rosalie for spending the day in the sun and getting a sunburn and chapped lips, the day before her wedding, no less! At the mention of her lips, Jacob's eyes had been drawn to them, and of course, Anton picked up on it.

"Put your eyes back in your head, brother. You're embarrassing those of us who are pure of mind and body." His siblings groaned and rolled their eyes.

In response, Jacob stood and bowed to Bailey, and then unabashedly escorted her to his old bedroom, followed by the catcalls of his brothers and protestations of his sisters. Ginny trailed behind them, relishing the part of chaperone, and was not dissuaded until Jacob produced a shiny quarter and a square of chocolate from his pocket and ordered her to get lost.

"Have you been carrying that around all day?" giggled Bailey, but he didn't respond; he pulled her close and kissed her, making her whole body pulse. He was determined to have ten seconds before the family descended.

And descend they did: soon the whole lot of them came tramping down the hall, banging away on pots and pans, and Jacob was bodily lifted by Johann and Anton and carried away to a waiting wagon: he was to stay the night at Marianna's and Miguel's.

"Why there?" he protested, craning his neck for one last look at his bride, who was laughing so hard she was wiping away tears as she waved at him.

"Are you kidding? We're not taking any chances." Johann poked him in the ribs.

"We know how it goes with you two," added Anton cheerfully. "I'm willing to wager that you've already had your wedding night a tad bit early."

Jacob gave up the struggle and allowed himself to be dumped in the wagon. "Sadly, no. Ginny saw to that."

"Well then you better rest up for tomorrow, brother. You're going to need it!" Miguel offered, and everyone shouted with laughter again.

The next day dawned clear and bright, the uncharacteristically warm weather holding; it was downright *balmy* for the first week of December, according to Gacenka, who was already fanning her merry red face. The women were up three hours before sunrise shuttling between the kitchen and the pantry, shouting instructions to each other and then shushing each other in turn, endeavoring not to wake Bailey.

They needn't have worried: Bailey had enjoyed the deepest, most satisfying sleep of her life. She didn't wake until well after eight o' clock, a late hour for her. She stretched and then lay still for a few more moments, listening to the sounds of the women murmuring, their hushed voices punctuated periodically by a sharp bang of a lid on a pot, followed invariably by a chorus of "*Shhhh!*" She grinned and felt her heart swell with love, imagining Gacenka and her small army laboring over mounds and mounds of food; food for *five hundred*, for pity's sake. She curled her body around a fat pillow and thanked the Lord again for Marianna, who had arranged for the wedding to be a simple affair attended by only family and a few close friends—and in a truly magical place! When Marianna had asked her where she would marry Jacob, if it could be anywhere, the answer had come to her instantly.

"In a sacred grove, just like your Mama and Papa. Surrounded by only family. And the birds would be invited, of course."

Marianna's pretty mouth had formed an O, and she had jumped up and whirled in a circle, talking a mile a minute in her excitement. "I know just the place! I know it—it's a cottonwood grove! Wenzel showed me once, when we were kids, but he told me never to go back there until it was for something special. I had no idea what he meant, but I knew better than to argue with Wen. This is it! This is it, Bailey! This is what he meant! And it was after you were here and you and Jacob—well, you know— fell in love, right in front of Wen. I just know he was thinking of you and Jacob!"

Bailey was unable to answer. She didn't doubt Marianna's words for a moment.

They had snuck out early the next morning before breakfast, before she and Jacob spent the day with Ginny, and when she saw the grove, she had let out a sob. There were joyful spirits dwelling here, perhaps. She didn't know too much about that sort of thing, but a feeling of overwhelming love and a sense of well-being and even giddiness rose up within her. The trees were huge and ancient, their thick, deeply-furrowed trunks a reddish brown. Beams of sun filtered through the bright gold and red leaves; cottonwood seed drifted softly down like snow.

She laughed aloud and danced, her arms akimbo and her face turned to the sun. She felt Mari do the same beside her, and it was a few minutes before they settled down and lay in the soft, fragrant grass, gazing up at the bright gold leaves of the bigtooth maple trees. They shared ideas for the ceremony, growing more animated by the moment, until finally they heard the breakfast bell being rung.

Bailey's heartbeat quickened to think of it. In just four hours, she would be standing there, hand-in-hand with the other half of her soul, the one true love of her life, marrying him. Marrying *him*! *Jacob*! The blue-eyed boy of her dreams, the boy she thought she may have just fabricated from a lovely childhood dream. He was real, and he was to be hers, for life.

She turned her face into her pillow and squealed, kicking her feet and pressing her fists against her chest, releasing some of the pent-up joy and anticipation that she felt would probably cause her to explode soon.

Rosalie brought her a tray but she couldn't eat a bite; instead, she took a steaming mug of coffee to the bathroom and soaked in the tub, attending to herself scrupulously, blushing at the thought of Jacob seeing *this* and touching *that*. Tonight! Tonight she would know him, at last, body and soul. She washed her hair with a lovely soap scented with lemon and vanilla, then washed it again, and again. He loved her hair, this incorrigible red mess; he would want to run his fingers through it, brush it perhaps. He loved to smell her hair and skin; she remembered him doing this when they were young, even though he didn't know she knew.

She stood at last when the water began to cool, and watched as the gooseflesh formed on her skin, her nipples puckering. He did this to her; made her body flush and become soft here and hard there, supple and yearning. She touched her breast and remembered what it felt like when he had touched her there. It had felt like she were on fire, like she would forever be bereft without his hands on her. Without her hands on him.

She toweled herself, smiling all the while, wondering if Jake were doing the same at this very moment.

He had been in Marianna and Miguel's clawfoot tub for over an hour. Unlike the bathroom he had constructed at the ranch house, this was the old-fashioned variety: he had hauled the water himself, dumped it by the buckets into a cast-iron pot over the fire, and heated it while drinking his coffee. "Miguel, my good man, it's time you let me build you a proper bathroom," he had commented to his jovial brother-in-law, who had nodded his assent.

"That would make Mari happy. She's always wanting to——." He had stopped, face reddening, and Jacob had enjoyed a good laugh, holding up his hand.

"Say no more. Please."

Miguel had left soon after, heading over to the ranch to help the men put up the food tents and finish preparing the barn for the reception. Jacob began filling the buckets once more, tipping the cast iron pot carefully and hauling the water to the tub. It was an arduous task, but when at last he sank down into its soapy depths, he realized it had been worth every moment.

His thoughts immediately shifted to Bailey. He wondered if she were bathing now, too, and felt such a swell of desire that he groaned, burying his face in his hands. Her face rose up before him, her dear, perfect face, with her enormous dark eyes, expressive mouth, and sculpted planes. He knew her face better than he did his own. He closed his eyes and lifted his hands, imagining he was touching it, and he could discern every feature. He moved his hands down to the column of her throat, her collarbone, and the swell of her breasts, which fit into his hands as perfect as the peaches he picked every summer from the trees on the north ridge.

Stop it now, damn it! He was completely aroused, sitting here by himself in quickly-cooling bathwater, and growing more— well—*agitated* by the moment. Time to get out and do something useful, but he had already gathered all of the items Marianna had instructed him to collect. He smiled as he thought of the grove of trees waiting for them this morning, and felt a deep sense of rightness with Bailey's choice. The ceremony would be intimate and truly personal: Wen would be there, and the birds, and everyone they loved the most. It was the perfect setting to begin their lives together.

He had been forbidden from going to the house until he was fetched, so helping the men set up tents was out. He wished he had thought to ask Kube to come over for breakfast: if anyone could distract him from thoughts of Bailey, Kube could. But then again, Kube would've teased him mercilessly, and Jacob didn't want to have to punch anyone on his wedding day.

He rose from the tub and wondered if she were doing the same, and when he imagined her body wet and soapy and puckered with cold, he felt his knees get weak.

After he had dried and dressed in the clothes Marianna had laid out for him, there came a knock on the door, and for a moment, his heart was in his mouth. Could she have snuck past watchful eyes? He yanked open the door, heart pounding, and then gaped in surprise.

"Stařenka! Why hello! Marianna's left already, I'm afraid."

His grandmother waved her hand impatiently and held up a purple velvet pouch. "I'm here for you," she smiled.

Marianna came to her room an hour later; Bailey had been sitting at the open window drying her hair in the breeze.

"Oh, Bailey! Your hair! It's gorgeous!"

Bailey lifted a skeptical eyebrow, looking for signs of Marianna's usual teasing, but her face was aglow and sincere. "Really? It's not the usual big frizzy mess?"

Marianna shook her head and stroked it, oohing and ahhing over the curls, which fell in profusion to Bailey's waist. "There's so much of it! You have *so much hair!*"

"Yes…and what are you going to do with it all? You only have a few hours, you know!"

"Nothing! Well, almost nothing. Are you kidding? I don't dare to touch it too much. It's perfect the way it is."

Bailey felt a twinge of alarm. She knew Marianna was aiming for a natural look, but her hair was truly—well—*wild!*

"Are you sure about this?"

"Sit. Here. Eat this and just let me do what I came to do." She shoved an egg sandwich into Bailey's hand and got to work, plucking flowers out of a basket and pinning them here and there. It was surprisingly quick work. When she was finished, Bailey begged to look at it, but Marianna shook her head.

"Gown next. Here it is, Bailey! And I knew when I found it that you're so very close to Mama's size when she married. Just a few nips and tucks is all I'll need to do." She helped Bailey to step into the gown, which had been lovingly preserved with careful hands over the years. It was still snow-white, made of the finest spun cotton overlaid with white lace of an intricate design. Bailey peered at it when Marianna let her: it was ivy and birds, all intertwined, covering every square inch of the dress, which gathered under her breasts and fell straight to the ground in layers of soft fabric. There was no train, but there could be no mistaking it for what it was: a hand-made wedding gown in a style that evoked images of ancient times.

"Did your grandmother make this?" breathed Bailey.

Marianna nodded, her eyes shining. "She did. I've told her about you wearing it, and she was so happy, Bailey, that she wept."

Bailey swallowed a lump. "I can't wait to spend more time with her. I barely have ever spoken to her."

"You will love her! She's very introverted—a real thinker. She's actually kind of the polar opposite of Ma! It takes a bit of effort to get close, but it's well worth your time."

Bailey nodded and stood patiently as Marianna brandished a needle and thread and deftly took the dress in. She had guessed correctly: very little alteration was necessary, *mostly in the bust area*, she thought forlornly.

Finally, Marianna put away the sewing kit and turned to open her cosmetics bag, which contained items that Bailey couldn't even identify. At Bailey's worried frown, she giggled. "Don't worry; I won't paint you like a doll." She kept her word: she applied a bit of light brownish powder to cover the last fading bruise, a dab of clear, goopy something-or-other to lengthen her lashes and moisten her lips, and that was it.

She stepped back and beamed, apparently delighted with her handiwork.

"Can I look now?" Bailey ventured. Marianna nodded expectantly, and Bailey slowly turned, deathly afraid to see what the mirror would hold. Whatever she looked like, that would be the bride Jacob would see, because they would leave for the ceremony in just a few moments and there was no time for revision.

She gasped when she saw herself and came perilously close to crying. "Don't you dare!" Marianna shouted, guessing that tears were threatening.

Bailey gazed at herself, amazed. She looked so much more like herself than the painted Moravian maid produced a few days before: she looked incredibly young, almost a teenager again! Her cheeks and lips were still quite red from yesterday's sunburn; her hair was left long and flowing to her waist, blazing, shining, red curls, with pink cherry blossoms and peonies and golden dandelions and linden blossoms pinned down the length of it. "In honor of Lada," she breathed.

Her gown lent her an ethereal, almost other-worldly air. *I look like a spirit*, she thought dazedly. *Like a beautiful ghost.* And she *was* beautiful; she finally felt it, for the first time in her life. Her wooden engagement ring and Gacenka's pendant were her only adornment, and they only served to accentuate the ancient, timeless look of her.

"Mari," she choked.

Marianna held up a hand. "Stop. No time for tears! Now step into these, and it's time!"

Bailey stepped into the simple white slippers, her legs shaking. It was almost time! *She said it's almost time.* In a few minutes she would walk to the grove with Mari: everyone else was already there, waiting, she knew. Waiting for her. Waiting for her to come and marry Jake.

CHAPTER THIRTEEN

Marianna led Bailey through an empty, silent house. It was eerie, really: over the past three days the house had been bursting with the noise of wedding preparations and restless children: pots and pans forever clanging, children barreling through the hallways, feet pounding, doors opening and closing, babies crying, mothers issuing threats; men laughing. Now it was silenced, and the house seemed to be holding its breath in anticipation.

Bailey realized *she* had been holding her breath, and she let it out slowly, following Marianna's quick pace, feeling a bit numb with excitement. It all simply felt like a wild dream now: time seemed to slow down and speed up: one moment she was in the hallway outside of Jacob's room, and in the next instant she was outside, staring in awe at her white slippered feet as they traversed the grassy trail, seemingly in slow motion. And colors were accentuated beyond description: surely the leaves of the oak tree couldn't be that ridiculously red and gold, and it wasn't possible for the sky to be that brightly blue. The red of Marianna's dress was so brilliant that Bailey had to look away, focusing on the grassy path again, and her feet upon it.

They walked on, Marianna instinctively silent, remembering waiting in the back of the church at her own wedding and being subjected to Rosalie's endless chatter. How she had longed for the chance to just absorb the moment, to live it fully and privately, to savor it and commit each instant to sensual memory, and so she kept her silence and gave that gift to Bailey.

And then suddenly—or perhaps, at last—they made the turn around the very last bend and stepped into the grove. Bailey stopped, remembering Marianna's directive, and Marianna winked at her and went to stand beside Miguel.

It was achingly beautiful: an ancient cottonwood tree at the far edge of the clearing sprawled majestically, its branches reaching every corner and releasing occasional delicate cottonseeds that the children reached out to catch and blow again from their hands. Around the tree was a double-ring of large stones; coal had been laid in the ring and a low fire burned, creating a majestic sphere of flame. The grove was bathed in soft yellow light, transforming the falling cottonseed into golden fluffs. The tree branches were heavy with birds; they were murmuring softly; a colorful, astonishing array. And the bluebonnets! The flower did not grow naturally here: someone had cut hundreds of them and scattered them; they carpeted the ground, their scent heady and sweet. And the deer! A delicate doe stood docilely at the edge of the clearing, held by Franz with a rope bedecked with magenta-colored peonies. Ginny stood proudly beside him, holding a large, white, ornate birdcage that enclosed a rooster, who was blessedly quiet. Everyone whom Bailey loved was there: Thomas and Gabby, Sister Anna, Karl and his wife and son, Hope, and all of Jacob's siblings and their families. They, too, were murmuring happily, milling about and visiting, the children wading in the bluebonnets, entranced. Each person held an unlit candle. The grove was full of life and love and promise and magic, and she felt it to her core.

As they entered and Marianna moved aside, a gradual hush fell over the assemblage as they turned to see the bride.

And then utter silence fell, punctuated only by a few gasps.

Jacob stopped breathing for several long seconds. He was standing in front of the ancient tree with Minister Jindřich Juren, the sole minister to those Moravians of the Brethren faith. Only

Jacob didn't know if he'd be standing much longer. He stared and stared, feeling something akin to a whirling panic. The girl who had entered the grove was surely a vision, a spirit from another place and time. She looked so much like the girl he had pulled from the creek fifteen years ago that he wondered if maybe Wenzel had arranged for some kind of time travel. Maybe that was the magic of this grove: maybe Jacob was fourteen again, and was getting a second chance to get it right. Or maybe this was a dream: it had certainly felt like a dream all morning.

He felt himself getting dizzy and he swayed on his feet. Minister Juren grabbed his arm. "Steady, Brother Jacob," he whispered. "Breathe."

Jacob obeyed, but he could not tear his eyes from her, the elusive, vanishing ghost girl of his dreams. He needed in the worst way to touch her now, to know that she was real.

She walked toward him slowly on Franticek's arm, the crowd parting, her hair flowing around her like a dazzling red cloud. Her face was so very young, so devoid of artifice. Her black eyes shown forth like specks of gleaming ebony, and her lips—they were parting in a smile now; her joyous, infectious smile.

His eyes. She focused on his eyes, two spots of blue that were more vivid than the sky. They seemed to pull her toward him; surely she wasn't making her own feet move. All conscious function seemed to have deserted her: she felt as though she were floating just slightly above her own body, pulled to him by some force beyond her own authority. He closed his eyes briefly and her gaze shifted: he was wearing an eagle's feather in his hair: it was magnificent, shining white and brown against the luster of his black hair. An intricate tattoo of ivy and birds—the same that adorned the lace of her own dress—was wrought in some sort of indigo dye, drawn onto his left jaw and extending down the side of his neck, disappearing under his shirt. Bailey found herself longing to touch it, to trace it. Had his grandmother done that? Yes, of course, she must have. His tunic was white and fitted, and there were the ivy and birds again, embroidered with silk so fine that the design was almost imperceptible. His brown trousers were high-waisted and simple, belted with an ancient-looking sash constructed of colorful beads and hemp. He looked extraordinarily wild and young, like some sort of ancient man-boy who had emerged from the woods to find a maiden.

Franticek reached his destination and leaned forward to kiss her cheek; still, she could not look away from her beloved, and the crowd broke its silence to titter.

She flushed. Jacob flushed.

The minister gently joined her hands to Jacob's, and it was the moment she had been waiting for. She was touching him!

He was touching her! *She was real!* And she was here, her hands were in his; they would say their vows and he would kiss her lips, and they would belong to each other forever and beyond forever.

Minister Juren, dressed in severe black, cleared his throat, smiled at Bailey and Jacob, who were supposed to be looking at him but were instead enthralled with each other, and began. "Dearly beloved, we are here assembled, in the presence of God and these witnesses, to join together this man, Jacob Franticek Naplava, and this woman, Bailey Faith Rose, in holy marriage, which is blessed by our Lord Jesus Christ, governed by God's commandments, and is to be held in honor among all men. Therefore it is not to be entered into unadvisedly or lightly, but reverently, discreetly, and in the fear of God. In Holy Scripture we are taught: that marriage was instituted by God Himself, and is therefore a holy estate; that, according to the ordinance of God, a man and his wife shall be one flesh; that, under the New Covenant, the married state has been sanctified to be an emblem of Christ and His Church..."

His voice seemed to fade away; Bailey, in fact, felt that she was floating. She wondered if she was about to swoon, but decided that no, she must instead have one foot in a different world of sorts. The sounds of the birds seemed to sort themselves out, all at once, and they spoke of love in elemental ways that she would never be able to explain her whole life long. She was floating, but Jake was floating with her, and she knew that he understood the birds, too. They seemed to travel somewhere else for a few moments, somewhere achingly perfect and timeless, to part the veil and glide effortlessly through, and though they would speak of it many times to each other over the decades to come, they never attempted to share it with anyone else.

"Into this holy estate these two persons come now to be joined," finished Minister Juren, and the pause in the liturgy snapped the two of them back.

Minister Juren raised his eyebrows at Jake, as if to say, *Are you quite all right?* Jacob gave a slight nod, and the minister cleared his voice again, wondering if he was dreaming and these two might be spirits after all. "Jacob, will you have Bailey to be your wife, to live together in the holy bond of marriage? Will you love her, honor her, and care for her, under all conditions and circumstances of life, and through the grace of God, approve yourself a faithful Christian husband to her so long as you both shall live? If this is your desire then answer and say, 'I will'."

"I will," Jacob answered so quickly that the assemblage laughed again.

"Bailey, will you have Jacob to be your husband, to live together in the holy bond of marriage? Will you love him, honor him, and care for him, under all conditions and circumstances of life, and through the grace of God, approve yourself a faithful Christian wife to him so long as you both shall live? If this is your desire then answer and say, 'I will'."

"I will," she repeated, her voice breaking, and more than a few of the women dabbed their eyes.

Minister Juren nodded, feeling the ceremony was back on track. "Jacob, please take Bailey's right hand and recite your vows."

Jacob, who had never relinquished Bailey's hands to begin with or turned his eyes from her for a moment, began to speak. "I, Jake, take you, Rosie, to be my wedded wife, and I do promise and covenant to be your loving and faithful husband; for better, for worse; for richer, for poorer; in sickness and in health; so long as we both shall live."

Bailey smiled at the sound of their pet names and repeated his words, her voice strong and clear, ringing in the grove. "I, Rosie, take you, Jake, to be my wedded husband, and I do promise and covenant to be your loving and faithful wife; for better, for worse; for richer, for poorer; in sickness and in health; so long as we both shall live."

"What token do you bring?" prodded the minister, turning to Jacob.

Bailey removed the wooden ring from her finger, handed it to Jacob, who in turn handed it to the minister, much to everyone's amusement. Minister Juren's eyebrows shot up for a half a second, but he adjusted well, realizing that there was going to be nothing ordinary about this ceremony.

"Take this ring and place it upon the finger of this woman and say: 'This ring I give to you, in token and pledge of our constant faith and abiding love'."

Jacob repeated the vow and slid the ring back where it belonged, feeling that his heart was about to pound out of his chest.

Minister Juren turned to Bailey, realizing he had no notion what answer would present itself to his question. "Do you have a token, my dear? No matter if you do not."

Bailey nodded and produced a wooden band; it glowed a deep, rich amber. She handed it to the minister, much to Jacob's astonishment—he had no idea she had a wedding band for him—who intoned the vow and handed it back to her.

"This ring I give to you, in token and pledge of our constant faith and abiding love," she repeated, and slid it onto his finger.

He gazed down at it and saw that on the outside was carved *JLR*.

Jake loves Rosie. The carving was nearly identical to the letters he had cut into his bedroom floor, and the tears that he had managed to hold at bay during this ceremony finally formed and overflowed. How on earth had she done it? Who had shaped the ring and so lovingly copied those letters? He looked at her with the question in his eyes.

"Your Pa."

They beamed at each other, and then at last dropped hands so they could accept a large beeswax candle from Minister Juren. Together they stepped forward and lit the candle from the ring of fire, then turned to light the candle that Gacenka held. They watched as Gacenka turned to light Franticek's. And throughout the grove the flame was shared from one candle to another, until every soul held a glowing candle. There was absolute silence.

"Let this flame be the love that burns brightly and fiercely forevermore in your hearts. Let this flame remind you of your love for each other and for your God." The minister smiled and stepped aside, bringing forth a tiny woman to take his place; Jacob's grandmother.

She smiled at them both, her strange gray eyes glittering, and waved her hands in some sort of complex pattern, muttering under her breath. Then she began to speak in a tongue so ancient that Bailey knew nobody would understand it; Marianna had told her it was to be the same blessing she had bestowed upon Gacenka and Franticek, in a Předmostí language, tens of thousands of years old that predated even the Celts. Marianna had promised that Stařenka would translate for her, if she made the request in just the right manner.

She bowed to Bailey, bowed to Jacob, and then rose on her tiptoes to make a mark upon their brows. Her fingers were bright yellow with mustard seed, and her touch was hot. *Lada's sun*: Now Bailey wore it, too. She felt a shiver, a surge of power run through her, and glanced up to see if Jacob felt it, too. The expression he wore was so awestruck that she had to look away again, afraid she would burst into tears at the expanse of joy she was feeling.

Minister Juren stepped forward again once Stařenka had moved away, and Bailey's heart tripped into a frenetic pace. It was about to happen: the pronouncement.

He smiled at them benevolently, his eyes glistening with tears. Never had he participated in such a moving ceremony as this.

Pagan elements, yes, but Christ the Lord was here as well: he could feel the Holy Spirit in this sacred place, perhaps even more than in his own church. He allowed that spirit to fill him before he continued.

"By the power invested in me by the Brethen unity, by the state of Texas, by Christ our Lord, and by—whatever spirits and unknowable power dwell here—I now pronounce you husband and wife. You may kiss your bride."

Jacob did not hesitate, not even for a brief smile or an acknowledgement to the minister or family. He reached for her and kissed her so long and so well that the family began to titter again, then laugh a bit louder, then finally plead to him to let his bride up for air.

They ignored it all, enraptured, consecrated, together at last, at long last.

The reception of Mr. and Mrs. Naplava—"Dr. Bailey Rose Naplava," as Jacob insisted at the formal introduction—was the party of the decade, to be discussed and gossiped about for years to come in the Hill Country. Food, wine, dancing, the infamous hide-and-seek game: it raged on throughout the night without ceasing. At daybreak, the women served breakfast under the tents and it was apparent that most of the five hundred guests had stayed.

It was a blur, an utter blur, to both of them. Three times they attempted to sneak off to the henhouse, only to be waylaid each time by well-wishers. They gave up on that idea and circulated amongst their family and friends, holding tightly to each other, stopping frequently for kisses each time the rowdy crowd banged their mugs on a table. They danced with each other as much as they could, but Bailey was in high demand: she was swung around the floor by Anton, Johann, Joe, Miguel, Franz, Franticek, Kube, Thomas, Karl, and a good number of men she didn't know.

She took a break at last, and as Jacob twirled around with Eveline, she gave him a little wave and strolled off with Gabby, arm in arm. "What are you still doing here?" Gabby laughed. "I mean, look at your man, Bailey. He looks like some sort of primitive warrior god. All of the eligible young ladies look as though they want to rip his clothes off—and a good number of the married ones as well."

Bailey bumped Gabby off balance and the two of them lurched around, giggling. "I honestly don't know. I can't wait to get out of here."

Gabby surveyed her friend. "You're not nervous at all? Not one tiny bit?"

Bailey shook her head. "No. I mean, not yet! Should I be? You know, Gabby, even though I don't have personal experience, I *did* grow up in a brothel. I think I know how it all works."

Gabby considered that and finally shook her head, smiling. "No, Bail. It's nothing like it. That was just sex. Believe me, I should know. Just friction; any two animals can do it." Bailey laughed again but quieted as she realized Gabriella was serious. "Making love with your soul mate—I can't even begin to describe it. I didn't know what to do. I was nervous as hell! You want it to be perfect, you know?"

Bailey stopped and stared at her. "Well now I *am* starting to get nervous. Thanks, Gabby!"

Gabby squeezed her hands. "Jacob's nervous, too. I can tell he's all keyed up." She pulled her back into a slow stroll. "Can I give you some advice?"

Bailey nodded, biting her lip.

"Don't worry about it being perfect. Don't worry about getting everything right. Just enjoy each other. Love each other. Everything falls into place."

Thomas approached them and bent to kiss his wife, and as Bailey relinquished her, Gabby's words reverberated in her mind. She wasn't sure if she was more or less anxious about the night ahead, but she was sure of one thing: she wanted it to happen *now*.

When she was reunited with Jacob, he kissed her as though

she had been absent for a year, and she knew he felt the same way. The hoots and hollers around them were deafening.

They separated at last, laughing, and he steered her to a smaller group of people at the edge of the crowd. "I want you to say hi to someone," he explained.

"Who?"

"It's a surprise." She smiled in anticipation and followed happily, having the time of her life but longing for the party to end so she could be alone with her husband. *Her husband.*

They reached the knot of people and a man stepped forward, causing Bailey to gasp in astonishment. "Mr. Duke? Oh, Charles!" She flung herself forward into his arms, and he returned her embrace, laughing with his deep, rich tone. "I just can't believe it! However did you come to be here?"

She stepped back and stared at him, still gripping his arms. He looked so different in his Sunday best: a crisp, stand-up white high-collar shirt under a dark indigo-blue-checked jacket, chocolate-brown striped trousers and a dark brown derby hat, which he had doffed to greet her. "Your man and I go way back, didn't he tell you? We're in thick."

She turned to stare at Jacob, dumbfounded. "How on earth?"

Jacob smiled, nodding. "Do you remember how I told you that a stranger approached me with a plan to break you out of prison in case the jury made the wrong choice? Well, it was Mr. Duke here, and I ran into him again at the train station the day we were in the Plaza." The day she was collecting mockingbirds! He had driven away to leave her in peace, and by some stroke of fate, had come upon Charles Duke again.

Charles grinned and turned to pull forward a stunning woman, perhaps in her forties. "Allow me to introduce Miss Lucille Brown." The woman smiled shyly and tentatively offered her hand.

"It's so very nice to meet you!" Bailey pumped her hand like a man, and the bashful woman blushed.

"Congratulations, Mrs. and Mr. Naplava," she murmured, and Bailey chatted warmly with the couple, thanking Charles for attending the trial and planning her jailbreak—they all had a good laugh at that—and she was delighted to learn that he had quit the porter business and was working as the Chef at Cubbie's.

"Thanks to a generous tip from a passenger," he said softly, and Bailey gave him another impetuous hug, no doubt setting a few tongues wagging at the sight of a white woman hugging a black man. Lucille beamed as Jacob asked her to dance, and Charles took the cue and bowed to Bailey, who took his hand and danced with her dear friend.

Bailey soon caught a glimpse of Gabby and Thomas and waved them over, and after making the introduction, was pleased to see them engage Charles and Lucille in an animated conversation. A doll was produced by a laughing Ginny, who had been charged with the custom of passing the doll to all of the guests and gathering money for a future baby's cradle. Thomas and Charles obliged good-naturedly with a few choice comments about the honeymoon, and Bailey blushed a brilliant red while Jacob beamed.

She was soon whisked away to throw her bouquet of bluebonnets, which Hope caught quite handily. She was rewarded with an introduction: Bailey grabbed her arm and dragged her to a beer keg where Kube was standing with several ranch hands.

"Vavrinec Kubin, I would like to introduce my sister, Miss Hope Miller. Hope, please make the acquaintance of Kube. He's not a cowboy, but he's as close to one as you'll find around here."

Hope was dressed in a gorgeous green silk that clung in all of the right places and yet still seemed dignified: the color accentuated the subtle green tones in her eyes. Her brown hair was caught up at the sides with beautiful diamond combs and allowed to hang in soft waves past her shoulders. Her features were delicate and refined, so like Adele's. She wore diamonds on her right hand, rubies on her left, and more diamonds around her neck. She looked exactly like what she was: a wealthy society girl from back east.

So Kube was all the more startled when she stuck out her hand

and pumped his enthusiastically, bellowing "It's about damn time! I've been picking at her to introduce me to a cowboy, and just look at *you*!" She drew out the last word and allowed her eyes to take in the measure of him, from the tip of his brown Stetson to his carefully pressed white Sunday best shirt tucked into a pair of dark blue Levi's to the tip of his brown boots, shined for the occasion. "And you have *blue jeans*! Oh, mercy." She took his arm and led him to the dance floor before he had a chance to say a word, and Bailey noted that Kube appeared to be simultaneously flummoxed and exceedingly happy.

"I do believe Kube has met his match."

Jacob gazed at her with a fond smile. "I didn't know you were such a matchmaker."

She returned his smile and stroked his arm. "There's only one match I want to make right now," she whispered.

"Do you think they'd notice if we took our leave?" he whispered back.

"Yes. The sun hasn't even set yet. It's only four o'clock."

"Do we care?"

"No. No, we don't."

And so they made their way casually to the livery stable, getting stopped no less than six times. Some of the questions folks asked were incredibly intrusive, the price of living in a small, close-knit community. "Where will you folks live?" "You're starting a family soon, I suppose?" "Will you continue your practice, Dr. Rose? I mean, Dr. Naplava? Surely not?" "Have they found that Vogler girl yet? Such a tragic story, such a shock for everyone. Poor girl must have lost her mind."

"I'm about to lose mine," Bailey whispered to him as the last of the horde moved away.

"Let's make a run for it!"

And they did just that: broke into a run, holding hands and laughing all the way. And when they found their rig, they laughed even harder: someone had festooned it with paper streamers and old pots and pans tied to the ends of ropes. While Jacob fetched the horse and harnessed him, Bailey flung open the rear doors.

In the space of five minutes they were on their way, the pans sending up a cacophony behind them, and as they looked behind them, they saw several family members laughing as they watched them escape, waving handkerchiefs and blowing kisses.

"I don't think that was much of a sneaky getaway," she observed, blowing kisses back to the well-wishers. "Hey, you need to turn around! I thought we were spending the night at Marianna's and Miguel's!"

He raised his eyebrows and shrugged. "Really? What gave you that idea?"

"You did! Yesterday, when you said, 'Hey, Rosie, Mari and Miguel offered to stay at the ranch house and give us their house for the wedding night'."

"Oh," he said, drawing out the word, as if it had only just occurred to him. He continued to drive in the opposite direction, past the ranch house and down a path that was barely a path at all, and certainly not a road. The wagon began to bump over uneven ground and roots, and she had to duck a few times to avoid getting swatted by sprawling branches.

"Jacob! How much wine did you drink? Where are you taking us? We're off the road, sir!"

"What?" He looked around as if flummoxed, and she took the opportunity to punch him in the arm, hard. "Ouch! What'ja do that for?"

"You're being obtuse."

"Now there's a ten-dollar word," he observed, leaning back and smiling at her from under his hat.

"Are you going to tell me where we're going?"

"Nah."

But just a few moments later, after an endless barrage of pestering from Bailey, the wagon climbed a rather large and very rough hill—she thought they may tip over backward, although Jacob and the horses seemed to be unconcerned—the wagon began to slow, finally coming to a stop on a plateau. She looked around and experienced a dawning sense of familiarity.

He turned to her and shifted, reaching down in a satchel to

pull out a handkerchief. "Now, Rosie, I'm going to have to ask you to trust me."

She raised an eyebrow. "You're not going to gag me are you? Are you some kind of maniac, after all? Because I still have Gabby's knife and I know how to use it."

He snorted. "I could disarm you in a blink of an eye." He waved the handkerchief as he said it.

Quick as a snake, her left hand darted out and snatched the handkerchief as her right hand delivered a solid right hook to that perfect square jaw.

He stared at her, astonished, rubbing his face, before an appreciative grin begin to break over his features. *"Damn, woman!"*

It was her turn to offer a derisive snort. "That was nothing. I just gave you a tap to prove my point. If I had meant it, you'd be laid out."

He continued to stare, speechless for a moment, and finally held out his hand. "The blindfold, please."

"Blindfold?"

He thrust his hand closer to her, palm up, and looked gravely at the hanky. "Yes, ma'am."

She shoved it into his hand, all the while making disapproving noises, and he ordered her to turn around so he could properly fasten it. When her eyes were covered and the hanky secured, she let forth with an exaggerated sigh.

"Happy now? Now, can you please tell me what's going on?"

He didn't answer, but she felt his warm lips briefly touch her own. "Trust me," he whispered, and she shivered. *I'm never going to survive this night,* she thought frantically. *I'm a dead woman. Death by passionate swoon.*

She felt the rig lurch as he jumped down, and then felt his hands on her waist. "Jump down, now," he commanded, and when she was safely disembarked, he put his arm around her and began leading her up the steep hill. She tripped once and squealed like a little girl, much to his amusement.

"I've got you! I won't let you fall! Such a fuss you're making," he scolded, his voice teasing and affectionate. "Honestly, I didn't know you could squeak like that. I'm not sure I want a wife who squeaks. I've had a lifetime of squeaking with my little sisters."

He received a surprisingly well-aimed punch to his mid-section for that, and it took him a few seconds to regain his breath.

"Remind me to talk to you about the virtues of non-violent expression." His voice was an exaggerated croak.

"Remind me to talk to you about the virtues of not mocking your wife's terror at being led blindfolded up a slippery hill! After all, I don't mock your unnatural fear of crickets!"

"Ugh," he shuddered. "Crickets."

She giggled and then flailed for his hand as she began to slip again.

"Jake! Honestly!"

"Sssshhh!" he issued, steadying her. "We're here. Stand still, now."

He carefully brushed her hair aside, raising gooseflesh up and down her spine, and untied the blindfold. As it slid away, Bailey gasped and then cried out, and the sound echoed in the glen like a hosanna.

CHAPTER FOURTEEN

They were standing in Jacob's expansive secret meadow. Feather Hill: he had shared it with her, all of those years ago, and she had named it. It had not altered with the ravages of time or the elements: it was as pristine as she remembered, as if it had been suspended in place by magic, although it had been in the full blush of summer when she had first laid eyes on it. The sprawling, low branches of several live oak trees reached everywhere, low to the ground, inviting a climb or a restful respite. She imagined fairies and sprites dwelling there, so ancient did it appear. Pecan trees, cypress, and sumac enclosed the glen in a rich, late-autumn canopy in shades of red and orange and yellow and faded green. A fair number of leaves had already fallen, allowing the golden afternoon sunlight to filter through. The floor of the clearing was tidier now: he had created a dazzlingly beautiful lawn. The entire left side of the clearing was given over to a meticulously-crafted garden: beds of primula and pansies with their delicate, tidy petals in all bright colors; violas, that so closely resembled the wings of a butterfly; red and pink geraniums with their dark, velvety green leaves, and cyclamen, which looked to Bailey like tulips standing at attention or a butterfly poised to take flight. The flowers were profuse and astonishingly bright, all planted lovingly in beds of varying heights and sizes. Some of the flowers bloomed from an odd assortment of items: an old black boot held a bright red geranium; a rusty child's wagon was filled to overflowing with pink pansies; a statue of an angel held a basket of cyclamen in each hand; a line of wooden buckets held violas. Small stone paths crisscrossed the garden, and stone benches were tucked in perfect corners for reading. She caught glimpses of other precious things: tiny stone figures that were indeed in the form of fairies and gnomes, peeking around flowers and benches; a grotto with a statue in the middle of a striking goddess of some sort: she held a stick in her hand and a tiny waterfall issued from her feet. A small creek meandered through the garden, and the tinkling, whispering sound of the water put her into some sort of heady trance. What on earth had her beloved conjured here?

"These are the winter flowers. Amalie helped me build this: she's a wonder with gardens. You should see hers! She said these flowers will bloom all winter if we don't get a frost. If you want to cut any, she's commanded us to use shears; see that little hutch over there? There's all sorts of gardening tools in there, and I have no idea what most of them are for. Your wildflowers—firewheels, prickly poppies, sunflowers—oh, and the bluebonnets!—they'll bloom again in March. See where they are? Amalie said to leave them for now, even though they look like a dead mess to me."

She could barely tear her eyes away, and when she did, her cheeks were wet with tears, although she didn't know it. The right side of the meadow had been cleared of flowers, the grass trimmed tidily, but the ancient trees had been allowed to stand proudly. A row of bronze hitching posts cast in the shape of rams' heads stood ready. A path of white cobblestone separated the garden and the grassy lawn; the cobblestone extended across the expanse of the meadow, which was at least four acres square, she supposed.

And at the end of the path was their home. She hadn't allowed herself to look at it closely yet, but she turned her eyes to it now, her heart thumping out of her chest.

Their home!

She let out a yelp, reaching for him for support, and he laughed and caught her arm.

"Jake," she said, her voice strangled. "Our house. You built it!"

"Steady there girl," he grinned. "You look as though you might faint. No fainting permitted."

The house was constructed of the light-colored limestone favored by the German and Moravian settlers in these hills. Unlike the homestead, this structure stood two tall stories high. Where the homestead presented a straight front with a wide, tacked-on porch, Jacob had constructed their home in an "L" shape. As they stood facing the house straight on, she saw the main front of the home in beautiful shades of gray, tan, and cream-colored limestone, bordered with fluffy green laurel bushes. An enormous porch—so deep it must have been ten feet, she guessed—graced the front of this house. The wide pine planks of the porch floor were painted dark gray, and four exquisite white wicker rocking chairs with mustard-colored, puffy cushions waited there for them, each with an accompanying white wicker table. Her eyes traveled to the large, deep windows; the gray wooden shutters had been flung wide and she saw cream lace curtains fluttering in the breeze. Beautiful plants in enormous stone pots were placed lovingly around the porch and in the yard leading up to it. She sucked in a breath as she remembered a boy's voice from fifteen years ago.

Now look. Imagine that the pile of stones is much bigger, say as big as that tree over there. Now imagine the stones are arranging themselves into a cottage: a really big two-story house with lots of windows, a deep front porch right there, and a tall chimney over there. Can't you see it? Isn't it beautiful?

"It's exactly our house, just how we described it!" She spun to him, grasping his shoulders, and gave him a shake. "It's like our words brought it to life!"

He nodded, his grin widening. "That about sums it up."

She stared at him a second longer and then suddenly tore up the path, and he laughed, running to catch up. She skidded to a halt before she reached the porch—he very nearly ran into her—

and turned to look at the portion of the house that stood at a right angle to the main part of the house, trying to take everything in at once. The oaken doors stood slightly open, and the room within seemed unnaturally bright, didn't it? What on earth? She turned to walk toward it, as though in a daze, but Jacob had caught up with her, and was pulling her by the hand. "This way, kid. Come into the main house first."

She followed him up the porch stairs, her hand lingering on a rocking chair, and waited, heart pounding, as he opened the heavy oak door. Jacob's mouth was dry and his own heart was banging away; would she cherish this place as he did? This was the home he had spent his life building for her, since the day he had returned to the ranch without her fifteen years ago.

She found herself frozen in the foyer, completely unable to take the next step forward. Beneath her feet was a smooth floor of cut travertine, she thought she heard him say, and above her head, ten feet at least, were thick beams of cypress.

"Did you build—all of this? Jake?" She reached back for him, her hand shaking.

"Yes." He gripped her hand tightly, his stomach in knots. Did she hate it, after all? "I needed—well—time alone when I was a kid. After you left. So I'd load the wagon and come up here and build. I've always loved to build things, you know." He knew he was babbling but found a sudden, desperate need to fill the silence. Maybe this had been a huge mistake, after all. She had seemed so happy when he told her the little fib about living at the ranch house. Maybe she needed Gacenka nearby since she was a new bride. He swallowed thickly and continued to rattle on. "I remembered how we planned it out, and when I got started— well—I just couldn't seem to stop. Everyone always teased me that I disappeared every day, but Wenzel knew where I went, because he helped me, then when it got to bigger things like raising walls and putting logs and stones in place, I needed more help, so by the time I was—I don't know—twenty-three or so— everyone knew about it and pitched in. They all knew I was building it for you, but no one ever said a word about it. First time in their lives my family hasn't butted in, I reckon." He paused and chuckled, but it was a strangled sound. "It kept getting bigger and bigger. So I kept clearing more land and adding on. This parcel's pretty big—five acres, maybe a little more…" He drifted off as she wandered forward, as if in a trance, and picked up a figure of a wooden sheep that graced the top of a rustic pine café table—she supposed he had made that, too. The sheep was intricately-detailed; standing in full wool and gazing slightly to its right. "I carved that," he said stupidly, and tried to stop himself from prattling on, but could not. "When I was out riding the range, when I was still a kid, maybe fifteen or so, there was this one sheep who followed me around. I kept her as a pet for a few years until she passed. She would always watch the sunset, with that expression on her face—you know, kind of like a goodbye. So I set her on this table next to the window facing west, so she can watch the sun set every night." It sounded utterly ludicrous now that he said it out loud.

There was a silence as profound as love itself, and while Jacob agonized with self-doubt, Bailey experienced an upwelling of love stronger than any emotion she had ever known in her life. *I could die now. It would be perfectly okay. I could die now and be ecstatically happy, because I love this man, and he loves me.* It quite took her breath away. She placed the sunset sheep tenderly back in her place, being sure to turn her so she could gaze out of the window, and in the ensuing silence, Jacob spoke again, his nervous words crowding together.

"So the layout of the house is a little—well—weird. I'm not sure it makes much sense. Pa said the design is a jumbled mess of everyone who helped me: Moravian, German, Mexican. I mean I never had a master plan, I just kept adding on rooms. Oh, and I should mention, it's not finished yet! I mean, we can live here, you know, until we move into town in a few months, but there are things you're going to notice that need finishing. A stupid way to build a house, really. It's like five or six houses put together…." He petered off, desperate now to hear her speak, but terrified of what she may say; so when she turned to him, her face radiant and her lips parting to answer, he rushed in to cover her words.

"Wait! Don't say anything yet." He pulled her by the hand, leading her through a French door out of the foyer. She gasped again and stared. It was fanciful, whimsical, and somehow— utterly familiar. The door opened to an expansive room; the ceiling soared twenty feet high, and she realized there was no second story to this section of the house. Colorful rugs covered the wide plank floors, and deep chairs and chaises created a cozy, inviting space, even within the expanse of the room. From the cypress beams high above hung three brass Rococo four-arm gas chandeliers, topped with cut-glass globes. There was a big, lovely card table set into a nook, rather like a booth, with a low-hanging red gas chandelier, and she could imagine the family playing a lively game of faro. There was a deep chair with a reading lamp by a window, and the east and north walls were lined with built-in floor-to-ceiling shelves, filled partially with books, complete with a rolling library ladder! *Wherever had he come upon a library ladder?*

He watched her drift to the shelves, her eyes shining as she stroked the ladder in wonder. "The library is a gift from Professor Greaves, back east. Took me under his wing; he was mentor when I was in Boston. A fine, fine man. When he passed five years ago, he willed me his library, complete with the shelves and books. And the ladder! Pa helped me get it all into place."

"Jake—" she found she couldn't really speak just yet, but she looked at him, her eyes full, and he felt the tightness loosen in his chest.

On the northeast end of the room close to the reading corner was a door; to where did it lead? She felt like a child exploring a castle—*her* castle! But as she rotated in a slow circle, her eyes were drawn all the way to the other end of the huge room, to the focal point: an enormous, walk-in fireplace on the far south end. She walked toward it, enchanted.

"Go ahead," she heard him say behind her, his voice tight with excitement. "Walk into it!"

She looked back at him, a stupid, stunned expression on her face, and walked into the fireplace, feeling like Alice walking through her looking glass. "I'm not going to meet the White Queen, am I?" she said, her voice shaking a bit with excitement. She realized too late that Jacob would likely have no idea to what she was referring.

"If you do, you must believe six impossible things before breakfast," he smiled, proving yet again that she had much to learn about her new husband.

The fireplace was dark, but there was enough light to see that the back was solid. There was enough room to step around a grate laid with wood and through a small hallway to the left—a *hallway*, in the fireplace! She needn't even duck; the brick above her head was a good seven feet up. She stumbled through, touching the walls for support, Jacob behind her with his hands on her hips, steadying her, talking on and on about chimneys and flues and bricks and stone and mortar and downspouts and proper footing. Honestly, she had never heard him talk so much, and she had to stifle a laugh at his enthusiasm and nerves.

"...and so here we are!" he finished exuberantly, and they emerged into a bright kitchen. Bailey laughed and clapped her hands in sheer appreciation, blinking furiously to adjust from the darkness.

"Whatever made you think to have a secret passage? I love it!"

He grinned and rubbed the back of his head sheepishly. "Well, actually, you're going to think I'm a colossal idiot, Rosie. I told you that I built this house room by room, literally. The room in front was the second room; there was just the foyer and the front room for a long time. I built them before I went to law school; well, the library wasn't there yet, of course."

Bailey marveled at that piece of information. By the time he was eighteen, he had already constructed that beautiful foyer and expansive room! She was dying to explore the kitchen, but she turned her back to it and gave him her full attention.

"So when I came home and started building again, I realized I had no idea what I wanted the house to look like. I was kind of lost, to be honest with you." Bailey nodded sympathetically, touching his arm. They had both been lost for so long. "So instead of figuring out how many bedrooms and where to put them, I added a hallway to the fireplace and built the kitchen back here."

Bailey nodded, smiling, eagerly turning to explore the kitchen. Tongue-and-groove wainscoting in a cheerful lemon-yellow covered the walls, and the floor was white pine covered with some sort of gloss that she suspected would mop well. The shiny range sported the "White, Warner & Co." label, and she ogled it; there was a hot water tank behind the stove! No more heating water on the stovetop, which meant no insufferably hot kitchen during the sweltering summer months. A highboy icebox, a fine piece of oak furniture, stood on the other side of the kitchen, and she ran her hands over it, her eyes shining. "Is this..."

Jacob nodded eagerly. "It's an icebox! I'll stock it with ice from the icehouse out back. We can keep milk and meat there; no running to the root cellar for every meal."

"Ohhhh..." The word was long and drawn out as she imagined preparing fresh meat that had not been smoked—a flavor she had never enjoyed.

The pièce de résistance, however, was the gargantuan butler's pantry that stood as a transitional space, accessed through swinging doors, between the kitchen and dining room, perhaps half the size of the kitchen. There was a small dresser with a pair of lead sinks with folder covers for hot and cold water, but her eyes were drawn to the floor-to-ceiling built-in cupboards featuring glass-faced cabinets, a wide counter space, and numerous drawers and cabinets below.

"There's not much in it yet," he said sheepishly. "I thought maybe you'd want to choose your own china, or we could do it together. There's linens, though, that Ma made, and plenty of canned goods."

She stood, shaking her head in amazement. "This is—this is incredible. You *built* all of this?"

He nodded, coloring and clearly pleased at her reaction. "You know I like to build things," he muttered, and then silently berated himself for sounding like a simpleton. "But there's a punchline."

"A punchline?"

He nodded miserably and led her back into the kitchen. "Do you notice anything missing?"

She looked around at the beautiful range, ice box, plentiful shelving, and movable table. Then realization dawned: she didn't recall seeing a doorway or hallway in the living area that could lead into this kitchen; only the door on the far northeast end of the room, and that one couldn't possibly lead to the kitchen, now that she thought about it.

He sighed and nodded glumly. "You've figured it out. There's no way to the kitchen..."

"...except through the fireplace!" she finished, chortling. "Oh, Jacob! That's perfect!"

He rolled his eyes. "You won't say that when we have the fireplace going at full roar on a frosty winter night. But don't worry; I'm going to knock a hole in the wall and connect the rooms, maybe with a pretty arch. I just haven't had time yet. Did I mention that there's other things that aren't quite finished with the house?"

She grabbed his hands and swung them, laughing. "Let's never say it's finished! I love the idea of adding to it. Let's promise that we'll add something every year! When we're one hundred years old we'll add an observatory with a telescope so we can see the moon—our children will be able to see men on it, remember?"

"You remember talking about that?"

"I remember everything we talked about!" She flung her arms around his neck and kissed it, breathing him in, and then pushed him away to explore the kitchen, letting him go on and on about the intricacies of the plumbing. Off the kitchen on the northeast corner was a small lavatory with a toilet and sink. "How wonderful! An indoor lavatory!" A door next to this room opened to the outdoors; she opened it and gasped at the view: she had caught a glimpse of an emerald yard with olive trees sloping down to a creek, but Jacob's arm reached around her to shut the door.

"Not yet," he whispered in her ear.

They returned to the south end of the kitchen and walked through the butler's pantry into a room that had somehow been built two steps up: it was a dining room, complete with a Russian Rock crystal chandelier, a long table with a pine plank top surrounded by ten Bavarian chairs with burl wood frames, carved and turned back splats, and beautifully painted faces. On the wall was one of Wenzel's paintings: the woman pouring the glowing honey. Bailey paused to wipe away a well of tears.

"Jake," she choked again, but could get no further.

"I mucked up this layout, too. The only way to get to the dining room is from the kitchen through the butler's pantry. Imagine us holding a fancy dinner. 'And now, I ask you all to allow me to extinguish the fire so we can walk through the fireplace, into the kitchen, and through the butler's pantry to access the dining room.'" He shook his head disgustedly. "I may be a builder, but I'm no architect."

"I think it's genius," Bailey answered promptly, her voice ringing with conviction. "It's absolutely brilliant and unique." She saw that he was not convinced. "And I think I saw a good three feet of clearance past the fireplace on the southwest corner of the living room. I imagine we could build a hallway that curves around the side of the house into the dining room. Or it could lead to a conservatory, you know, with glass walls! An observation room for birds and wild animals. Sun parlors are all the rage. And that room could lead to the dining room."

He stared at her, a smile breaking over his features. "You're crazier than I am! But that's a hell of an idea! And I know a man in Austin who has one of those in his house; his wife's a botanist."

She smacked her hands together and nodded briskly. "Then that shall be our next addition to the House that Never Ends."

"I love you," he said abruptly. The words were unexpected just at that particular moment, and her breath caught in her throat.

"I love you, too," she answered, and they stood and stared at each other for a beat, frozen in place, smiling stupidly.

"Did you make this table?" she asked finally, loathe to break the spell, but aching to see the rest of the house.

He nodded. "And the chairs are a wedding gift from Rosalie and her family. And you know who the painting is from." He was emotional, too, and he suddenly took her hand and pulled her back down the two stairs through the pantry and into the kitchen.

"We're not even close to being finished with this tour, madam," he announced brightly. "Follow me, if you will, and please forgive the indignity of exiting through the fireplace."

Back through the looking glass they went, into the cavernous front room, but as she headed toward the mysterious door, he steered her to face the west wall instead, the one that fronted the house. She found herself looking at a shelf full of Mr. Greaves' beautiful volumes.

"If you could choose any of those books, which would you choose to read first?"

She turned to look at him, crinkling her brow. "Honestly, Jake, can we read later? I want to see the rest of our house!"

He turned her by the shoulders again until she was facing the books. "Choose."

She sighed and began to look at the titles, and immediately knew it when she found the one, laughing in appreciation. "You have it! Verne. *The Green Ray.* Was it Greaves'?"

He shook his head. "No, I bought my own copy when you were—"

In jail, he had about said. *Now that's a perfect thing to bring up on your wedding night—one of her worst memories!*

"In the stony lonesome?" she smiled, turning. "It's okay, Jake. We're not going to pretend it didn't happen." She turned back to the shelf, reaching for the book. "And this book, it helped me to see my way so clearly—" She abruptly snatched her hand back and gasped, backpedaling so quickly that she almost knocked Jacob over. "*What the...*"

The bookshelves were swinging open!

She understood right away where the secret passageway led to: she was gazing into a courtyard! She took two steps forward and stood on the precipice, gawking. "I don't believe it! I just don't believe it!" she whispered.

"Aw, it was no big deal to make it. I just built bookshelves onto French doors, and added a mechanism that triggers them to open. Pulling that book off the shelf just unlocked the doors, so to speak."

She stared at him, dumbfounded. "Are you a spy?" She finally asked, and he snickered.

He took her by the hand and stepped around her, leading her through the doors onto a lovely stone path that looked very much like the ones in the garden. She followed him, her head swiveling comically as she tried to take it all in at once.

"This part was Mari and Miguel's idea," he admitted. "Every proper home in Mexico has a courtyard, you see. And it was as good a way as any to connect the two houses."

The path led to a patio on which stood a wrought-iron table and chairs, all covered over with an umbrella in stripes of yellow and pink. He showed her how the umbrella could be adjusted to provide shade from the hot Texas sun as it moved across the sky. The rest of the courtyard was covered in impossibly soft grass, and she knelt to feel it. Yes, it was as soft as it looked!

"It feels like silk!"

"It's Zoysia grass. I planted it because it's so soft; I thought our dogs, and later on, our babies would love to play here. It's all enclosed as long as we keep the doors shut, see? A nice big space for them to run. We can put a swimming pool out here if we want. Or maybe we'll never want a pool," he amended quickly, realizing the horrible associations they both had with pools.

She smiled up at him. "I would love a pool; I'd like to learn to swim, and our children, too." He was reminded again of the steeliness of her will. He could only ever hope to be that brave. "Jacob, it's an amazing, wonderful courtyard."

He beamed. "Well come on. I don't have any more secret passageways, I promise, but I want to show you something I think you might like." He led her across the courtyard in the opposite direction of the main house, and they passed under a lovely stone arch and through a door into a very large room. It was completely empty, and was markedly different from the unique, beautiful space of the big room in the main house. The floor was tiled in here, and the walls were a pristine, shiny white. A hallway at the back of the room beckoned, and she crossed the room and entered it, thoroughly confused. Off the hallway were three smaller rooms, all of them identical to the main room, and at the end of the hallway was a slightly larger room which contained the only furnishing she had seen thus far: a stunning Samuel Oxford desk with five drawers, black leather on top, and carved dolphin legs. She stood and stared at it, her mind working frantically, wondering what to say to fill the silence. Were these the bedrooms, then? But they were so stark! And the smaller rooms were so *very* small; how would they ever fit a bed and furnishings into the space?

And then the light bulb illuminated in her mind, and she gasped and swung around to face him. "Jacob! It's—why, it's a clinic! A clinic for me!"

He grinned and rolled his eyes. "Well, of course it is, dimwit. What did you think it was? Our *boudoir*?" He roared as he read the answer in her face. "Well, dammit, if I would've known that, I would've teased you much longer."

She started to swing at him but ended up hugging him again instead. "I love it. I love it! It's so—big! And three exam rooms! And this is my office, right?"

"Unless you want it to be our bedroom. I can haul the desk out and see if the bed will fit."

This time she did swing, but he was ready for her, capturing her hand and spinning her around.

"I can't believe it! I wondered how I would practice medicine, once we get to live here for good. I thought maybe I'd just be a circuit doctor making house calls, but the hardest part about leaving my clinic in the city was going to be leaving a space that was all my own. This is just *perfect.*" She was already moving back through the hallway, inspecting each corner, imagining what she would put where, and Jacob felt a twinge of deep regret knowing that his election would take them away from this house and from the start of her new practice for a full four years. He hadn't even shopped around for a townhouse to rent; he had wanted her to be a part of that process, but he could already see that leaving this place would be downright painful for them both.

"But it doesn't matter. We'll be together."

She had come back to the office and had taken his hands.

"What?"

"You were missing this place already; I can tell. I know we'll have to leave it soon. But we have a few months; let's make the most of each day. And living in the city will be loads of fun. We can go to the theatre and go dancing and out for dinner. We can go to San Pedro Springs and steal kisses in our special spot. We'll find a pretty little house and make it cozy."

"I forgot that we seem to be able to read each other's minds."

"A dangerous thing, I'm sure."

They lingered in the clinic for a while longer, and he surprised her with stairs leading up to a spacious loft. "Just in case we ever have any relation who need to live with us for a while."

"This house, it never ends!" she gushed.

"Well, it does, but you haven't seen the best part yet."

She knew what the best part was, and color flooded her face as she followed him down the stairs, out of the clinic, through the courtyard, and back through the bookcase. She turned to face the unexplored door, practically skipping across the room to get there. "I think I know where that leads," she grinned.

"After you, m'lady," he gestured grandly, and she sucked in a breath of excitement as she turned the knob.

"It's a staircase!" she announced.

"Very astute."

She began to climb, Jacob on her heels, and murmured in appreciation when she reached the landing. It was a spacious area with a cushioned bay window overlooking the beautiful backyard, and she sat in it, sighing with pleasure. "I could sit here all day, gazing out of this window, reading a book, writing in my journal."

He cleared his throat meaningfully. "You are welcome to dream away your days here, my love, but just maybe not *today*." She could have sworn she saw a flush rise in his face before he moved away. "Come on, now. The rest of it!"

The rest of it was grand beyond her daydreams. First, he showed her the rooms to the north of the landing; a hallway led them to four bedrooms, each spacious with large, bright windows, bead board wainscoting, and pine floors and beautiful hooked rugs with figures of horses and sheep, flowers and ivy. "Ma made all of the rugs and curtains," he added. "She's been working on them for years. She stopped when I started courting Caroline, but you know, she started right up again when you came to help Clarissa." Bailey felt warmth seeping through her.

They made their way back down the hallway, stopping to inspect a lavatory, which drew gasps of surprise and pleasure from Bailey. The room was spacious and included a sizable roll-top, enameled, cast-iron claw foot tub with a round shower ring, a toilet with a bowl boasting a decorative blue china pattern ("That was Rosalie's idea, I swear!"), and a white pedestal sink over which hung a round, gilt and wood mirror. The thought of her bath earlier that morning, and the images she had harbored of Jacob sharing it with her, made her blush. She felt him looking at her quizzically, but he didn't say a word.

"Did you do this plumbing yourself?" she ventured, desperate to dispel the images of a wet, sleek Jacob. "I can't believe we have a lavatory *upstairs*!"

"Ya, and now Marianna is insisting I build her one!"

"I've never had a shower," she said shyly.

"I prefer a bath." He smiled at her and she smiled back, and their gaze held for a long, silent moment.

"One more thing to show you," he finally ventured. "Follow

me, if you will."

She knew where they were headed, and though her pulse drummed with nervousness and she felt her face begin to stain again, she quickened her step. He was ahead of her a few steps, and she could not help but stare at this man, her beloved. She was dying to explore that indigo tattoo. Her eyes traveled down the length of him. The beaded belt moved against his thigh with each step, and she felt a pull. He would be removing that belt soon, and the trousers, and the white tunic that was a bit too tight across his broad shoulders. And everything underneath it as well. Or maybe he'd want her to remove his clothes.

She felt a sudden surge of panic. *I have no idea what to do.* Of course, she knew what to do, and five hundred ways to do it, thanks to conversations at the bordellos and the clinic, but she didn't *know*. It was akin to learning about how to perform a caesarean section from a lecture and actually performing it herself: why, it wasn't the same thing at all!

When it came right down to it, she didn't know anything. *But he did.* That somehow made it worse, didn't it? She didn't resent his experiences; she suddenly resented her own inexperience. He would see, perhaps very soon, how much she didn't know, and maybe he would be disappointed on his wedding night. She could learn, of course. *But tonight is supposed to be perfect.*

She didn't realize she had stopped walking until he turned around and came back for her; she was staring rigidly at the floor, awash in self-doubt.

Jacob took one look at her face and his stomach lurched. *She hates it. She hates this house with its strange passageways and missing doors. She hates the bedrooms. Or she hates that damn blue China toilet bowl.* Her whole countenance had changed very suddenly, and he swallowed thickly, wondering how to proceed.

"Can I show you the last room?" he finally said hesitantly, his voice betraying his anxiety, and she snapped to attention, keenly regretful for having made him worry.

She smiled and squeezed his hands. "Of course!"

He recovered some courage and led her by the hand to their

bedroom, his words sticking in his throat.

His nervous energy had carried them through the grand tour of the house, and she let it, longing to put him out of his misery but understanding that his soul was in these walls: his dreams of her, his longing for a life with her since he was fourteen years old. It was almost unbearable for him to let her speak, she realized, for what could she possibly say that would make this all right— the grandeur, the sheer fearlessness of his vision?

For in front of her was the bed—*the bed*! A replica of the canopy bed he had carved in miniature for Ginny, down to the very last detail of floral etchings. It was masterful; breathtakingly beautiful. And above it was another of Wenzel's paintings: this one, the flamingo sky, his masterpiece: Bailey as the sunrise, Jacob, the sky. They stared at it for a moment in silence, and she felt the tears on her face again.

She lowered herself limply onto the massive bed, stroking a precious hand-stitched quilt in shades of deep red and mustard yellow, watching him pace the room, listening to him explain about every last detail.

"I wanted to be sure there was a deep bay window, and I really like the arch in the ceiling; do you? It's unconventional, so I wasn't sure about it....."

"Jake."

"And I told Marianna to find paper with bluebonnets for the walls; she looked everywhere, but I finally found some in Indianapolis a few years back...."

"Jake."

"I left this wall bare." He gestured stupidly at the wall the bed's headboard was butted up against. "So the painting would have its own place. But we can paper that wall, too. I still have extra paper and paste."

"Jake."

"And if the wardrobe isn't big enough, we have plenty of room for another one. I wasn't sure how many things you'd have." He paced to the wardrobe and peered into its emptiness, and stayed there, his shoulders tense.

"Jake!"

And finally, at long last, he stopped, letting silence settle around them, letting the moment happen that he'd been waiting for most of his life; dreading it, aching for it.

CHAPTER FIFTEEN

"Come here." She patted the bed and he came stiffly, perching on the bed as though it were covered with eggshells. He turned and moved toward her. She took his hands and placed them on her face, and left her own there, covering his. She looked into his eyes and saw all of the pain and fear and doubt and hope and love that had composed his life since she had stepped into it so long ago. She had no idea what she was going to say. She took a deep breath and spoke what was in her own heart.

"I've had four homes in my life. The first was under the porch of a whorehouse. I shared it with mice and spiders and snakes and lizards and the occasional raccoon. I shared it with a boy one night." They both smiled at that. "The second was a cot in a convent school, shared with many, many girls over the years. I guess you could say the convent was my home, but it never felt like home; there was the refectory and the chapel and the schoolrooms—but only my little cell and cot was home, really. And the third and fourth weren't homes, either; just rooms in sparse boarding houses for women as I finished medical school and internship. And then back to the convent and my cot." She paused as another tear escaped, and he brushed at it with his thumb. "But from the time I was twelve, and I met a magical boy, *this* was my home, Jake. *This house.* It was *this house*, down to the last nail. We built it together, and I lived there, in my mind, with you. When I was in prison, I would curl into a ball on my cot and go to our house, and it was *this house*. I sat on the porch; I wandered in the garden; I cooked in the kitchen; I rested by the fireplace, in your arms. I made love with you, on this bed. Do you understand?" She tightened her grip on his hands, her voice quavering with intensity. "I was *here,* with you. When I walked into this house today, it wasn't for the first time. I have lived here, always, with you, and will live here always, with you, long after we have passed away to the other place. *This home is my heart.*"

The expressions parading across his face were a marvel to witness: shock, relief, wonder, tenderness, and love. And then something else—an emotion that preceded movement by the barest of margins—passion, desire. Hunger. She saw it only for an instant before his lips were on hers, his hands moving from her face to her hair, and she drew him in. For a long moment they drank from each other, reassuring themselves it was real; it was really happening at last—the inauguration of their lives together.

She shifted at last, just a tiny movement, but enough to make him draw back and smile at her. "Too early in the day? Are you hungry? Should we wait until dark?" The uncertainty and tenderness in his voice made her flush.

"No, it's not that, Jake. I was just wondering—this may sound silly—but could you gather some flowers for me? Maybe bring a little of that beautiful garden into our bedroom? And maybe a bottle of wine, if you have one handy?"

He mentally smacked himself for not thinking of those details. "Of course! I'll be right back!" The swiftness with which he launched himself from the bed, out the door, and tore down the stairs made her cover her mouth with her hand to suppress another giggle; he wasn't wasting any time getting back to her! And she was glad! But it would give her barely enough time to get everything ready...

She bolted from the bed and rummaged through her satchel: there it was, her very own "brown paper bag," identical to the package she distributed to her patients. She lifted her dress, pulled down her unmentionables, and squatted on the floor, wondering why her hands were shaking so. She had practiced this, for goodness sake, and counseled her own patients about it time and time again! Still, she was dreadfully nervous. If she did it wrong, it could be painful or ineffectual. She inserted the womb veil and followed it with her own concoction of muriate of quinine and Vaseline—quite an effective spermicide—and pulled her knickers back into place, her face red, her hands still shaking. This would *not* be something she would hide from Jake, and there were plenty of condoms in that bag for him; but just for this first time, it was something intensely personal and private, an action she wanted to take alone, with her own body.

And now for the fun part.

In my dreams, I'd come in the house and find your lace collar. A few steps more, and I'd see your shoes, then your dress, then your unmentionables, all laid out like a trail leading right to my bedroom. I'd be sure I'd get there and you wouldn't be there; you'd just be a ghost, but you were always there, waiting, sitting by the window, your skin glowing in the moonlight. You always stood up when I walked in and held out your arms to me...

She scurried back across the room and began rummaging in a table next to the bed, and there it was; the lace collar! She smiled tenderly and rushed to the hallway, placing it gently several feet from the bedroom door, her face shining with anticipation. Her slippers were next, followed by the precious white lace dress itself—thankfully, it was rather easy to shrug it over her head; certainly not the feat of disrobing Rosalie's wedding dress would have been—her camisole, garter and stockings, all leading in an orderly line to the door of the bedroom.

Too orderly! She stared at the tidy arrangement and realized how ridiculous this all looked. She hastily picked the garments up and threw them back down, striving for a haphazard look, as though she were peeling her things off as she ran to the bedroom in a frenzy. She giggled out loud, feeling incredibly foolish and excited all at the same time. She really had absolutely no idea what she was doing!

Now what? She was down to her chemise and bloomers. Should she take those off, too, and sit by the window buck naked? A nervous giggle erupted again. She attempted to arrange herself seductively at the bay window, guessing that maybe Jacob would like to remove that last bit of her clothing. The moonlight wasn't exactly shining on her skin, seeing as there were still a few good hours of daylight remaining, but her hair was long and wild, and she had left a few of the flowers in for good measure. She turned to the door, arranging her arms just so, then shifted a bit so her profile would be to him, then leaned all the way back on her elbows, her breasts thrust forward. *Yes, that's it. Look just like a prostitute.*

She sat up abruptly, panic threatening again. What in the name of all things holy was she doing? How should she sit? Should she be standing? Should she get in bed, under the quilt? Was this all a big mistake? Maybe she should pick up her ludicrous display of clothing and put it all back on; what on earth would he think, finding her like this? Would he maybe wonder if she hadn't been a soiled dove, after all? Her eyes grew as round as saucers and the flush crept up her neck and into her sunburned cheeks. She clutched her hands together in her lap, suddenly realizing she had made a dreadful mistake, wondering if there was enough time to correct it. How long had he been gone? Five minutes? Ten? And was the womb veil slipping? Everything felt slippery down there—clearly, she had overdone it with the ointment. Did she have time to check it?

And that was how he found her, coiled in the bay window like a cat about to spring, her hair a bright, untamed corona speckled with flowers, her shoulders, legs, and feet bare, toes curled, eyes wide, mouth open in dismay.

"Rosie?" he finally managed, quite sure that he must have knocked himself out somehow and entered into a dream. "Are you real?" The flowers in his hand scattered to the floor, and he fumbled the bottle of wine comically, nearly dropping it before he managed to set it on the table by the door.

She's a ghost. This has all been a dream, after all.

"A real fumbling nitwit, maybe!" she choked, and burst into tears.

He reached her in two seconds. "Stop," he chided, smiling but alarmed, wrapping his arms around her, wanting to comfort her, aching for her. "Why are you crying?"

"Because I don't know what I'm doing!" she blurted. "I tried to—" she flapped her hand in the general direction of the door— "to make your fantasy come true, and I've made a mess of it. I bet the Bailey in your dream didn't act like *this*."

He moved her away from him and squeezed her chin with gentle fingers, forcing her to look at him. "Are you kidding? You have it perfect, right down to the lace collar. When I came down the hallway I thought I'd died and gone to heaven."

She managed a tremulous smile and took a few deep breaths. She might as well be honest with him; she could see that she was worrying him terribly. "Jake. If I'm acting funny—"

"Oh no, you're not acting funny at all," he teased, and was rewarded with a soft laugh.

"It's just that I don't know what I'm doing. You might have the idea that I know what I'm doing, but I don't, really. And I know you do."

He sat back a few inches to regard her better. "Is this about other women I've been with? Because Bailey, there've only been—"

She put a finger to his lips. "No! It's not about that at all. It's that I'm an old maid! Here I am, twenty-seven, and I may as well be a maid of sixteen!"

Jacob gulped and tried heroically to banish the image of the two of them together, like this, as teenagers. "I feel like I'm sixteen, right at the moment," he confessed. "Nervous as hell and ready to—." *Ready to explode*, he had almost said. *A hell of a poetic sentiment to impart to my wife on our wedding night.* But he could sense immediately that his words seemed to have had a calming effect on his bride: the tension left her face as she gazed at him, and she lost the tightly-sprung pose of a panther, relaxing against him.

"You're nervous?"

He nodded.

"*Why* are we so nervous? We've always been so easy with each other. Being with you is—it's like we've always been together. Like we're the same person, almost. Why should this be any different?"

He reached down and entwined his fingers with hers. She noticed that his were stained with green; she imagined him tearing the flowers of the beds in a tremendous rush, forsaking Amalie's proper gardening shears, and she squeezed his fingers hard, the familiar swell of love coursing through her; a great, rolling wave of longing.

"I don't know," he whispered. "But I don't think we'll be nervous for long. Maybe it's just the whole business of getting started."

They stared at each other for ten long, breathless seconds.

"How about we just jump in?" Her pulse pounded in her throat madly.

"Yes. Okay." He tried to swallow and found that he could not, and wondered if he would choke.

"On the count of three."

They both laughed at that, but stilled at once. The air in the room had grown heavy and electrified.

"*Three,*" they both said, and lunged at each other, promptly knocking heads and falling back again, laughing, each with a hand to the forehead.

"That was exciting but painful." Jake rubbed the tender spot and shook his head.

"My family will wonder what in the world we did to each other, with matching bruises on our foreheads."

Bailey giggled and then the room grew quiet again. "Maybe we're making this harder than it needs to be," she finally offered, and reached forward. "Can I maybe just take this off, for starters?

Remember that day you washed up at Glory Creek, fifteen years ago? You just took your shirt off and waded right in like it was nothing, and all the while I was swooning on the shore, trying not to let Wenzel catch on that I could barely breathe for watching you. I wanted so badly to touch the dragon wing on your chest that Wen drew there."

She ran her fingers gently over the embroidered ivy and birds on his white tunic, and Jacob was sure that his heart would stop after all. He closed his eyes and had to remind himself to breathe. *Breathe. Breathe. Breathe.* Johann had given him some brotherly advice for tonight: he and Lindy had remained chaste throughout their courtship, and he confessed that on their wedding night, he had come damn close to passing clean out on the bedroom floor. He advised his younger brother to focus on one thing: breathing.

He felt her warm hands travel down the front of him, grasp the bottom of his tunic, and raise it, slowly, baring his abdomen (*was it jumping on the outside like it was on the inside?*), then his chest, and he raised his arms so she could draw it over his head.

Then she was touching him, and her hands were like fire on his skin. She traced his tattoo from his jaw, down his neck, and over his collarbone, and across his chest: every strand of ivy, every tiny bird, and then she leaned forward to kiss it, starting with the bird that perched on his jaw, and ending with the last leaf of ivy that lay over his heart. His skin smelled of fresh outdoors and warm spice, and she sat up, feeling drunk with him.

He was staring at her, his blue eyes dark in the gloaming, his lips parted as if to ask a question, and by way of answer, she shifted from the bay window and stood before him, raising her arms.

He leaned into her, burying his face in her stomach, his arms reaching around to stroke her back, then gently lifted the chemise over her head, and it floated to the floor behind her. "I'll give you the tattoo now," he whispered, and began tracing the design with his finger, starting with her jaw, moving down the side of her neck, across her collarbone, and around her heart. And then he retraced the path with his lips, just as she had done, and her eyes wanted terribly to drift shut with the pleasure of it, but she looked down instead, watching his dark head below her. She grasped his broad, powerful shoulders, anchoring herself, as his lips took the path of the ivy, finally reaching the point over her heart, his beautiful mouth closing over her breast. She let go of his shoulders and sank her fingers into his thick hair, making a sound she was quite sure she had never made before.

"Jake," she managed. "Can we lie down?"

He caught her as her knees gave way, and as he lowered her onto the bed, the fire was lit; that fire that had consumed them twice before, and there was a fierce straining all at once, mouths, tongues meshing, limbs entangled with clothes, hands striving to feel every inch of bare skin, gentleness morphing into urgency. He tugged gently on her bloomers and she pulled away from him long enough to kick them down her legs to the foot of the bed, and then she sat up beside him, suddenly realizing that being naked with this man was—well—just as *normal* as being clothed.

"Can I—" she managed to start, and then gave up making the request and began groping at his belt, which had been tied in a damnable knot of sorts. "I can't—" she began, but he had pushed her hands aside and had the belt off in the space of two seconds, then lifting his hips to make brief work of his pants and everything underneath them, all of which went sailing the entire length of the room, narrowly missing a picture frame on a table by the door.

"Sorry, did you want to take those off?" he laughed softly, turning back to her and gathering her close, and her whole body quaked at the feel of the bare length of him against the bare length of her; his legs twisting around hers, the soft hair on his chest creating a novel friction against her bare breasts, and the hardness of him down below, pressing against the softness of her.

She made some sort of answer, she supposed, but then they both grew quiet and still, each learning the feel of the other.

Slowly, slowly, ever so slowly, he kissed her, sucking gently on her lips, his tongue finding the beloved dent before venturing deeper, and she responded in kind. Kissing had always seemed to be such a strange thing, she had thought, lips mashing together, tongues poking here and there in a terribly unhygienic activity, but this wasn't strange at all; it was—essential, as if she could kiss this man forever, and perhaps *must* kiss him to survive. She felt his left hand leave her hair and begin to explore the length of her, now slowing the feverish pace to take his time, stroking her face, her lips, one finger resting on the dent; her collarbone, her breasts, shaping and re-shaping them, circling the center until finally he shaped that as well. And then he sank down and his mouth took the place of his hand, and she sighed and stretched her body toward him. His hand caressed her stomach, her ribs, and bypassed "down south"—a term her patients used that had always made her smile—to massage her thighs, and then he sunk lower and kissed the hollows of her stomach, taking such sweet time, then he raised his head and inched back up her body, and began over again, kissing her mouth until her lips were swollen; bathing her breasts with his lips and tongue, and then, oh, *then*, she felt his hand trail down her stomach once again and slip inside to the warm, wetness of her, and her muscles locked. She froze; he froze.

"Is this okay?" he whispered, lifting his head from her breast.

"Yes," she breathed, incredulous at such a question. "Don't stop, Jake."

He didn't stop. His gentle fingers explored the depths of her, and then he found the very softest and most exquisite spot in all the universe, she was certain, and as his tender hand created a rhythm, she began to feel that maybe the universe would soon explode, right within her body. The force within her built and built, and when she began to thrust against his hand, he withdrew it and grabbed her own hand.

"Please, Rosie, can you touch me? Like this. And I'm sorry if I don't make it very long. I've just been waiting so long." He led her hand to the place it needed to be, teaching her to encircle him, to stroke him, and she found that he was hot and hard and his skin was like silk. She looked down at him and was moved to tears.

He groaned and thrust against her, just as she had done, but after only a few seconds pulled her hand away.

And then she didn't need his instruction anymore: she grasped his hips and rolled him on top of her, opening herself to him, and he paused for a brief second, reverently, looking down at her, his eyes shining with love and passion and tenderness. "I love you, Rosie," he choked.

"I love you, Jake."

When he entered her, she gasped, not from pain, although there was a bit of that, but from utter fulfillment. They had been right: there was nothing to it: their lovemaking was an extension of their uncanny affinity, utterly natural and simple and nourishing beyond measure. *Oh, this is what it's like, I know this feeling.* It was an extraordinary sense of homecoming, of rightness with the world.

As they moved together, the rhythm growing more urgent and fierce, she felt strange liquid waves jetting through her, and the universe didn't shatter after all but tapered to one tiny point. She heard herself cry out again and again, and he was crying out as well, their voices blending together, and with one last magnificent thrust they lay together, gasping, spent, replete.

For long moments they didn't move, sealed together, sensing the world coming to rest again just as the cotton seed had settled in the sacred grove.

He finally shifted from her and lay beside her, arms still wrapped tightly around his bride, gazing into the dark depths of her eyes, yearning to say something properly profound but faltering, knowing that no words could suffice.

"Rosie?"

She raised her eyebrows, smiling. "Mmm?"

He smiled in return and shook his head ruefully, his knuckles stroking her cheek. "I don't know what to say."

Her smiled deepened. "Well, I do!" She propped herself up on one elbow. "That was really, *really* fun! *Spectacularly* fun, actually!"

He stared at her for a beat before the laughter bubbled to the surface. How, *how*, did he get so lucky as to spend his life with her, this mercurial, unpredictable, bright flash of a woman?

"It was fun for me, too!" he laughed, shaking his head and pulling her back down.

"I do have a serious question, though," she said soberly after the hilarity had died down a bit.

A tiny crease appeared between his eyebrows. "What is it?"

She stroked his jaw, trying not to smile. "How long do you suppose until we can do that again?"

At some point deep in the night, after the two lovers lay murmuring and sipping chokecherry wine by candlelight, eating cheese and bread and delicious chocolate-dipped strawberries prepared by Rosalie, Bailey sat up, perched excitedly on her knees.

"Okay then. Close your eyes and count to one hundred, and then come and find me."

"Find you? In the house?"

"No." She looked down at her left hand, at her beloved wedding ring, and slid it from her finger, turning it to him to remind him of the engraving inside.

"Green meadow," he said obediently. "Does someone have a fantasy of their own they need to tell me about?"

She grinned seductively and nodded, and leaned forward to whisper the whole thing in his ear.

He sat back when she was finished and nodded gravely. "Yes. Yes, I believe I can make that happen, Mrs. Naplava."

She clapped her hands in delight and hopped from the bed, vanishing like a fiery sprite—damn, she was quick—and he smiled after her, counting silently as he donned his Levis and the soft blue cotton shirt she loved so much. He pulled on his boots and his black vest before turning to fetch one last thing from a hook beside the wardrobe.

He pulled the Stetson low over his eyes and went to fetch his horse.

It was time to find his girl in the green meadow.

"Jake!" There was a squeal of laughter and a splash, and the two of them tussled a bit before finding their footing.

"I could have got in on my own, you big turd!"

"Looks to me like you were chicken."

Bailey kicked water at him and then screamed as he lunged at her, forcing her deeper into the wide, swollen creek.

"Okay now, hold on to me. We're about to go over your head, but I can still touch. Creek gets deep this time of year."

"Not to mention cold!"

"You said you wanted to learn to swim, young lady."

"In the spring, maybe! Not in December!"

"It's seventy degrees today; Ma's thermometer said so."

They continued to bicker as he carried her around, and while she clung to him at first, within a few minutes she was floating on her stomach and back, supported by his strong hand.

"Watch where you're reaching there, mister," she teased.

"What? My hands are behind my back," he answered innocently, reaching around her and groping one small breast through the bathing costume she had borrowed from Mari.

But she didn't bat his hand away; she turned and pressed herself against him and found something to grab as well, and they lit the fire, right there in the chilly creek. They laughed and kissed and staggered backwards toward the shore until they were prone upon the banks, and soon the only costume she wore was the strange pendant, which glinted powerfully in the sun as her lover moved over her.

In the depths of the water a creature was curled behind a mossy rock, tightly coiled into a ball of misery, not wanting to watch the lovers but unable to look away. Her body began to spasm with pain; and she unhinged her jaws to release her agony and loss; over and over she screamed, the sound piercing through the water like a thousand sharp daggers, detectable only to the creatures of the creek, filling them with dread and terror and driving them away for miles. When she could scream no more, she turned away, and with a flash of green iridescence, she vanished into the murky depths.

EPILOGUE

1910

T he party was in full swing: the new barn had been specially constructed for parties such as this, giving up any pretense of usage as an actual, functioning barn. Jacob Naplava had designed it himself, and the best part was the huge stage that stood at the far end, complete with a velvet curtain. The stage served well not only for the lively band currently playing a rousing version of "Some Day, Melinda," but for school and community theatre, musical productions, debates, and spelling bees. There was a loft filled with romantic hidey-holes, and many a couple "climbed the ladder" at some point in the night, often eliciting jeers and whistles from the crowd below. The rest of the building could be filled with chairs when needed, but tonight most of the floor was cleared for dancing, with the exception of the northeast corner, which was devoted to tables laden with food and a nifty bar complete with beer on tap and bottles of homemade wine and ginger ale.

It was hot and noisy, the air filled with laughter and singing and excited chatter, the swishing of ladies' dresses as their men whirled them around the dance floor, their boots stomping on the hard oak.

The band took a breather as a handsome man in a battered

black Stetson took the stage, and after the crowd roared approval, they finally quieted as he waved his hand, laughing.

"All right then, rascals. I'm happy to see everyone we love here tonight. Are you having a good time?"

The crowd roared again, stamping their feet, whistling, and clapping their hands.

"Well, the last I saw of my nephew Silas, he was *climbing the ladder...*" The crowd hooted, hollered, and whistled again. "So I know *he's* having a good time."

"I am!" yelled a voice from the loft, and it was a good three minutes before Jacob could get them quiet again.

He gestured a few times to someone in the crowd, finally clasping his hands in a plea, a dimple flashing, and a lovely woman sprung lightly to the stage, a baby on her hip. Her red hair was tied partially back with a black velvet ribbon, but it exploded from her head in a fiery display, and every woman there felt a twinge of jealousy as she reached her husband and turned her face up to him to receive a full and lingering kiss. The crowd heartily gave its approval.

"Dr. Rose and I thank you for being here tonight, and so does Big Frankie here." The baby waved as if on cue, and everyone in the crowd could see that he was the spitting image of his Papa, with his black hair and piercing blue eyes.

"Thank you ever so much for helping us to celebrate our eldest child's sixteenth birthday! Most everyone we love is here: most of my rotten siblings, for starters." He scanned the crowd and found Anton and Alice and Mari and Miguel, both couples holding their latest babies; and Ginny and her new husband, a fellow from New Jersey she had met at college. Joseph and Clarissa stood clustered with their four children, three of whom were adopted. Eveline had married a cattle rancher and moved to Montana, and Franz was back east, married to a society girl in New York City and working for her wealthy father in finance. But there were Johann and Lindy, Rosalie, Amalie and Anna and their husbands; all standing together, clapping and cheering. And Thomas and Gabby, arm-in-arm, beaming.

The absence of Wenzel still made his heart squeeze.

"Adele Naplava, come on up here, baby." Jacob gestured to someone in the crowd again, and soon he and Bailey were joined by an astonishingly beautiful young girl. She had her mother's red hair—although it was smooth and cooperative where her mother's was disorderly—and Bailey's trim, athletic build, but she had inherited her father's flashing blue eyes. When she smiled, she looked so much like Bailey that it still made her Papa catch his breath.

"Hey! What about us?"

Two rambunctious boys tore onto the stage and plowed into a laughing Adele, lifting her in the air in triumph, and where other teenage girls would perhaps be mortified or shrieking, Adele laughed and played along, holding onto her brothers' shoulders for dear life. They looked identical to each other and to Adele: even though the twins were only ten, they were big already: all blue-eyed red-heads, the perfect blend of mother and father.

Jacob whispered something in Bailey's ear, his eyes scanning the crowd, and she shook her head, whispering back to him. He nodded and smiled fondly, and turned to signal the band, and they launched into a rousing rendition of "Happy Birthday to You," followed by further loud cheering and shouts of congratulations. Every unmarried boy under the age of twenty-one stormed the stage to get to Adele: she looked a bit alarmed but then laughed and stood calmly, speaking politely to each one in turn, handing her dance card around until each boy was satisfied. She looked at her mother and rolled her eyes and winked, and Bailey felt enormously blessed and relieved that she had raised such a kind, level-headed young woman.

"Let's go dance, Rosie," whispered Jacob in her ear, and after all of these years, she still felt the flesh on her arms raise.

She responded by pulling him down for another long kiss, and then shifted the baby to consult her card. "I'm sorry, love, but I'm dancing with Kube, and I believe you're dancing with Hope."

Gacenka materialized and whisked Frankie away for a piece

of birthday cake, and they went in search of Bailey's sister. They found her swaying to the music with a tall, wiry man, pressed just as close as they could possibly be, and Jacob smirked.

"I don't think we're going to be able to pry those two apart. You'd think they were newlyweds the way they're going at it."

They weren't newlyweds: they had married just one year after Jacob and Bailey, but they had been inseparable ever since, riding the range, camping out for months on end. Kube was a changed man: gone was the edginess and disdain for life: he was devoted to the woman in his arms, and she to him. Bailey's heart swelled. To have her sister right here in Hill Country with her was a dream she had never thought possible.

Bailey turned gladly into her husband's arms, and they swung away, dancing madly with the lively tune, spinning and dipping and laughing like two children; then the music slowed and they clung together, enthralled with each other, utterly lost to the world, and the couples around them craned their necks to witness the precious sight of it.

Down by Glory Creek, sitting underneath Wenzel's favorite tree, was a girl of twelve. She had black hair, not gloriously curly and untamed like her mother's nor straight like her father's, and certainly not smooth and shiny like her older sister's. It was rather thick and dull with only a hint of a wave, nothing very interesting, and braided carelessly into a ratty tail that hung down her back. Her eyes, as black as her mother's, were trained with a laser-focus high into the trees. She spent most of her life outside, alone, roaming the hills or swimming in the wide creek, day in and day out, and her skin was tanned to the color of the walnuts that she harvested, staining her fingers every autumn. Her knickers were always covered with dirt and grass stains; thank goodness Mama let her wear pants and boots, no matter how Granny Naplava frowned.

Some of the children at school called her a "mangy Mexican" when her brothers and sister weren't around to defend her. They whispered in her ear that she was adopted, found abandoned on the doorstep of Dr. Naplava's clinic; that she was a foundling, a dirty Mexican foundling. She knew it wasn't true. She could see for herself, when she looked in the mirror, that the dent in her full lower lip was identical to her mother's, as were her strange dark eyes, and her hair was the color of her father's. But she didn't really blame the other children for their confusion: she looked nothing, absolutely *nothing*, like her siblings. She understood their incredulity when they learned that the spectacular Adele was her sister. She was incredulous herself, to be honest.

She really didn't mind any of it. Her outsider status had given her a sort of freedom: where the other children played together and inevitably caused trouble, she could slip away with Rue, her border collie, and wander to her heart's content, as long as she was home by dark. She knew how to catch, clean, and cook a fish—she could start her own fire with a bow drill—and the berries and apples were abundant. She always had her gun on her and she could hunt and dress a rabbit or squirrel with ease; she had even shot a few bucks. "You were born a wanderer," her mother would always sigh.

Even her name was strange. *Cassidy.* She knew it was some long-ago family name, but she sure didn't know any other girl who was called Cassidy. All of her siblings had family names, but the others were easy to explain: Adele was named after her mother's mother; John after her mother's father, Wen after Uncle Wenzel; Frankie after Grandpa Franticek. Cassidy was a great-grandmother's surname, she had been told. *Surname.* They had given her a last name for a first name! "Olivia" had been her great-grandmother's given name. She knew another girl named "Olivia" in her church. That name wasn't right for her either, though: it was pretty and melodious, and she was not. She often wondered why her parents hadn't named her something regular and non-fussy, like "Joan" or "Paula," a name she had read in a magazine once. *Paula.* That would have been a fine name for her, because it rather sounded like a boy, and she guessed she acted like one most of the time.

"Because you *are* different," her mother had told her once when Cassidy had summoned the courage to ask her. "You are unique and extraordinary. I knew it the day you were born."

She thought about that now as she gazed up into the tree and listened to the birds. They were chattering about the wild raspberries on the south hill, giving each other directions and orders; establishing boundaries and quantities. This was something new. Just this summer she had discovered that if she listened closely enough, she could understand what the birds were saying. It had come as a quite a surprise.

Yes, she supposed she was very different. She also supposed she better never tell anyone just how different she was.

She knew she should probably get back to the party. Today she had actually changed out of her knickers and was wearing a light blue dress, a hand-me-down that had looked utterly breathtaking on Adele when she wore it a few years ago but made her younger sister look rather—well—*frumpy*, she supposed. She was smaller than Adele had been at twelve, flat where Adele was curvy, and the dress hung on her like a sack. Mama had wanted to fix it for her, but Cassidy could see she had her hands full planning the party, chasing the baby, tending to her patients in the clinic, and scolding the boys, so she had politely declined. Cassidy had kept her boots on today, though, and Mama and Daddy hadn't said a thing; just laughed and hugged her something fierce. They were the best, really. They never tried to change her.

She really didn't care much about how she looked; there was not much improvement to be made, and the party wasn't for folks to look at *her* anyway. Adele had made sure she was not upset about wearing the dress; Adele was always careful about the feelings of others. She was the kindest, most wonderful girl on the planet, not at all conceited even though she looked like an angel, and Cassidy loved her with all of her heart, even though they had absolutely nothing in common. Cassidy herself usually cared not a whit about hurting the feelings of others: she was plain-looking and plain-spoken where Adele was exquisite and eloquent. Adele wished to stay inside and care for the baby and play the beautiful grand piano; Cassidy couldn't wait to escape each morning, hastily kissing whomever was nearby and promising to be back by dark. She would whistle for Rue and vanish, exploring every inch of the hills and creek for miles and miles. She had stayed out for a week all by herself this summer with the somewhat nervous permission of her folks, shooting off her gun every evening at dusk as a signal that she was okay.

She stood up and sighed, brushed the dirt and twigs from the blue dress as best she could, and made her way back to the party. When she arrived, she saw that they had already introduced Adele and sung the birthday song: the cake had been cut and Adele was twirling around the dance floor in the arms of a tall, freckled boy who had graduated from school last year. A line of other boys was waiting nearby, furtively consulting their dance cards, and Cassidy hid a grin behind her hand. She had a dance card too, somewhere; maybe she had left it on the creek bank. She had stood patiently for thirty minutes when the band started a few hours ago, obeying her father's request to "stick around 'til half past five, at least," but no boy had even glanced her way, let alone asked to sign her card. She hadn't minded; she'd been happy to slip away from the hot barn with plenty of daylight left to burn on this beautiful summer day.

And now here she was again, standing on tiptoes and waving to make sure her father saw her present and accounted for; she smiled delightedly as though she were having a smashing time and then waved again and spun away, as if she had somewhere pressing to go.   She didn't; she just found another corner, this time out of her parents' line of vision, and leaned against the wall, her mind a pleasant, fuzzy blank. She stood for several long moments, watching Adele adroitly manage several boys until she lost track of her, then switching her focus to her cousin Libby, who was wrapped so tightly around her beau that she would surely get a scolding from her mother Lindy at any moment; yep, there it was! And it was a good one, too, Lindy shaking her finger and whacking the boy on the butt, who straightened, terrified, and bolted in the other direction, much to Libby's ire.

"Hey! Cassidy, right?"

She looked up, startled, to find a girl she knew from school. Not a nice girl, either, but one who spent her days snubbing every girl and writing notes to every boy, and then vanishing with one or another during lunch. She had overheard the boys say that Josie was a *sure thing*, but she tried not to listen to garbage like that. Josie was only a few years older than Cassidy, but she might as well have been ten years older: she was developed and rouged and lipsticked, her honey-blond hair curled into a high pony-tail secured by the biggest, most obnoxious blue bow Cassidy had ever laid eyes upon. "Hi Josephina," she said tonelessly, using the girl's full name to annoy her, her dark eyes barely making contact before they skittered away to some point over Josie's shoulder.

"I was sent to give you a meeeessaaaage." She sang the last word, drawing it out suggestively, and Cassidy's eyes snapped back to the simpering girl. She said nothing, waiting, and Josie frowned.

"Well, don't you want to know what the message is?"

Cassidy yawned in a most unladylike fashion, not bothering to cover it, and leaned her head back against the wall, closing her eyes. "No, not particularly." She bent her knee and settled one crusty boot on the wall.

The older girl huffed and stammered. "Well, I—I'm going to give it to you anyway! Jesse Stanton wants you to meet him outside behind the hen house."

Cassidy felt her stomach roll over and struggled to keep her face neutral and disinterested. Only she *wasn't* disinterested. If there was one boy who could make her blush and get all squeezy on the insides, it was Jesse Stanton. They were actually quite good friends; they had even hunted rabbits around the creek beds behind his father's ranch a few times. Just friends, is all; she happened to know he had it bad for Adele, and he was Adele's age, after all. He was too shy to do anything about it, but she knew by the way he asked about her. But it didn't stop her from imagining what it would be like if he were to take off his dodgy straw hat, lean down from his height, brush his light brown hair out of his light brown eyes, and kiss her.

She swallowed thickly. This could be a trick; it probably was, but she couldn't back down now, or she'd be a chicken. And everyone who knew her knew that she didn't back down from anything.

"All right then. I guess I'll see what he wants. He probably wants me to get him a dance with Adele. Where is she, anyway? Can you see her?"

This distracted Josie long enough for Cassidy to slip away.

And so on shaking legs she made her way to the hen house, moving cautiously, tense for a fight, hands balled into fists. When she arrived, she skirted her way around it, moving silently, but after several long pauses and trips around, she was satisfied that nobody was here. She began to relax; this was a lame trick, even for Josie, and a rather confusing one. Maybe Jesse *had* been here and got tired of waiting.

She heard a rustle from inside the hen house and froze in her tracks: it was probably just the chickens shifting around; but no, she thought she heard a low murmur of a male voice. Was he inside that shithole? Waiting for her in *there*? She smiled to herself and made her way through the sludge to the dark door, peeking inside.

A lantern was turned low, but the light was bright enough for her to see. Jesse *was* in there. With Adele. Kissing her. Not just a tender embrace, like the one Cassidy had naively daydreamed about. It was a passionate act she was witnessing: heads were moving, tongues were involved, and hands were disappearing into clothing.

Cassidy raised her hand to cover her mouth, unable to stop a tiny sound of pain, but they didn't hear her. She backed out silently and then ran at full speed in the opposite direction of the ranch, her eyes dry but her heart aching.

She was just over the first hill and out of sight of the barns when she was tackled from behind. She instantly coiled and rolled, then struck out with her fists and feet, connecting with her left foot and causing her assailant to release a string of obscenities. She jumped to her feet and raised her hands: she was confident she could take whomever this was. Kube's right-hand man was an immigrant from Japan who had been teaching her and the twins to fight with punches and kicks and balance using techniques they had never seen before. As big and strong as the twins were, she beat them every time they sparred. Chin Lu made them promise to use it for defensive purposes only, and she had kept that promise: she had fought this way only once, before school last week, when she came upon Vincent Jorgen—a big boy of fifteen—beating a boy the twins' age for his lunch money. She had dispatched him with a few kicks and punches, and news had gotten around fast, making her more of a pariah than ever.

And here he was, of course. Only there was more than one, she saw now. There were three boys: all of them members of Josie's fan club. It all certainly made sense now.

She tried to remember everything Chin had taught her, but they hadn't really progressed to fighting more than one assailant at a time. *That's unfortunate*, she though hazily as two thugs managed to pin her hands behind her back. *This is going to hurt like hell*.

Vincent was a terrible fighter. Most of his punches were ineffective and aimed at her stomach, which she kept clenched as tightly as she possibly could. It hurt, but nothing was breaking. The boys hissed the usual insults.

"Filthy fucking whore of a Mexican rat!"

"You're an embarrassment to your family! How do they stand to look at you?"

"We heard you like girls, not boys, isn't that right? You look like a boy, anyway, you freak."

"Well, you punch like a goddam sissy," she gasped, and was immediately sorry. Vincent reared back and punched her in the face, and as the blood started to spurt, the boys holding her began to panic.

"Not in the face, you stupid moron! Her Pa's gonna kill you!"

217

Vincent froze, watching the thick red blood squirt in impressive arcs, splattering the blue dress. His face contorted with fear. He was clearly drunk and had not thought this through. "If you tell him who it was, you'll be sorry." But his voice held no real threat any longer, and his cronies dropped her to the ground like a rag doll and took to the hills.

"Don't tell him, okay? Here." She heard him rustle around and then felt something soft hit the side of her head, and then the sound of his boots in the grass as he sprinted away.

She rolled to a fetal position, stomach aching, blood pouring from her nose. It was a pretty good bet it was busted. She felt her ribs gingerly; painful, but not broken, she didn't think. She turned her head and vomited into the grass, and only then did she see the roll of cash. She stared at it. He was paying her not tell her father. *Now that's a reputation*, she thought proudly. Even at the ripe old age of forty-seven, her old man could kick anyone's ass, and still did, when the occasion called for it. She stuffed the money in her boot, already devising how to blackmail Vincent and scare the hell out of him at the same time.

What to do now? She would not ruin her sister's party or worry her parents. She had been in her mother's clinic long enough to know that she didn't have any serious injuries. She staggered to her feet, and made her way as stealthily as she could back toward the ranch, and when she saw her cousin Silas in the shadows with his girl, a plan began to form. She gave a quick *psssst*.

"Silas! It's Cassidy. Tell Mama and Pa I went to Granny's, okay? I'm going to sleep there tonight."

Silas turned, startled, and started to come toward her. Cassidy sank back into the shadows.

"You all right there, Cass?"

"Yeah, of course. Just bored."

Silas nodded his head wisely and she imagined he was grinning. "Oh I see. You got into the wine, did you? Had a bit too much? This was your first time?"

She laughed but stopped abruptly as her nose throbbed.

"That's it, all right. Will you tell them you spoke to me, and saw me go in the house? Give me a head start, though. Maybe in twenty minutes or so?"

"Sure thing." He chuckled again and gestured toward the barn. "They just started *schovávačka*. You've got a big head start, I'd say."

She breathed a sigh of relief and began walking, giving wide berth to the party barn and staying in the shadows, whistling softly for Rue. She reached the big porch and was relieved to see that nobody was here; they were all in the barn or out in the hills, playing the game. She stumbled inside, the dog by her side, grabbed a lantern, and headed for the lavatory first, and when she hung the lantern on the hook and looked in the mirror, she gasped. Her nose was swollen to twice its normal size, and was still trickling blood. She touched it gingerly and her knees buckled. It was broken for sure, and she was going to need ice. She'd catch hell for this tomorrow.

After washing up as best as she could, she made her way outside to the ice house: no fancy electric ice chest here like at home. She chipped off a chunk and wrapped it in a towel she found in the kitchen, and finally made her way to Aunt Ginny's old room, which was always made up for the grandkids whenever they cared to stay.

She kicked her boots off and stepped out of the ruined blue dress, not wanting to pull it over her head for fear of bumping her nose, and curled under the quilt, Rue soft and warm sprawled over her feet, and held the ice to her face.

Well, she had done it. No one would bother her till morning.

Come to think of it, no one would probably notice she was gone for quite some time. There were no friends to miss her, no beau to find a dark shadow with. Adele was quite occupied with Jesse, wasn't she? Cassidy felt a hot sear of moisture build behind her eyes and blinked furiously to stem it. Her parents were hiding together somewhere in the hills, no doubt having at it like two teenagers.

It was of her own doing, of course, this isolation. She could try harder to fit in: she could put on a dress more often, let Adele brush her hair, and learn how to flirt and be charming. She could stop spending her days outside and spend more time in the clinic, perhaps training to be a nurse or even a doctor like her mother. She could invite girls over—she had plenty of cousins who were friendly and tried to include her—she could *let* them, for once.

For the first time in her life, a great, black heaviness settled somewhere around her gut, right under where the blue bruises would appear tomorrow. She didn't know how to do those things. And would she still be herself if she did try to fit in? Maybe it wasn't so bad to try to be someone else for a change. She had been alone for so long, and being alone with Rue and the birds and the creek and the hills had been sweet and exhilarating and blissful. *Alone* had been good.

Lonely was not.

The rain was gray. The boy wasn't sure this was possible—gray rain—and he removed his black leather glove and held out his hand, cupping it, trying to catch the rain to detect its color, but the wind was blowing too hard.

"Ticho!" His mother murmured. *Quiet!*

But he hadn't said a word.

He understood that she meant he was not to move; he was to stand like a statue. This was not in his nature. He put his glove back on and she took his hand. He liked the feel of his hand in hers: she rarely touched him. He offered a little pressure, a squeeze, but her hand was limp and lifeless.

His eyes shifted restlessly. There was not much to see: a gray yard devoid of vegetation surrounded by a rusty iron fence, with small rectangular stones thrusting up here and there like fingerless stone hands.

The boy was too old to be made to stand still. Or at least too big. At twelve he was already taller than his mother, although admittedly, she was a very small woman. He liked to think that he'd be tall and big, like his father.

The boy's eyes shifted again. He hadn't wanted to look there, but now he couldn't seem to help it. The hole had already been dug and the casket lowered down into it when they arrived, and after his mother had stepped forward and delivered a brief, whispered speech in that language he had only heard once before, she had stepped back and nodded to the man in the black trench coat holding the shovel, who began to fill the hole up. It had taken quite some time. The boy knew that the sound of the dirt hitting the casket was a sound he would never forget. It was a dull thumping sound, followed by a trickling as the dirt skittered across the top of the casket and down the sides. Then the rain had started to come down harder and sideways and gray, and the sound of the dirt being thrown into the hole turned into the sound of squelching mud, which was much, much worse.

Finally the gravedigger had scattered a few handfuls of grass seed on top of the mound of mud, tipped his hat and left, peering at them curiously over his shoulder as he hurried away, back bent against the rain.

Now he and his mother stood alone, for no one else had come to his father's funeral.

He had loved his father, a tall, lumbering, sweet-natured man who spent hours hunting and fishing with him. His father never said much, but he had loved the boy with all of his heart. In fact, the boy was quite sure that his father was the *only* person on the whole earth who had loved him.

The grief and rage suddenly surged inside him, taking him utterly by surprise, threatening to erupt. He had to let it out, didn't he? He felt that he must howl or he would break apart.

But he uttered not a sound, moved not a muscle, not wanting to disturb the feel of his mother's hand in his own. For long moments he stood thus as the gray rain thickened and blew sideways, slicing icy ribbons into his cheek.

He dared a glance at his mother. She was gazing off into the far distance, her eyes unfocused. She stood stiffly, her back straight, in her black hat and veil: he could see that she was soaked to the bone like he was. She was not crying and did not appear to be distressed; and why should she be? She hadn't cared much for her husband, an *oaf* is what she called him, the boy thought bitterly. When the news came about the accident at the fishery, she had barely managed to register shock; her expression had been more of a resigned *of course he's gone and mucked things up again, as usual.*

Maybe she was sad because now she was utterly alone, thought the boy. Her parents were dead and he knew nothing of his father's family, who apparently lived in Poland somewhere. She had no one. Except for him.

He had a terrible thought then. He wondered if he were to just walk away from her, from this spot, right now; would she even notice? Surely, she would notice! She must love him! He was her son; her only family in the world. She would call out for him, wouldn't she? She would hug him fiercely to her, beg him not to leave her. Perhaps it was the only way to awaken her from this appalling trance.

Ever so carefully he eased his hand away and was dismayed to find that his hand was slipping out of his over-size black glove. *Even so, she must feel it. She must feel that the glove is empty now.*

He lowered his arm and turned to her; she stood unmoved, holding the empty black glove where his hand used to be, eyes unfocused, unseeing.

"*Matka*," he breathed softly. She did not look at him or move.

"*Matka*," he said with more force, his heart pounding.

Still nothing.

"I'm leaving," he said in English. She didn't like it when he spoke English; surely this would get a rise out of her. But nothing.

He took one sideways step, just like one of the crabs down at the river, and stopped, gauging the effect, only there was no effect. He took another and another. She didn't move.

"Goodbye mother," he called. The sound of his voice, insignificant and bereft in the wind and rain, frightened him. He turned and strode away; five determined steps, arms swinging. *One more time. Just one more time. Surely she will call for me.*

She did not turn or call for him, but stood straight and frozen, an exquisite statue with her gaze caught upon something distant he could not see, holding an empty black glove.

This time when he turned, he did not look back.

ABOUT THE AUTHOR

Jenny Haley is the author of the *Bailey Rose, M.D.* series. As a writer, she was shaped by the works of LaVyrle Spencer, immersing herself in compelling stories of strong women in authentic and relatable situations within rich historical settings. Jenny's genre is tricky to define: historical magical realism paranormal romance, perhaps. You will not find bodice-ripping stories with helpless, flawless protagonists in her books, but stories that deeply resonate, featuring courageous, imperfect women and the men who love them.

Jenny makes her home in the American Upper Midwest where she lives with her husband, teenage daughter, her young adult son close by, and two retired racing greyhounds. In her spare time, she works as a college administrator and writing instructor at a public university.

Jenny loves to hear from her readers! Visit her website at www.jennyhaley.com, where you can watch the latest book trailer, read her blog, and connect via email. If you enjoyed this novel, the nicest way to say "thank you" is to leave a favorable review online!

Made in United States
North Haven, CT
20 July 2023

39304005R00139